LIV,
FOREVER

LIV,
FOREVER

Amy Talkington

WITHDRAWN

SOHO
TEEN

Published in the United States by Soho Teen
an imprint of
Soho Press, Inc.
853 Broadway
New York, NY 10003

Library of Congress Cataloging-in-Publication Data

Talkington, Amy.
Liv, forever / Amy Talkington.

HCISBN 978-1-61695-322-5
PB ISBN 978-1-61695-479-6
eISBN 978-1-61695-323-2
[1. High schools—Fiction. 2. Schools—Fiction. 3. Murder—Fiction.
4. Ghost—Fiction. 5. Supernatural—Fiction. 6. Artists—Fiction.
7. New Hampshire—Fiction.] I. Title.
PZ7.T154398Liv 2014
[Fic]—dc23 2013038270

Interior design by Janine Agro, Soho Press, Inc.

Printed in the United States of America

10 9 8 7 6 5 4 3 2 1

To Robbie
for truth and humor

Ruth

Chances of a girl like me ending up at Wickham Hall were next to nothing. I was a farmer's daughter, and neither of my parents even finished grade school. But I loved to read. I read every single book I could get my hands on. And, fittingly, it was in a novel that I first heard of Wickham Hall.

I can't recall which book it was. Fitzgerald's new one, maybe? But it said something like, "Presidents go to Wickham Hall." And that sounded dandy to me. A girl could do worse in life than become a president's wife, especially if he was dreamy like Calvin Coolidge. Oui! Oui! A president's wife would just go to parties and entertain, with oodles of free time to read books.

I wrote a letter to the school, asking for admission, dramatically explaining my plight in life, and several weeks later I received a letter back from the headmaster himself inviting me to join the student body. Can you imagine la joie?! I never filled out an application. I didn't even know there were such things until I heard everyone complaining about how long theirs had taken. Mon Dieu. I was lucky, I thought.

It's hard to tell by looking at me now, but I was a happy girl and not bad looking. The boys just adored my red hair, and I was pretty witty, too. You'd have thought I'd have more sense than to fall for an anonymous note, a request to meet at the weeping willow tree. But no. Silly me. I thought, "Quelle coincidence!" I'd always loved those kinds of trees. And there were so many handsome gentlemen at Wickham Hall. It was just too intriguing an invitation to decline.

As I got dolled up—pin curls, of course, and my sole, fine-beaded dress—I started to hum that "Weeping Willow" song. It was very popular at the time. Then I strolled over. I leaned against the trunk underneath those willow branches and looked up. They made a silhouette against the moonlit sky. From below, those weeping arms looked like suspended streaks of rain.

Then something grabbed my forehead from behind, pinning my back to the tree, and I felt the chill of a blade gliding across my neck. It didn't exactly hurt. It was just cold. And terribly shocking.

I didn't even know I was dying until I looked down and saw the blood soaking into my dress. To think, the very last thing I wondered—while still a living, breathing girl—was, "How am I going to get this dress cleaned in time for Fall Festival?"

CHAPTER 1.

A man in a black suit was waiting for me. He had polished shoes and white gloves and held a sign that read WICKHAM HALL. It was written in the same font I'd seen on their website. I'd call it "ye oldy worldy." But that's just me. It's the kind of font you can't really read. The kind that screams to the world, "We're so important, we don't care if you can read our logo." It's the kind of font you'd see on a gravestone in London. Not that I've been to London. But I'm into fonts. It's part of what I do.

The man looked at me with—well, pity might be a little strong. But it was certainly on the pity spectrum. Perhaps it was just sympathy. He noticed my fingernails and asked if I needed to go to "the powder room."

"It's not dirt. It's ink," I told him. "It's permanently there." The pity turned to something more like poorly veiled disgust. "No, not like tattoo ink. Like pen ink. I draw things." He nodded his head like he couldn't care less.

I'd said, "I draw things," as if it were no big deal. Just something I do, like take a shower or go to school. But it's *all* I do. Or at least it's all I do that matters. I was certain it was the reason I was standing at baggage claim in Boston's Logan Airport headed to the best prep school in the country for my last two years of high school. My grades certainly didn't get me into Wickham Hall. I assumed it was my portfolio. I'd worked on it for months. I knew it was my only hope of getting out.

The man was surprised by how little I'd packed. One duffle bag for my clothes. And one very heavy suitcase.

"Shoes?" he asked as he lifted the suitcase with effort from the carousel.

"No, books, vintage magazines. Ink." For my collages. I brought as much as I could carry. I wasn't going to take any chances with the Wickham Hall school store.

As he rolled my bags to the car, I got my first taste of humidity. I'd always heard about it, and now it was hitting me in the face, as thick as the paint on a Monet canvas. I'd never been east of the Mississippi. I'd never even been east of the Grand Canyon. Fine, I'd never been east of Las Vegas. I'd hardly been out of Las Vegas. We went to Reno once. That was our biggest family vacation to date. My parents aren't big on vacations. Not because they don't like not working—they *love* not working—but vacations cost money. And that they never have.

So you can imagine what I thought when the man approached a limousine. I'm not kidding. A black stretch limousine. With tinted windows. "I was kinda more expecting a good ol' American school bus. You know, the yellow ones?"

"Not at Wickham Hall."

AFTER WE LEFT THE Boston area, I tried to roll down my window, but it was locked. I could see in the rearview that the man had noticed, but he didn't offer help. Finally I asked. He obliged. I stretched out across the back seat, lying on my back so I could look straight up toward the sky. The sky and trees became blurry fields of color—blue, white, and green—stacked like a Rothko painting. Except Rothko almost never used green.

When I sat back up, we were already in New Hampshire, where LIVE FREE OR DIE is on every license plate. What a state motto. Much better than Nevada's ALL FOR OUR COUNTRY—what does that even mean? LIVE FREE OR DIE is something I could get behind, and not just because it contains my name (phonetically). It's passionate and romantic. I like all things Romantic. And I don't mean mushy, cheesy romantic. I mean truly Romantic with a capital R. As in Byron, Shelley, Keats, and of course, William Blake.

LIVE FREE OR DIE. It made me think of how Modigliani's muse Jeanne Hébuterne jumped to her death while pregnant with their second child the day after he died from tuberculosis. Or how the French painter Léon Bonvin hanged himself when he realized he would never be able to make a living from his art.

There are countless stories from days past, but it's hard to imagine someone actually dying for freedom or even for love these days—in this country at least. Everyone I know is way too apathetic to consider it. My parents rarely bother to vote. Even the guys at school who talked about joining the army only care about job security and free college. No one says he wants to do it for his country or for freedom. But maybe that's because they think it'd sound lame. It wouldn't sound lame to me.

Would I die for freedom? For love? I liked to think I had that in me, but how can you die for love if you've never felt it? And I don't just mean I'd never had a boyfriend. I mean I'd possibly never felt love at all. The social worker said it was a protective mechanism. Maybe it was. I'd had four different foster families before I was finally adopted. I was practically bred not to love.

Or maybe it's just that I got matched with the wrong family. It could happen, couldn't it? Just ending up with the wrong parents the same way you could end up with the wrong guy on an Internet date.

Headed to the far north finger of the state, we passed through Salem then Concord, and after several more hours, penetrating deeper and deeper into woods that were more dense than I'd seen before, we approached a tall stone wall. I recognized it immediately from the website. It's something they tout: fully enclosed within a wall built in 1781. I think it originally had something to do with the Revolutionary War. We drove along the perimeter for some time. It was so much bigger than I'd imagined. I wanted to say something to the man, but to be honest, he kind of scared me. So I saved it. Instead, I pulled out my Moleskin notebook and ink.

WE WERE RUNNING LATE. The man made sure I was aware it was not his fault but rather due to my plane's delay.

"Tardiness is not tolerated at Wickham Hall," he snipped. He told me he'd take me straight to Main to join the transfer tour. I asked him if I could skip it. But he said it was required—then shut the window between us, ending the conversation.

I looked at my reflection in the tinted glass. Just a trace of me but enough to see the unfortunate circles under my eyes and a silhouette of my dark, tangled hair. The locket I always wore around my neck glimmered like a disco ball as the light came and went. I started to raise the back of my sleeve to wipe the shine off my nose, but we turned and the gates opened as we passed a security booth. My focus shifted from my reflection.

A stretch of perfectly manicured gardens unfurled as far as I could see. I've always questioned the so-called perfection of surfaces. If you looked close enough, there was always a flaw. And sure enough, in the distance beyond those gardens, the jagged outline of an old cemetery crowned a plump green hill. That was more like it. Out the other window was a cluster of big colonial buildings. We'd studied Mount Vernon in history class, and they looked just like four Mount Vernons—each imposing and symmetrical, painted white with black shutters and capped with a pointed cupola.

Then we passed a spectacular Victorian mansion, its gingerbread trim delicately elaborate. And another one.

And another. Signs out front announced these were faculty housing. I wanted to ask him to stop, but then I saw the Art Center. This one I'd studied of course. It was the reason I wanted to come to Wickham Hall. Designed by Philip Johnson, it was, according to the website, their only modern building. The school had called it a "perfect celebration of art." They were right about that, at least. To me it looked like an explosion of everything I loved. I couldn't wait to go there, unpack my suitcase, and actually have a studio.

Up until now, I'd worked in my room. I'd had to cover my floor with painters' drop cloths because our apartment had wall-to-wall carpet. My mother said if I got a single drop of paint on it, I'd have to pay for it myself. When it wasn't too hot, I'd work in the alley or in a park nearby. But it was almost always too hot.

I'd just spotted a Gothic chapel in the distance when the limousine stopped in front of the main building. The man came around and opened my door before I thought of it. He waved me toward a small gathering of students at the top of the stairs.

"Your things will be waiting in your dorm: Skellenger," he said, then closed the door and drove away.

There was a small group of five or six students halfway up the steps of Main, following a girl with straight blonde hair. They were all dressed similarly in what the school website called "class dress"—dress shirt, tie, and sport coat for guys and for girls, a knee-length skirt and a blazer.

I called out to the blonde. No response. So I ran up the stairs.

"Olivia Bloom. You're late," she snapped once I'd caught up. Not exactly the warm greeting one might have hoped for after coming clear across the country to attend a new school.

"Sorry, my plane was delayed."

"Well, we're on a tight schedule." She got back to her tour, perturbed to have been interrupted. "Where was I?"

One of the fawning male transfers said, "Presidents."

"Yes, as I was saying, two of the most illustrious presidents of the United States lived in those rooms," she said, gesturing up to the windows of Main. Then she motioned over to the Mount Vernons. "And two others lived over there. Google it if you don't already know. The point is: Wickham Hall has a rich history, renowned alumni, and a powerful network that extends around the entire world." She spoke as though delivering a soliloquy for an unseen camera. "Now, come along. We have a lot to see."

She turned her back on us and scaled the stairs. From behind, I couldn't help but stare at her hair. I'd never seen such straight hair cut in such a straight line. Surely some blog would proclaim this the perfect bob. But to me it looked like a piece of tracing paper wrapped around a head.

We entered the lobby of Main, a stately, masculine sitting room with a hand-carved fireplace and a massive pewter chandelier. It looked like the kind of place where cigars were smoked . . . or pipes—definitely pipes. Strangely, there were no students lounging in the deep leather chairs. I realized I hadn't yet seen a single student on the campus aside from our small group.

Perfect Hair led us through the lobby to a small door and then down a spiral staircase that was so narrow we had to walk single file. I was last, so by the time I reached the bottom of what seemed like hundreds of steps, I'd missed the beginning of her speech. Not that I really cared.

"And you may or may not have heard the frivolous rumors that Wickham Hall is haunted. Students have passed ghost stories down from generation to generation, mostly as a means of diversion. And non-Wickies like to snicker about our ghosts because frankly, there is nothing about us in the *real* world they can snicker at."

"*Wickies?*" I asked.

"Yes, Wickies," she replied, completely without humor. She turned to lead us down the dark hallway. I lingered back and looked around. I paused at an arched doorway and looked inside—a small nook—as she continued. "We call these the catacombs. They connect all six of the original academic buildings. And, as you can see, they are not, in fact, haunted."

Right then, the lights went out. Pitch black. The group had moved several yards ahead, but I could hear our guide trying to remain calm. I laughed quietly—because it was as if a ghost were protesting its nonexistence (not that I believed in ghosts)—but right then, I felt it. I turned quickly to look. It felt like someone had opened one of those giant freezer doors at the grocery store—that cold burst of air. Except here there were no doors. No windows.

"Hello?" I called. I waved my arms.

The guide assumed I was talking to her. "Is that Olivia? We're up here! Please don't get separated from the group!"

I moved toward her shrill voice and the general rumble rising from the group of nervous transfers. "Everyone follow me," she barked. "Stay close!"

Just as I caught up with the group, there came a long and anguished howl. A textbook howl, really. One of the transfers screamed and grabbed me. Their chatter got louder. The panic was palpable. The guide had to yell to be heard. "Everyone calm down! Please! I'm leading us out the fastest way!"

We started up some steps, rough and uneven underfoot, as if they were stone. And I could smell the dankness. While the other transfers whimpered and whispered, I remained silent. We were inside a protected fortress, after all. What could happen? I had no idea I'd be so still in the face of fear. I just listened to each pulse of my blood, surprised I could actually hear it pounding in my ears. And I felt my heart banging through my chest like in an old *Loony Tunes* cartoon.

As we mounted the stairs, a faraway shriek rose eerily from somewhere deep in the catacombs. One of the guys pushed me aside to save his own life. Nice. We all moved to get out of there as fast as possible, piling on top of one another.

"This way!" the guide yelled, sounding quite overcome herself. We came around a bend to blinding bright lights and thundering noise. Oxford shirts. Blazers. Laughing faces. Perfect teeth. Lots of them. Kind of like those paintings by Yue Minjun—everyone laughing hugely and wearing the same clothes—except all these people weren't Chinese. In fact, none of them were.

I looked up and saw Gothic arches. To my left were some men and women, all delighted, and a pulpit. We were in a chapel. On stage. In front of the entire school. One of the men onstage approached a microphone, stifling a chuckle. "Welcome! Welcome transfers to Wickham Hall! Did you get a fright?"

I looked to my fellow transfers. They were all quick to smile and play along, pretending that was absolutely the most charming greeting they'd ever received. I stood in disbelief. Disoriented, but mostly shocked.

The man at the microphone, wearing a stiff blue suit, went on. "I'm Headmaster Thorton. We always welcome our new transfers with a grand prank. And, thanks to our star thespian Abigail Steers, we got 'em good!"

Our guide, apparently named Abigail, stepped forward and took a bow. And then another one. The students cheered, and I noticed some adults I had to presume were faculty members also clapping and cheering for her.

"So that was supposed to be funny?" I didn't plan to say it. The words just fell out of my mouth. It wasn't accusatory. It was a sincere question. I was truly grasping to understand why they would do this. The headmaster went silent, and I knew he had heard me. Everything went silent, and everyone was looking at me. Accusing me. Or so it seemed. I'm sure it wasn't that bad, but I'm not the type to stand onstage. I'm the type who hides in her closet, drawing. For an instant it all felt very dramatic.

But the headmaster ignored me, turned away as if I'd said nothing, and looked out to the student body, continuing his well-oiled speech. "As I was saying, welcome.

You, transfers, are the chosen few, carefully selected to fill the scarce open spots at Wickham Hall. You will spend your remaining years in preparatory school getting the best education this country has to offer. But be fore-warned, we are an institution of traditions. Big and small. From our beloved Headmaster Holidays to our secret societies, we are founded on a tradition of excellence, of high performance, of, dare I say, *perfection*."

That's when I noticed him. He was standing next to the headmaster, still looking at me even though the others had turned away. Dirty blond. His expression was dif-ferent than the others'. Not disapproving or shocked. It almost looked like wonder. I noticed his shirt was partially untucked. And his teeth were *not* perfect; one buckled ever so slightly in front of the other. Our eyes met, and I quickly looked away. But I could feel his gaze linger. I des-perately willed my face not to flush, my lips not to purse. Suddenly I was aware of every single muscle in my face. I even think I invented some. I tried to focus on the head-master's words.

"As you all know, this is Wickham Hall's sesquicentennial. We're celebrating one and a half centuries as the country's premier secondary school. We celebrate Wickham Hall's birthday every year with Fall Festival, but this year, we have a *very* special alumni celebration planned."

He kept talking, but I no longer heard him. I looked up at the Gothic ceiling, but all I saw were those mesmeriz-ingly imperfect teeth.

CHAPTER 2

When I got to my room, my clothes were already unpacked, and whoever had done it felt leggings deserved to be hung up. I couldn't decide if that made me feel fancy or violated. I was trying to appreciate Wickham Hall, so I decided to feel pampered, like I'd checked into a hotel so lavish they unpacked your bags. And this invisible valet had made my bed, too. The crisp white sheets and pillowcases had *WH* monogrammed on the edge. I wasn't used to having my bed made for me. Or crisp sheets for that matter.

It's not that it was so bad at home. My parents were nice people. Nice people—I always spoke of them as if they were someone else's parents. Legally, they were mine, and it's not that I wasn't grateful they got me off the foster-home circuit; I was deeply grateful. But I felt about as close to them as I did to my chemistry teacher. And chemistry was not exactly my favorite subject.

My dorm, Skellenger, was one of those Mount Vernon

buildings in the stretch known as Dorm Row, but the style inside wasn't quite as presidential. The room was simple and small. A bed, a desk, and a giant wardrobe with a mirror. Cold linoleum floors.

The first order of business was to rearrange the furniture. I always did this. My foster parents had always been so surprised when they'd come to see how my first nap was going, only to find I'd rearranged the room. Some would laugh; some were impressed by the strength of such a slight girl. But usually they'd get angry. I guess it was my way of making those short-term rooms feel like my own. Or, if you want to psychoanalyze, you might say I did it as a way to assert some control over my erratic life. Or it might just be that I've always liked things to look a certain way.

I decided to move the giant wardrobe so that it blocked the view of the room when someone entered. It provided some mystery and privacy. I pushed the bed into a corner and the desk beneath the window. Then I pulled out my homemade cardboard portfolio. I'd brought a few collages to hang on the walls to create some semblance of home.

My collages were mostly black and white with an occasional streak of color, and always very precise. I used text from old books and magazines, pencil, ink, and acrylic paints. Sometimes I wrote in big words. Not big as in fancy, S.A.T. vocabulary, but small words that represent big ideas. *Love. Truth. Beauty. Death. Home.* Stuff like that. I always avoided God, not because I was afraid of some divine retribution, but because I wasn't yet sure where I stood on that particular issue. My parents belonged to a Bible church where they dragged me as often as possible, but I could just never get with the being-gay-is-a-sin thing. I mean, does Jesus love you or not?

I liked to use duct tape to hang art, but we'd been specifically instructed to use only poster tack on Wickham Hall's historic walls. They were so serious about this rule that they provided me with two packages of Elmer's Tac N' Stik in the welcome pack I found on my desk. As if they knew. Had my parents told them?

I should call them and tell them I'm here and safe.

I tried to get through several times, but the signal wouldn't hold. So much for the omnipotent iPhone I spent six months saving up for. Finally, I just texted. Then I sat down and started something new—a picture of a girl floating. A self-portrait. Almost all my drawings are self-portraits. They don't necessarily look like me—in fact, they rarely do—but they represent me. It doesn't take a degree in art history to imagine why I'd draw myself floating. I jumped, startled, when someone rapped on my door. "There's a mandatory dorm meeting in the common room," a clipped voice announced from behind my wardrobe.

THERE WERE ABOUT TWENTY girls draped in a variety of relaxed poses over the chairs and low tables in the common room. I never realized people could look so uptight and so relaxed at once. Abigail Steers sat in the center of the most central couch, surrounded by the others. They seemed so at home, and considering most of them had been living at Wickham Hall for at least two years already, they probably *were* home. It's a feeling I'd never felt, and I certainly didn't feel it then.

But there was something else. You know how they say girls who live together will start to get their periods at the same time? Well, it was like these girls had started to *become* the same. They dressed the same. Their hair was almost identical. Their skin was milky with the occasional bout of freckles. Their noses even turned up in the same way. But mostly, they all talked the same. They talked about prefects and proctors and coxswains. Harkness. The Tuck. I didn't have a clue what they were talking about, but the Head of the Charles sounded pretty gruesome.

The dour dorm mistress, Mrs. Mulford (think pitch-fork lady from *American Gothic,* but in ill-fitting slacks and a Wickham sweater) introduced me to the disinter-ested group of Sloans and Charlottes and Elizabeths. She announced that Abigail was our appointed dorm prefect. "A student monitor," she explained to me, as if I were three years old. Then she went over the standard safety issues and quizzed me on Wickham Hall's strict code of conduct. Just me. When I couldn't tell her the exact pro-tocol required to leave campus, the girls tittered. Mrs. Mulford suggested I reread the student handbook. She went over the main dorm rules: curfew at 9 P.M. and no boys allowed in our rooms. Period. Then she excused us to get ready for dinner.

I THOUGHT I WAS dressing properly for dinner when I changed into my vintage sundress. Big mistake. When I arrived at the dining hall, I found all the girls in sleek cocktail dresses and the guys in dark suits. I quizzed a cus-todian-looking person near the entrance. "First Dinner," he sniffed. Another phrase that had no meaning. No one had told me about First Dinner. Was it a Wickham Hall tradition for the students to dress formally for the first dinner back at school? The word "perfection" rang in my ears.

The dining hall *was* perfect, with dark, wood floors and a hand-carved vaulted ceiling. Students sat at dozens of round tables, served by waiters. Waiters? What kind of school had waiters?

In an effort to avoid the dreaded looking-for-a-seat-in-a-new-cafeteria moment, I decided to walk with purpose until I saw an empty seat or a friendly face. The problem was, I didn't see any empty seats. Or friendly faces. So I kept walking, and the more I walked, the more I began to hope I'd see a back door I could just slip through. No door, either.

But at the farthest end of the room was a table with just one person. His wasn't a friendly face—he was looking down, his darkish long hair hanging over his eyes. But it was a seat, so I took it to spare myself the embarrassment of having to parade, underdressed, back through the enormous dining hall.

Just as I sat down, everyone in the room started to stand up. *Perfect*, I thought. I stood back up. The guy at my table also stood, and I could see he was dressed even more shabbily than I was—beat-up cargo pants and a dark hoodie over an old, indecipherable band T-shirt. They all raised their hands to their hearts—all except the guy at my table. I expected to hear the Pledge of Allegiance, but instead they started to sing, "*Wickham Hall, oh Wickham Hall, our joy and our pride! Wickham Hall, oh Wickham Hall!*" Then the guy leaned in close so I could hear him defiantly change the lyrics, *"You've got nowhere to hide!"*

I pulled away from him.

"Don't be afraid of me," he snarled. "Be afraid of *them.*"

I thought he was making some sweeping generalization about the student body, but then he gestured across the room and I looked. There was a group of four students carrying a giant silver platter with a dead animal draped across it, and they were followed by five or six other students, all swinging silver carving knives back and forth to the beat of the song.

"What is that?"

"A *boar,*" he delighted in telling me. I had to laugh, which immediately put him more at ease. "I'm Gabe," he offered.

"Liv," I said.

He was skittish and intense, but his brown eyes were gentle. Still, I wanted to keep at least three feet away. He was almost exactly how I'd always pictured Vincent Van Gogh—in other words, pretty crazy.

While everyone continued to sing the Wickham Hall alma mater, the students placed the boar platter onto a table in the center of the hall. The students with the knives quickly and deftly carved it up. Then everyone clapped and took their seats. All I could think was, *There's been a terrible mistake. I need to go home. I don't belong in this place.* I didn't know people ate boar or that they even still existed.

Gabe turned to me and said, "It's crazy, right? Am I crazy, or is it crazy?"

I cringed. "It looks pretty crazy to me."

The headmaster approached a microphone (clearly one of his favorite things to do) and announced it was time for the First Dance.

"Exactly one hundred and fifty years ago, Wallace and Minerva Wickham stood in this very hall." His voice boomed and echoed, enveloping the crowd. "It looked much the same as it does today. Their son Elijah carved the boar, and then they celebrated the beginning of their school's first year with a waltz. They were very romantic, the Wickhams, and commenced every school year with that same dance. And, thus, after Wallace and Minerva passed, it became Wickham Hall tradition for the president of the student government to lead a waltz in commemoration of the Wickhams. This year, I proudly present to you: Malcolm Astor."

I glanced at Gabe. His lips were tight; his forehead was creased and sweaty. He looked truly disturbed. But when he saw me looking at him, he switched to a mocking look.

"What's going on?" I asked.

"He's trolling for a partner. I call it the Snob Trot. Yet another archaic, sexist Wicky tradition. They only pick one another, dance with one another. Just watch. It's disgusting."

I turned around to check out this Malcolm Astor. He was blocked by the headmaster, so I craned my neck. When he stepped out from behind the headmaster, I saw it was him. The one with imperfect teeth. The one I couldn't stop thinking about. The one I'd already made a drawing of.

The students clapped and cheered as he started to stroll through the hall, proud but not cocky, his eyes searching.

He took his time, basking in the moment. And I could see girls' faces warm with hope as he approached. I felt Gabe looking at me, so I tried to look disinterested, even disgusted. And part of me *was* disgusted; this whole scene felt like something from a fussy John Singer Sargent painting from the nineteenth century. But another part of me didn't want to take my eyes off him.

As Malcolm wound his way through the hall, all the guys were egging him on, chanting, "Astor! Astor!" I noticed Abigail sitting at a table with several girls from the dorm. As he headed toward her table, she turned to her blonde acolytes, excited. They giggled, patting her. Primping and pumping her up. Surely he was headed to her. She touched her hair expectantly to make sure it was just so, with full tracing paper effect.

But then he made a dramatic turn the other way. Students hooted and hollered. Abigail's eyes flashed. The curt smile couldn't conceal her annoyance.

I could see his face as he turned and thought I saw a mischievous glimmer, as if he knew he'd faked her out, and it gave him some pleasure. Maybe they were exes. That definitely seemed like potential ex behavior, but I wouldn't have known. I'd have to have had a boyfriend to have had an ex.

"Look at this guy," Gabe scoffed. "It's like he wants to grace every single girl in the school with his perfect presence. And all the pathetic girls are eating it up."

I nodded my head. I did agree on some level, but when I looked up and saw him approaching, I got a sick feeling in my stomach.

"Look, he's even coming back to the Pit," Gabe huffed.

I nodded again and then looked down, took a bite of the dinner that had appeared in front of me. I had to chew something. Maybe I was starving, and that's why it felt like my stomach was collapsing into itself. Was that meat wild boar? While I was looking down, shoving a roll into my mouth, there was a shift in the room. Everyone went silent. I looked up, mouth full of bread, to see what had happened and . . . he was there.

He stood in front of me and asked, "May I have this dance?" He looked sincere. Even nervous. I had to finish chewing and swallow. I'd never realized swallowing took so excruciatingly long. It gave me time to look around and see the entire student body was staring at me (again)—a field of baffled faces, including Gabe's.

"I don't know how to dance like that," I whispered so only he could hear.

"I can lead you." He saw I was taken aback. "Or we can dance however you want."

I didn't say yes, but he could tell from the look on my face that I wouldn't argue. He took my hand and led me away. I couldn't bring myself to make eye contact with Gabe. I didn't know why I even cared what Gabe thought.

As we reached the dance floor in the middle of the great hall, a waltz started to play. He held my right hand and my waist firmly, and somehow, without realizing it, my feet started moving. At first I had to silently count the beat: *1-2-3, 1-2-3*. I watched my feet and willed them to be graceful. I felt uneasy being up there but also defensive. I did not want to fail in front of those faces. Those people.

And, at some point (probably once I stopped thinking about all that), I realized I was actually dancing with him, enjoying the strength of his hands silently leading me. I never would have thought I'd want to do this—waltz in front of all these people—but this I wanted.

What I remember most of all is that he looked into my eyes. We were only a few inches from each other, yet he held my gaze. He looked at me intensely, like he wanted to catch every thought or emotion that flickered through me. We locked eyes, and I forgot where I was. I felt completely free. Then I stumbled on his foot. When he heard the snickers from the crowd, he released my waist and spun out and away from me, striking a disco-meets-flamenco-meets-*Dancing with the Stars* pose. There was a brief wave of stifled chortles across the room. And I giggled, too, grateful that he'd taken the attention off me. But when I looked into the crowd I saw displeased faces. Girls who felt cheated. Guys who looked confused or appalled. I even sensed dissatisfaction in the eyes of the headmaster as he, once again, approached the microphone.

"Now, Sixth Form Honors gentlemen, you may select your partners."

Ten or twelve guys stood up and approached girls, bowing in front of them. The girls all curtsied, and then the couples joined us on the dance floor, waltzing. A blond guy—textbook handsome with blue eyes and a smile that seemed oddly familiar—passed us, chuckling over his partner's shoulder, "Astor, you sneaky devil."

"Shut up, Steers."

What was sneaky? Suddenly I felt self-conscious. Stupid.

Obviously this guy had some ulterior motive. "This isn't really my thing," I confessed, as if it wasn't already obvious, and looked around for an exit plan.

"We don't have to dance," he whispered as he slowed us down until our feet weren't moving, only our bodies swaying.

"I'm Malcolm, by the way," he said softly.

"Olivia. But people call me Liv."

"Like 'live' without the e?"

I nodded.

"Nice. My name's so boring. Completely uninspired. Unabridgeable."

"Yeah, I guess Mal isn't the best nickname, huh?"

"Or Colm. But Liv . . . it's a name, a verb, a command. A notion of mortality. That's a name ripe for some epic poetry."

I smiled. "I guess." No one had ever put it quite like that.

"If I could write, I'd write you one, a poem."

I gave him a look. I mean, *seriously*? But he really seemed to mean it. "You don't even know me," I said.

"But I know I need to."

Need, not want.

I was glad we were no longer moving our feet, because I wouldn't have been able to dance through that. I looked into his eyes, semi-expecting to see a glimmer of something, like he was teasing me or purposely being over the top, but he wasn't. He seemed sincere.

"Well, you talk big," I said, and he smiled, taking it as a compliment. He pulled me a little closer, gently turning my head to rest on his shoulder, and we just moved together.

I imagined seeing us from above. I did that some-times, pictured things from different angles. Maybe it was because I was always trying to decide how to commit an image to paper. From up there, we looked like two people united, resisting tradition. Like Klimt's famous lovers in *The Kiss,* we formed a single unit, as if we were wrapped in that same glistening golden robe, protected. We were an island in a swirl of waltzing couples, a steadfast island amid a swarm of conformity.

But then the song ended and everything was normal again. By normal I mean awkward. We were, after all, not wrapped in a golden robe. We were two total strangers who'd just waltzed together in front of the entire school. Before we could say anything, that blond guy and a few others were all over Malcolm, laughing about the First Dance, what a stupid tradition it is. I gave Malcolm a quick wave and rushed away. When I got back to my table, Gabe was already gone.

AS I WALKED BACK to the dorm, Abigail came running after me. "Olivia! You missed the announcement earlier about the transfer gathering tonight. It's at Old Homestead at eight."

"Thanks, but I'm pretty tired."

"No! It's really fun! Plus, it's *mandatory.*" I wondered if she'd decided to befriend me after what Malcolm had done. I knew it was more likely she'd decided to hate me. But it seemed she had some duty dealing with the transfers, so it was her job to tell me about it. She was the "prefect," after all. Weird how close that word was to "perfect."

According to the school map, Old Homestead was Wickham's oldest landmark. Built in 1861, it was the actual home of the school's founders, Minerva and Wallace. It was on the other side of campus from my dorm, about a half-mile away.

I purposely chose the route that passed through the cemetery. I love cemeteries. I love their stillness. I love their beauty, uniform but random. For a little while, I went to a cemetery to draw, but when my mother found out, she said it was "unholy" and forbade me from going back. As I crossed through Wickham Hall's cemetery, I realized that my mom's opinion didn't really matter anymore. I lingered and glanced at a few of the old headstones. They looked ancient, all the names mossy and illegible. I was tempted to sit down and draw, but I was late. The sky was darkening, so I hurried on.

Approaching Old Homestead, I passed an old well that looked like it'd once served the house. I felt in my pockets for a penny—I'm always one to knock wood or make a wish, I mean, why not, right?—but I didn't have one. I stopped anyway just to take a look. On the outside it was perfectly maintained, but when I leaned over and peered into it, I saw it was scarred and cracked. It faded into pure black, seemingly bottomless. As I leaned into the well, I felt a gust. Colder than the air. I whipped around, but nobody was there. No wind brushed the leaves. It was unnaturally still. Suddenly I felt very alone. I pushed on.

CLEARLY, THE FACULTY HOUSING had been modeled on this house. It had the most exceptional woodwork of all, as if the house had been draped with dark lace. I had to stop on the porch to inspect the detail. Looking closely, I saw so many images emerge: angels, bees, fire, and even strange creatures. The style reminded me of William Blake, like the etchings from *The Marriage of Heaven and Hell.*

The front door was unlocked. The entryway was creaky and opulent (like everything else here), presided over by a large framed portrait of the Wickhams: Wallace and Minerva—or so I assumed. They were not the stiff-lipped Victorians I'd expected. Her beauty was somewhere between Dora Maar and Mona Lisa—exotic and mysterious but elusive. And he appeared dignified, but gentle. I heard music coming from upstairs, so I headed up the curved staircase.

"Hello?" I called.

No answer.

I followed the sounds of Katy Perry or some other piercing pop singer who didn't belong in this house. It was like a museum, exquisitely preserved. The beds were made perfectly. Pillows fluffed. There was even a crystal tumbler on the bedside table in the master bedroom. Behind what looked to be a closet door I found another set of stairs, long and narrow. Finally I came to a small circular room where the music was loudest. It was painted a deep dark red, but most of the walls were lined with books. As I stepped inside, the door slammed behind me.

When I turned, there was no door.

I was surrounded on all sides by curved, floor-to-ceiling bookcases. My pulse quickened. I banged on book spines. I could see the faintest outline of a door, but there was no latch or handle, no way out. I yelled for help and grabbed at the books, seeing if one might be a secret lever, but they all just slipped off the shelf into my hands. The song kept blaring—something about a party—and I couldn't take it anymore.

I found the spot in the room where the song blasted loudest. I seized books and threw them to the floor, completely ignoring the fact they seemed quite old and precious. Finally, there it was, underneath a vintage copy of *Paradise Lost*: an iPhone. I flipped off the song (it *was* Katy Perry), breathed in the silence, then realized I was holding something that might be useful.

I quickly navigated through the phone. Jackpot: it belonged to Abigail Steers. I checked her phone favorites. I saw Mom, selected it, and put it on speaker phone.

"Abigail," I yelled, "I'm calling your mother!" But the phone immediately lost signal. I'd forgotten you can't really make a call at Wickham Hall.

"How about I read a text exchange instead? Let's see," I quickly glanced over her texts to find something juicy. "Here's one about someone named Malcolm . . ."

An instant later, the hidden door swung open, and Abigail stormed in with several others—some of the girls from the dorm and that smiling blond guy from the dance. She snatched the phone from my hand and snapped at me, "What are you doing in here?! You're not allowed in here. This is a private room!"

"Are you serious? You invited me . . . I think you *know* what I'm doing in here!"

She looked astonished by my accusation, an almost convincing performance.

"And, let me guess," I added. "It's a Wickham Hall tradition." I turned and stormed out. At least the anger had trampled my tears.

As I ran down the final flight of stairs, I noticed him slumped on the bottom step. I could tell from behind it was Malcolm. You couldn't mistake his messy-haired silhouette. Seeing him, I could feel my emotions starting to rise up, so I gathered speed and blasted right past.

"Hey, wait!" he yelled.

But I kept running. I could hear that blond guy yelling after him. "Astor, what are you doing?! We have a meeting!"

Malcolm was running after me, but I didn't look back. I ran as fast as I could through what was, by then, darkness. When it seemed I'd lost him, I slowed down, catching my breath, but then tripped over a small headstone and wiped out right onto another one. I hadn't even realized I was back in the cemetery. When I turned over, a figure towered above me. He was there.

I stood, dusted myself off, and turned away from him. "Just go *away*!"

"I wasn't part of that. I didn't have anything to do with it."

I turned back to face him. "Then what were you doing there? With your friends?"

He was silent. So I started to walk away again.

"I can't talk about it," he said after me.

I kept walking. He ran ahead to get in front of me. He put his hands on my shoulders, stopping me. "I'm not just saying that. I really cannot talk about it. There's an oath involved."

"Of course there is," I snapped. He laughed at that. And so did I, surprisingly. "But seriously, this place—is it all traditions and pledges and oaths? Doesn't anyone want to do anything new? Or unexpected?!"

"I do!" he exclaimed.

"Me, too!" I yelled, louder than necessary.

Then neither of us knew what to do, until he leaned in and kissed me. It was just a peck, really, but it took me aback.

"There's something new," he said.

"And unexpected," I added, pulling away. I could feel my face flushing. I didn't want to like him. I wanted to turn and walk away, but I couldn't.

"I'm sorry they did that. If it's any consolation, it's just what they do. Pranks are big here, especially on the new students."

I didn't respond. I wasn't going to say something like "it's okay," because it wasn't.

"Can I show you something?" he asked. "Something amazing."

"Why?" I said it without thinking but then realized that's what I really wanted to know—*why*? *Why did you follow me? Why did you just kiss me? Why are you even talking to me?* But I couldn't ask him any of that.

"You'll see. Come," he gestured to the big mausoleum in the middle of the cemetery. "It's the Founders Tomb."

I hesitated.

"You're not afraid, are you?"

"No," I said. I wasn't afraid of the tomb.

As we walked silently toward the vault, I heard my blood pulsing in my ears. My heart was thumping so loudly I worried Malcolm might hear it as we slipped into the narrow entrance and stood alone in the darkness. He stopped in front of the farthest slab wall. As my eyes adjusted to the gloom, an artwork slowly revealed itself, as if being painted by an invisible artist.

I gasped. It was extraordinary: a landscape—a view of a seemingly endless lake with one protruding rock on its horizon—faded from years trapped inside the dank stone vault.

"Edward Hopper," he said softly.

"Seriously?"

"Did you know he went here?"

I was stunned. I had no idea. But then I smiled. Why should I be surprised at anything I learned about this place?

"They never talk about it because he got kicked out. But, rumor is, he did it."

"I can't believe it's still here," I breathed. "That no one's removed it or tried to sell it somehow."

"No one dares touch the Founders Tomb," Malcolm said. I couldn't tell if he was being serious or sarcastic.

I searched my pockets to see if there was a scrap of charcoal. There usually was. I found a stub. I stepped back from the painting to look at it again, take the whole thing in. Then I leaned in very close and started to draw. I didn't draw *on* the painting—I'd never do that—but I drew above it: an angel in flight appearing as if she was emerging from the mist on the lake.

I stepped back to take a look. It was only then I saw Malcolm's face. That sublime, defective smile. "It's incredible," he said.

I looked down, embarrassed. Then he seemed a little uneasy as well. I wasn't sure why until he hesitantly asked, "You wanna see something I did?"

I nodded, and he walked me to the other side of the chamber. There was a small intricate drawing of a forest.

"Is it in ink?"

He nodded and I looked closer. The trees were all the same or nearly identical. There was one tree in the center that appeared to be like the others at first glance. But coursing through its roots—its veins—was a streak of red. Bright red ink.

"It's a self-portrait," I said with certainty.

He looked surprised, but then not at all.

"So you're an artist, too," I added.

He shook his head. "No."

"Yes," I insisted.

He smiled, as if grateful that I thought so, but insisted, "It's not something I can do."

"What do you mean 'can'? You obviously can."

"Expectations, you know?"

I shook my head. No, I did not know.

"There's just a lot of pressure to be a certain way. Do the same things my dad did. And that doesn't include making art."

"What *does* it include?"

"Wickham Hall student government, crew team captain, Harvard, Yale Law School. There are a *number* of things I have to be a part of."

"Like . . . now?" I didn't get it. His list sounded like a resume for some job application.

He shrugged. He wasn't going to elaborate.

"But why is it so important to your dad?"

"Because I'm an Astor."

"What's that?"

His face broke again into the most perfect imperfect smile.

"*What?*" I asked, starting to feel self-conscious.

"I think I've been waiting for you my whole life."

"It must've been a pretty boring life."

"It was. Then I met you."

CHAPTER 3

Day one of classes and the first thing I learned is that I was not, in fact, a junior in high school. I was a Fifth Former or, if talking to an outsider, "a Fifth-Form Wicky." Someone said it's something they do in England. The Wickies had different words for lots of things. Not that anyone spoke to me much. I felt the entire campus was looking down on me. Or, rather, looking *through* me. No one noticed me. And I'm not just talking about the students—the teachers, too. I wasn't expecting a parade or anything, but after the public humiliation of the first day, I thought they might soften toward the transfers. At my old school, the new students would always at least be introduced in homeroom. Of course, Wickham Hall didn't even have homeroom. They probably considered it too common or something.

I can't say I minded not having to stand up and introduce myself, but a simple acknowledgment might've been nice. It was like the teachers already had their favorite star students and had no interest in a new one.

My first class was English literature. The teacher, Mrs. Winslow, explained that Minerva and Wallace Wickham had personally established the Wickham Hall curriculum. And because they were great lovers of Romantic poetry, we'd spend the better part of the first semester on it. We'd start with the "big six" writers. William Blake first.

Blake was one of my favorites, always, because he was a poet *and* an artist. He illustrated his own poems, mixing text with imagery. And that's what I liked to do. I never wrote actual poems, but I used text. Also, he was almost as obsessed with angels as I was.

We read "A Little Girl Lost" aloud. The first stanza always got me:

> *"Children of the future age,*
> *Reading this indignant page,*
> *Know that in a former time*
> *Love, sweet love, was thought a crime."*

He was so certain things would have changed for us "children of the future age." But had they? Had we even come close to attaining Blake's vision of "free love"? At Wickham Hall they wouldn't even let you be alone with a guy.

When Mrs. Winslow asked what the father in the poem might stand for, I raised my hand. I was pretty sure I knew. Social restraint, conventions, rules. But she completely ignored me. One of the Sloans from my dorm got called on instead and guess what? I was right.

Then Malcolm's blond friend piped up. "But couldn't love be a crime?" he asked, smiling incessantly. "If you loved the wrong person?"

From snippets of conversation around campus, I'd gathered that his name was Kent Steers and that he was Abigail's twin brother. It made sense. He had her same straight blonde hair. And I'd known his smile seemed familiar when I first saw him in the dining hall.

"Fascinating concept, Kent. Not a theme that's central to the poem, but very, *very* interesting," Mrs. Winslow fawned.

But none of the teacher's favorites—the Sloans or Charlottes or Dylans or Kents—seemed to notice the irony of reading this poem at Wickham Hall.

I CHECKED MY SMALL metal mailbox in the Student Activity Center on my way to lunch. I found one piece of paper, a memo marked URGENT. It read:

To: All Wickham Hall Transfer Students
From: Headmaster Thorton

Each of you needs to check in at the infirmary today for your start-of-year physical exam. Nurse Cobbs will be available all day.

I consulted my campus map and discovered the infirmary was located in one of the oldest buildings on campus, not far from Old Homestead, about a ten-minute walk. I headed over immediately, beyond relieved to have a reason to skip lunch.

Someone must have been watching as I approached the door of the old stone structure because I got buzzed in before I even knocked. I entered a hallway, long and dark, passing room after room—all empty.

"Wickham Hall is more than two hours away from the nearest hospital, so we have to be prepared," snapped the officious Nurse Cobbs, startling me as she exited one of the rooms and started to escort me down the hall. "Back in the day, with tuberculosis and small pox rampant, we needed our own miniature hospital to serve the students and faculty. These days, it's not so busy." She almost sounded disappointed.

We entered a small examination room, and she sat me on a table and did the usual: temperature, blood pressure, reflexes. She banged my knee with that rubber hammer and nothing happened.

"Maybe my nerves stayed in Vegas," I joked. She didn't laugh but instead used the moment to catch my leg off guard, successfully making it jump.

Finally, she moved me to a little school desk to take my blood. I warned her that my veins were terrible. "Most years I showed up to school with bruises because my doctor's nurse could never hit the vein. Usually they ended up sending me to the lab at the hospital."

"I'm quite skilled at this task," she snapped. And, sure enough, she was. She smiled, pleased with her handiwork as the small vial filled. But I had to look away. I couldn't stand the sight of blood.

ALL WEEK, I APPROACHED every new class—and every walk in between—thinking I might see Malcolm. But I never did. Occasionally, I thought I saw him in the distance, part of a cluster of Wickies, but as I drew closer, it was never him. I wished he'd asked for my last name or my number, but he hadn't. I wished I'd sent in a picture for the student directory instead of being an invisible "no picture provided" girl.

The only bright spot of that first week was finally getting to set foot in the Art Center. Close up, it looked like a massive spiral staircase around a giant sunken outdoor fire pit where the school apparently held an annual bonfire: the centerpiece of Fall Festival. The exterior was made of glass and metal. When I stepped inside the atrium, I was shocked to see several of my drawings in one of the galleries. As I approached, I saw a sign that read WELCOME NEW ARTISTS!

Finally, a real welcome.

"Do you approve?"

The voice startled me. It came from behind—the throaty voice of an older woman, one who probably smoked about a thousand unfiltered cigarettes a day. I turned around. She was smaller than her voice. Tiny, in fact. And ancient, but with that cool, weathered, I've-seen-the-world look of Georgia O'Keeffe or Louise Bourgeois. She was dressed like a bohemian—patterned stuff from India, Central America, Africa—nothing resembling anyone else I'd seen around here.

"I was saving your portfolios for your arrival," she said. "I decided I should celebrate the work."

I smiled, but I didn't know what to say. I'd never seen my stuff hanging up anywhere except my own wall. This was like a real gallery. It was exhilarating. But also overwhelming and terrifying. I felt exposed.

She could sense my discomfort. "Your art *should* be up there, Liv, for all to see," she stressed. "But, unfortunately hardly anyone ever comes in here." And it was true. This magnificent building was weirdly deserted.

"I'm Ms. Benson, the head of Wickham's art department."

"I'm Liv Bloom. But I guess you know that."

"Yes. May I take you to your studio?"

"Yes, please. I've only been waiting sixteen years for this moment."

MY STUDIO. IT WAS perfect. It was the kind of studio you dream about having someday, after you make it big—with high glass ceilings and natural light and a sturdy wooden easel and flat files where I could store my work.

"It's all mine?" It really didn't seem possible, but she nodded.

Ms. Benson pointed out all the materials she'd stocked for me: several different inks, every variety of charcoal and pastel, a set of oil paints, a complete double-ended Bristol marker set, and some discarded magazines and newspapers for collage. There was even an old typewriter—just like the one I'd used at home but left behind because it was too heavy.

"I looked at your work carefully and tried to anticipate your needs."

I had to prevent myself from bursting into spontaneous laughter. No one had ever been quite so thoughtful or generous with me. Not even Santa. I'd made out painstakingly detailed lists every year asking for each of the specific pigments I needed—phthalo green is expensive!—but my parents had always ended up grabbing something like a Crayola paint kit from Target, thinking that was close enough.

"I don't know what to say."

"Say you'll work. Hard. Say you'll push yourself and try things that are uncomfortable . . . like making a big mess. Drawing with your left hand. Losing control. Breathe *life* into your work. Put yourself out there. I'd like to see you try bigger canvases that would make your art—and you— really *seen*." She turned to leave but then paused by the door. "And . . . say you'll keep your eyes open and be safe. Don't find yourself alone at night."

"They're pretty strict about that around here, huh?"

"Yes, they are," she croaked. But I could tell that hadn't been what she meant.

I WAS SO ENGROSSED in my drawing I almost missed my 5 P.M. scholarship meeting. I had to rush across campus clutching the Wickham Hall map with my dirty hands. When I finally arrived, I discovered the work-study advisor was Mrs. Mulford, my dorm mistress (aka Pitchfork Lady). She snapped at me; I was eleven minutes late. She reminded me that my scholarship at Wickham Hall was dependent upon successful completion of my work shifts. Then she informed me with near glee that my work-study job partner was Gabriel Nichols.

I looked over. Of course. Gabe from First Dinner.

"The students paired off, choosing partners they felt were well suited. Mr. Nichols was not yet selected."

Gabe: the weirdo in the corner no one picked. Imagine, even the scholarship students were this judgmental. He gave me a little wave from the corner of the room, then held up his arms triumphantly, shaping his thumbs and pointer fingers into *Ls*: the universal symbol for "loser." I smiled.

"Great," I chirped to Mrs. Mulford. "That's who I would've picked anyway."

Part of me wanted to let her know she hadn't won, part of me felt sorry for him, and part of me meant it. He kind of scared me, but he also seemed more real than anyone else around here. At least he owned his weirdness. It was brave. Being at Wickham Hall kind of made me feel like a loser, too, but I'd never wear it as a badge.

Mrs. Mulford made us wait until the other teams had their assignments. Then she explained our first job was to catalog all the alumni names carved into the bricks of the catacombs. We were to start immediately. Gabe shuddered. Like, actually *shuddered*. As if he had some physical reaction to the thought of the catacombs. I asked him what was wrong, but he shrugged it off.

WE STARTED AT THE bottom of the circular stairway, the same one Abigail had led us down the day I arrived. If you looked closely at each brick, there was a name and year carved into it. Supposedly, this had been a tradition for many years, until all the bricks were carved. On the occasion of the 150th anniversary of the school, they'd decided to log all these names and create a map of their locations so visiting alumni might easily find their ancestors' bricks. So it was our job to trudge like rats through the dark underground hallway and record these names on a laptop they'd given us. It seemed like an absurd task to me, but compared to what I'd expected—having to do dishes or scrub floors Cinderella-style—it didn't seem so bad.

I read out names, and Gabe typed them into the laptop, names like Archibald Cumberland and Willfred Pinfolds. I almost giggled a few times. You could just picture these people holding lapdogs or muskets while posing for a somber Gilbert Stuart portrait like that one of George Washington on the one-dollar bill.

But Gabe was edgy, constantly looking over his shoulder. He kept jerking at the tiniest sound.

"Are you okay?"

"Fine," he said unconvincingly as he clicked on the computer. "Did you notice this laptop is completely blank and Internet disabled?"

"So?"

"They obviously don't trust us."

"Or it's a new computer and they didn't put anything on it yet."

He huffed but then lurched, apparently hearing something down the hall. His edginess was making me feel uncomfortable, too. I tried to distract him.

"Prudence Goggins. Class of 1939." I put on a crackly old voice. "I studied needlepoint and tea-making at Wickham Hall and then went on to marry the ketchup baron . . . Haverford Heinz, Class of 1938."

Gabe managed a chuckle. We turned the corner into a small nook off the hallway, and he suddenly screamed— at the top of his lungs. He grabbed my shirt and lurched backward, pulling me away from something hideous. Something horrible. The school laptop hit the floor and smashed. I fell right on top of it.

"Run! Now!" he shouted at me. And then he turned back to the darkness, addressing whatever was there. "No! Stop! Go away!"

As I was gathering myself up and pulling away, I couldn't help but quickly glance back into the dark nook—the way you have to look at a car accident as you pass—and I saw it.

Nothing.

There was nothing there. But nothing has never been so frightening.

THE BROKEN LAPTOP SAT on the table between Mrs. Mulford and us. Needless to say, she wasn't pleased, especially with Gabe.

"Considering you're on Final Warning, this incident warrants a conversation with the headmaster and could possibly precipitate your expulsion."

He stared at his lap, his hair shielding his eyes. But I could tell from his expression that, as much as he despised Wickham Hall, home was worse. I understood. I felt for him. So, without really thinking, I started to talk.

"I dropped the computer."

She glared at me. "That's not what you previously reported."

"He was just trying to be nice. To help me. Because I'm new. And I let him because I didn't know about Final Whatever."

"*Warning*," she clarified.

"But he can't be expelled for something I did. It's not fair."

I could feel his eyes on me, but I refused to look over. I was going to stick to this story. I was not on Final Warning. I had nothing to lose.

"Is this the truth?" she demanded, shifting her stare to Gabe.

"Yes," I said firmly, before Gabe could reply.

"Well, in that case," she said with a smirk, "You'll *both* receive an appropriate punishment."

OUTSIDE, GABE QUICKLY THANKED me. We walked across the quad silently for a good while. I caught a few glimpses of his face, and he was clearly wrestling with something. Finally, once we were far away from everyone, he stopped. So I stopped, too.

"Do you want to know?" he asked.

I nodded. I was prepared for the worst: A) He was mentally ill, B) He had an imaginary friend, or C) He took bath salts—not that I ever really understood exactly what bath salts were.

"I saw Lydia. She's gruesome. She was coming at us."

I nodded again. It was definitely C.

"I hear the voices of ghosts at Wickham Hall. And there

are certain places—dark, cursed places—where I can see them, too. They haunt me. All of them. I don't know what they want." He bit his lip, seeing I didn't believe him. "Wickham Hall *is* haunted. It's not a 'silly myth' like they say. Ask me questions. I'll tell you about any of them."

I was silent.

"Lydia's in the catacombs. She's the only one whose name I know. Sometimes she repeats it again and again. Her neck's kind of tweaked like it was broken or something. She wears a Smiths T-shirt, and she's insane. There's another one in Main, in the lobby. And there's one by the weeping willow tree near the well. And there's a bloody one on top of Skellenger . . . and . . ."

He stopped when he saw my face.

"Let's go to the infirmary," I managed to say. "Let's get you help."

He recoiled. "No!"

"Did you take some drugs?"

"No!"

"Do you have, you know, a medical history?"

He started to almost shake with frustration, but then he paused. Calmly, he said, "I understand why you think I'm crazy. I thought I was crazy, too. But it's too consistent. Always the same voices, the same faces in the same places. I'm telling you it's *real.*"

I paused. How do you even respond to something like that?

His demeanor changed. He was nervous now, almost desperate, and bargaining. "Look, it's fine if you won't believe me, but please, you *have* to promise me you won't tell anyone.

I've never told anyone else here. I don't even know why I told you. I was just grateful. I thought you'd understand."

I couldn't pretend I believed him, but I did promise I wouldn't tell anyone. I only hoped he wasn't dangerous. He didn't seem the type to ever hurt anyone, but he definitely seemed capable of hurting himself. I'd hate to be the person who failed to report that kid before he snapped.

He didn't want to let me walk away. I could see he felt vulnerable. But there was nothing more to say.

I'D NEVER THOUGHT MUCH about ghosts. I certainly didn't believe in them. I'd been taught when you die, you go to heaven—that is, if you've accepted Jesus into your heart. So, let's just say that is true, then what about everyone else? What about the kind man in Timbuktu who never even had a chance to hear about Jesus? My mother never had an answer for that one. My parents' church had confused me. It'd actually driven me away from God, if there was one.

But I couldn't stop thinking about Gabe's description of Lydia. What did a ghost look like? I didn't know. Did it look like a Francis Bacon painting, distorted and ethereal? Or tortured, like Munch's *The Scream*? Was a ghost more like the chubby cherubs of Titian or the horrific devils of Hieronymus Bosch?

The thought of her haunted me, so I did what was natural. Alone in my studio, I drew her. I covered the paper in black charcoal and erased her out of the blackness: a ghoulish veil. I was interrupted by a text chime. I looked.

At first it just said:

hi liv. malcolm here.

Just seeing the name made my chest thump. Seriously, like out of a Keith Haring painting—a giant heart, neon and throbbing. Before I could reply, another bubble popped up. He'd been looking for me. He finally got my number from the admissions office. He wanted to meet.

I texted back, told him I was drawing.

He offered to come meet me in the studio.

I told him another day would be better.

I wanted to see him, but my head was full of ghosts, and I couldn't possibly tell him Gabe's secret. Plus all that thumping. That rush like I had stood up too fast. Why did he do that to me? Excitement. Fear. I honestly didn't know. For all I knew, that's what love felt like. I just hoped I wouldn't fall over or—God forbid—faint the next time I saw him. Avoiding him seemed the best course of action, at least for the moment.

I made it back to my dorm just in time for Hand-shaking, the nightly ritual where every student has to shake hands with the dorm mistress and the dorm pre-fect, who, in my case, was Abigail. When she looked down and saw the charcoal I'd smudged on her palm, she huffed off to the bathroom.

I just smiled and went to get my toothbrush. I was exhausted.

EVERYTHING WAS BLACK. I could feel myself moving through the darkness. It was thicker than water, more like oil. As my eyes adjusted, I could see subtle colors in the murkiness: browns, purples, reds. It felt like I was being born or like

I was a piece of film being developed . . . until I emerged
and found I was kissing Malcolm.

My eyes were closed, but I knew it was him. I could *feel* it.
He was warm and gentle. And it felt good. I wanted it, but
I felt out of control. I couldn't have stopped if I'd tried.

I separated from myself, imagining what we looked like.
From above, I could see we were lying on a deep red velvet
blanket, two teenagers making out in the dark Founders
Tomb. But then images started to emerge from the darkness around us. At first they were pleasant: a Titian cherub,
a Chagall angel. But then one of Bosch's devils appeared.
And Munch's screaming terror. Francis Bacon's agonizing
Pope. And one of Basquiat's jagged skulls. We were surrounded by ghouls and ghosts, yet we were still kissing,
oblivious.

Then another ghost appeared. She was from a
painting I didn't recall ever having seen—glamorous
but haunted. She could have been painted by Kirchner
or Emil Nolde. She was so vivid, a beautiful girl about my
age with her copper red hair in pin curls and a beaded
flapper dress. But the dress was caked with dark blood that
had clearly drained from a slim wound across her neck.

She leaned down and tapped my shoulder. "Stop yourself!" she whispered to me. But I kept kissing Malcolm. So
she shook me harder until finally I pulled away. At once,
I was back in my body, and I looked directly at her as she
warned me, "Stop yourself or they'll get you, too!"

Suddenly I realized what was happening. It was a nightmare. I was plagued by nightmares as a child and had
learned long ago how to wake myself from one. I blinked

my eyes several times—that usually did the trick. And it worked.

I bolted upright in bed, panting with thrill and fear. It had seemed so real. But it wasn't. I flipped on the light, grabbed my notebook, and started to draw what I'd seen.

Lydia

I should've known something was horribly wrong when Cyrus Huckle came to the woods with us to sneak a cigarette. Cyrus Huckle didn't smoke. None of the Preps smoked, at least not with us.

At first he kept to himself, pacing, but then he sat next to me. I ignored him until he offered me a swig from his flask. I didn't even know what it was. I didn't care. I had two. I played Echo and the Bunnymen on my boombox—"The Killing Moon." I remember he laughed when I told him the name.

It was unusually cold for October, and someone had a blanket so we all shared it. Under the blanket, his hand reached out for mine. Our fingertips touched. And even though he was a Prep whom I despised on principle, I held his hand secretly. All my friends—the Freaks (at least that's what the Preps called us)—were sitting right there, and none of them had a clue.

As we all walked back to campus for curfew, he quietly asked me to meet him at the nook in the catacombs under Main. At midnight.

I checked into my dorm. I had to fake out even my roommate. I *couldn't tell anyone I was meeting Cyrus Huckle. No one would've believed it. Not possible. Not real. So, I put on my pajamas. I even ate a Tastykake like I did every night, just so no one would think anything was off. That was my last meal. A butterscotch Tastykake because Katie Milton was out of chocolate.*

I hid an outfit in the shower. At eleven forty, I slipped into the bathroom and put it on—my crimson Doc Martens, well-worn Dickies, my favorite Smiths T-shirt, and a flannel. I grabbed my Walkman and listened to more Echo and the Bunnymen while I stole across campus.

When I got to the nook, he wasn't there. I started to think it was a joke. Of course. Just as I was about to leave, he walked up. He grabbed my waist and pulled me deeper into the nook. We kissed, but I didn't stop the music. I really wanted to finish the song because I kind of felt like I was in a music video.

He jammed his tongue into my mouth forcefully. I noticed a bitter taste as he put his hand down my shirt. The music was so loud, I didn't hear what came up behind me. But I heard the snap of my neck while Ian McCulloch sang:

. . . the killing time
unwilling mine . . .

CHAPTER 4.

It was weird how little I saw Malcolm during those first weeks. Considering we were confined within the walls of the campus, you'd think we might have collided more often. But we had no classes together. His dorm, Pitman, was at the other end of Dorm Row from mine. And boys and girls ate all meals in separate dining halls except for Saturday Supper. And I just might've skipped most of those to work in the Art Center.

When he texted me, I was always busy, headed to class or the studio or my work-study job, where Gabe and I would enter ridiculous names into the growing database, both of us awkwardly trying to pretend that I didn't know about his delusions.

And Malcolm was busy, too—classes, meetings, sports, and whatever sorts of things it was an Astor had to do. There was little time for flirtation at Wickham Hall. The school practically seemed designed that way.

Our only shared activity was the weekly morning Chapel. Once I bumped into him there, but he was being pulled in the opposite direction by his friends. And I was quick to tell him I was headed to the studio and would see him soon. I noticed his group—Abigail, Kent, and the others—always sat in the exact same spot near the front of the chapel, so I always sat in the back. This way, I managed to avoid Malcolm (without totally avoiding him) for a few weeks. I told myself I was playing hard-to-get like all the other girls seemed to do. But, as I watched the leaves turn from green to yellows and oranges as brilliant as Cezanne's fruits, I couldn't stop thinking about that spontaneous kiss he'd given me and wondering what exactly it had meant.

At Chapel, I kept waiting for someone to come out and talk about God, until finally a girl in my art history class told me it wasn't a religious thing. It was just an all-school meeting thing, and they only called it Chapel because it was in the chapel. Every week the headmaster came out and made various announcements, most of which were boring and braggy: Wickham Hall had won This Award, so-and-so alumnus had been appointed to That International Whatever. I was already in the habit of tuning him out and counting blazers in the pews or pieces of stained glass in the windows.

But on this particular day—now early October but before summer had totally thrown in the towel—the headmaster went up to his podium. He silenced the room, took a good long dramatic beat with all eyes on him, uttered two words, and walked away.

"Headmaster Holiday" is what he'd said.

The normally reserved students jumped out of their seats, hooting, hollering, and high-fiving—behaving almost like *normal* high school kids. I remained seated. I didn't know what Headmaster Holiday meant, but I was beginning to get an idea. I looked around and caught a glimpse of Gabe as he slipped out the door, alone as usual. I considered going after him. I wanted to help him, to befriend him, but he'd told me he saw ghosts. That kind of complicated things.

Then I saw Malcolm walking up the aisle. Abigail hooked arms with him and started to drag him toward the door, but he broke away from her and gestured to his friends he'd see them later. Abigail pursed her lips. She had that look of poorly masked outrage. The others all sauntered out the big, pointed wooden doors, but she lingered and watched as Malcolm paused, looking around.

I quickly realized he might be looking for me, and I busied myself. I stood up and clicked on my phone, as if it were utterly urgent to know what the weather forecast was. My stomach started to contract into a black hole. All of a sudden I realized I hadn't been playing hard-to-get; I was nervous. Really, really massively nervous. What if he'd had a change of heart? What if he'd gotten back together with his girlfriend—he must have one, right?—and he was just coming over to tell me about her. What if it was Abigail? What if he'd been drunk or on drugs that night? What if he actually had liked me, but when he approached he realized I was not pretty after all? Or if, when we spoke, he realized I was not all that interesting? Or, worst of all, what if he'd realized I was untalented and he hated my art?

In my peripheral vision, I could see him drawing closer—a blurry apparition in a polo shirt and blazer—but I kept looking down, eyes glued to my iPhone as if I didn't have a clue he was there. Eventually he got so close, he could see the weather page.

"What's the high for today?"

Busted. I wasn't even looking at the numbers, so it took me a second to read the temperature and reply, "Sixty eight and *not* humid. For a change."

"Perfect," he said. "I've been waiting for this day."

"Oh, have you? Why?"

"Headmaster Holiday is an unexpected day off. Happens twice a year. No obligations—no homework, no practice, no pressure. A day when you couldn't *possibly* say you were too busy."

I gave him a "don't be so sure" look, but he just smiled, almost daring me to say it. I didn't. So, he put out his hand. I hesitated.

"Consider it a military mission," he said sneakily. "Two spies in enemy territory. A covert action operation. Must proceed incognito."

I joined the game immediately, peering around with narrowed eyes. I noticed Abigail, still watching us. I raised my eyebrows, gesturing to Malcolm that a rival was nearby. We grabbed hands, slinked through the gabbing students, and slipped right out those big Gothic doors.

As we hurried across campus, Malcolm let go of my hand and took out his iPod. He clicked it on and then handed it to me. A playlist called Liv, Forever was cued up.

"I made it for you. Obviously."

"Hate to tell you, but I'm not going to," I said, master-
fully concealing my shock and delight.

"Not going to what?"

"Live forever."

"Your art will. That means you will, too."

"You really talk big."

"It's your fault, Liv Bloom," he smiled. "Your epic name
brings it out in me."

We kept walking. We took a trail behind some dorms.
I began to wonder where Malcolm was leading me. He
wouldn't say. We were alone. I heard Ms. Benson's voice
echoing in my head—those strange words of warning: *Keep
your eyes open and be safe. Don't find yourself alone at night.* But
it was daytime. And I wasn't alone.

"So, are you gonna play it?"

Oh, yeah. The iPod. "Yes," I said as I glanced at the playlist. There was Nirvana, The Velvet Underground, Arcade
Fire, Bon Iver, Fleet Foxes, Bright Eyes. Even The xx.

"Not exactly what I expected."

"What did you expect?"

"Something more like *you*, I guess."

"What am I?"

"An Astor?" I said iffily, quoting him. "Whatever that
means."

"Music is something I can control. It's one place where
I can do what I want. Listen to what I want. It's invisible, so
no one else can contain it."

"No one can control your thoughts, either," I said.

"That doesn't stop them from trying. But you're right.
And they can't control what I read or the art I like. I guess

that's why I'm so into all that stuff. They can make me do certain things, but they can't make me who I am."

I nodded. I thought I understood, but I didn't really. I didn't know what it meant to be an Astor or what it felt like for someone to expect something from you. And who were "they" anyway? I really needed to Google "Astor." A normal person would've done that already. But part of me wanted to learn who he was the old-fashioned way, and part of me didn't want to know because I was pretty sure it'd scare me away.

I unraveled the earphones. I took one earbud and handed him the other, then played the first song. So we walked along the path, shoulder to shoulder, listening to Bright Eyes's "First Day of My Life."

Once again, I stepped out of myself. I flew up ahead on the path, stood on a perch, and looked back. It was the me I knew, wearing my favorite vintage red jacket. Nothing about me had changed except I was with a boy—a gorgeous boy, perhaps you could even call him a man—the kind you'd see in an Abercrombie and Fitch catalog. Or maybe J. Crew, if they were lucky. And he was playing me a song, a romantic song he'd picked out for me alone. A song I'd heard a hundred times before, but I'd never heard at all. And he was looking at me as if he liked me, like he *really* liked me. And it did feel like the first day of my life, or at least the first day of something big and new.

"This is okay, right?" he asked, speaking over the music a little too loudly. "Just walking and listening?"

"Yes, this is perfect," I said.

And we walked along a sun-dappled path, comfortable

like two people who'd known each other forever. If you'd shown me this image a few weeks ago, I wouldn't have believed you. I'd never felt particularly comfortable with guys, especially not these kinds of guys. And these kinds of guys had never been particularly interested in me. It was like Michelangelo's sculpture of the perfect male specimen *David* holding hands with a lanky, odd Giacometti figure. Not that I'm putting myself down—I like Giacometti, I really do—but I'm no *Venus de Milo*.

And, joined like this, connected by two feet of cable, Malcolm took me on what he called "The Secret Agent Tour of Wickham Hall." We heard The xx's "Crystalised" as we tiptoed through the catacombs. Bon Iver's "Towers" walked us down a secret staircase in the back of the chapel. The Velvet Underground's "I'll Be Your Mirror" sneaked us along the muddy banks of the school's massive lake. Nirvana's "Come As You Are" escorted us into the crew boathouse, and Arcade Fire's "Awful Sound (Oh Eurydice)" hummed as Malcolm paddled me across the lake in one of the sculls.

We arrived at the edge of the campus, bordered by piney wilderness, during Fleet Foxes's "Your Protector." As if Malcolm had planned it, the landscape looked just like the video. I was visibly overtaken by the view. Think Turner—expansive and magical—with strokes and dabs of vivid fall colors.

"It's the Minerva Wickham Nature Preserve."

"You guys have everything here," I said, unable to keep the awe from my voice.

He nodded. "And you're one of us now, by the way."

I smiled, a little uneasy. I wasn't quite sure how I felt

about that yet. I looked out over the terrain. Lush and seemingly endless. And we walked right into it, serenaded by the Beatles's "I'm Looking Through You."

IT WAS MID-AFTERNOON BY the time we arrived at the mountain. It wasn't a mountain, really. That's just what the Wickies called it. It was the top of a ridge overlooking the lake. Maybe fifteen feet above the water.

We sat near the edge, leaning against a tree with our shoulders touching, and looked out.

"Look familiar?"

I scanned the horizon and realized out loud, "It's the view from the painting in the tomb."

He nodded.

"So, Edward Hopper sat right here. Took all this in."

"Pretty cool, huh?" he said.

I giggled.

"What?" he asked.

"I just can't believe you're as big of an art dork as me. Not possible."

"Try me."

"Okay. What's *Guernica*?"

He sniffed. "Please, that's insulting."

"Okay, what's *Saturn Devouring His Son*?"

"Goya. It's intense. A father eating his own son. Goya painted it on the wall of his own house right before he died."

I giggled again. I couldn't believe he knew all that.

"It always reminded me of my dad," he added, his tone a little serious. "But, come on, give me something hard," he challenged before I could ask more about his dad.

"What was Marcel Duchamp's alter ego?"

"Rrose Sélavy. With two *R*s."

"And why?"

"Phonetically, it says, '*Eros, c'est la vie.*' Or 'Love, that's life.'"

"Impressive," I said, downplaying the fact I was dying inside. Brain exploding like a Pollock. Heart melting like one of Dalí's clocks.

I could see a lone boat in the distance, far, far out in the middle of the expansive, glassy lake.

"You like paddling?" I asked.

He smiled. "We call it rowing. And, yeah, I don't mind it as much as some of the other stuff. It's peaceful out there. The repetition calms my mind."

"Calms it from what?"

"Thinking too much. Worrying about my future."

"Drawing does that for me sometimes."

We were silent for a moment, and I suddenly became hyperaware of the fact that we were touching. My shoulder and hip and thigh started to warm up, burning where we were connected. My eyes wandered, looking for anything to distract me from the fact that half my body was melting into lava, and I noticed a carving on a tree next to us: someone-plus-someone in a heart. I wondered if it meant this was the Wicky make-out spot. Maybe that was why Malcolm had brought me here.

Then, as if on cue, he said, "There's something I want to do." My stomach knotted up immediately. I wasn't a good maker-outer. And I didn't know if I was ready for it because I still couldn't really believe any of this was happening.

But—he did *not* kiss me. He stood up, took my hand, and walked me to the edge of the cliff.

"You swim, right?"

"Yes, I swim," I said, acting bent out of shape by the question.

"Well, you never know. I'm not a very good swimmer, and I spend about half my life in a boat."

He stepped us right up to the edge of the cliff. I looked out.

"Do you want to?" he asked.

I nodded. "But wait." I took off his iPod and put it on the ground at our feet. Then we jumped.

I'd always been afraid of heights, but Malcolm was so sure, I forgot to waver or worry—or even wonder—before I jumped with him. We continued to hold hands as we fell. Or flew. It felt like we were flying more than falling. Like we were weightless, a single airborne object. It's true that when you do something like that time slows down. I could see us from the distance, our jump forming an arched line down the landscape—a trickle of red paint dripping into the glassy water.

Hitting the lake felt like a slap in the face, much colder than I expected. But when I surfaced, I was laughing. I couldn't help it. It just happened. Malcolm started laughing along with me. He swam over to me and took my hand again. I shivered and shook out my hair. We swam to where the water was about four feet deep and stood in it, close to each other, both still wearing our shoes. Our clothes stuck to our shoulders and chests. My feet sunk into the soft sludge.

"I knew you'd do that with me."

"That's funny, because I didn't."

"But you didn't hesitate."

"It's like you have this idea of me, and I become it," I heard myself say. But I didn't regret it. "I'm not the girl who gets up and dances in front of the entire school or jumps off cliffs."

"Yes, you are."

He was right. I suppose I was—or at least was starting to be.

He reached up to my neck, touching my locket. "I like this."

"Thanks," I said, looking down, opting not to tell him where it came from, why I never took it off.

We stood there so close to each other. The water made us sway ever so slightly, as if we were dancing again. I felt he was going to kiss me, and I quickly swished onto my back in the water. There's nothing I wanted to do more than kiss him, but it scared me that I wanted this person so much. This person I still hardly knew.

He moved onto his back next to me. We floated and looked up at the sky. Looked up at the sky and floated. Until our fingers felt like "seersucker."

That's what he said. I didn't know what seersucker was.

LATER, AFTER IT WAS dark and our clothes had dried and we'd shared a grilled cheese and black-and-white milkshake at the Tuck Shop (which, for the record, is the student snack bar), we headed toward our final stop on the tour. Old Homestead.

As we approached the house through the cemetery, I felt uneasy. Malcolm insisted no one would be there. But I told him I'd rather wait in the cemetery while he went and checked. When he dashed off, I took out my small Moleskin notebook and looked around for inspiration. As I glanced over my shoulder, a girl was suddenly there. I stood up, startled. She looked oddly out of date, kind of fifties or sixties—like one of Warhol's famous *Jackie Os*—sporting a jet-black bouffant, a smart suit, and skin that was almost as blue and pasty.

"I didn't see you there," I said.

"But you see me now?" She seemed anxious.

"You just surprised me." I studied her face. I thought I'd become familiar with all of the faces on campus, but I did not recall this peculiar girl.

"You see me? You do?!" She looked down at herself, touching her limbs excitedly as if she'd just grown them. Then I saw her wrists. Both had gashes. They were bleeding. I sucked in a breath.

"Are you okay?"

"No, I'm not. I'm not at all okay."

"Should I get someone?"

"Yes! We need to get someone! But not one of them," she said, eyeing Old Homestead.

I looked down, fumbling in my bag for my phone, and when I looked back up she was dashing away.

"Hey, wait!" I rushed after her, weaving through the tombstones, but she vanished into the woods. I paused at the edge of the dark forest.

"Hello!? Are you going to be okay?!" I yelled out after

her. But no response. No girl. I immediately started to text campus security, as Mrs. Mulford had instructed us to do in the event of an emergency outside the dorm. I typed:

wounded girl in cemetery ran into woods.

"Hey! What are you doing way over there?" Malcolm said from behind, jolting me.

I turned to him, rattled. "The strangest thing just happened. This girl was here—dressed all retro—acting really weird. And her wrists were all bloody, then she just ran away."

At first he looked confused but then he sighed, kind of annoyed. "Must've been a prank. It's Headmaster Holiday. Wickies go *nuts* with pranks on this day."

I nodded. Of course. What else would they do with a day off? Looking down at the text, I realized how absurd it was. It obviously wasn't real. I deleted it.

"Ha. Ha. Very funny!" I shouted toward the forest, just in case she (or one of her conspirators) was still lurking nearby. "I bet it was Abigail," I said, remembering the look on her face as Malcolm abandoned her earlier. "Or maybe even Gabe." He didn't seem like the pranking type, but maybe he was still mad and just trying to freak me out.

"You're friends with that Gabe guy?"

"Well, we do work-study together."

"He kind of weirds me out."

I nodded—if Malcolm only *knew*—and Malcolm smiled, brushing any thought of Gabe aside, and gestured toward Old Homestead. "But come on. The coast is clear."

"OKAY, THIS HAS TO be against the rules," I said as Malcolm unlocked the front door to Old Homestead. He had the keys; I didn't ask how.

"Don't worry," he assured me. "I promise, we can't get in trouble for this."

"It just feels wrong."

Being there reminded me of that night. And that room with no door. And his friends—Kent and the others. And Abigail laughing at me.

Malcolm sensed my reluctance. "I swear to you, if there's another prank waiting in here, you can disown me forever. But I have to show you this. It's worth it. Trust me."

And so I did. He led me into a small room I hadn't been in before. It was painted a dark velvety brown. And the walls were empty except for one small artwork. I recognized it immediately and rushed over.

"It's a William Blake," I breathed.

Malcolm nodded. "Supposedly Minerva's parents knew him."

"But he wasn't famous while he was alive." I knew Blake's story well; I'd read two different biographies. "He didn't mingle at all with the upper class. People thought he was completely insane."

"Okay, Livipedia."

I looked down, embarrassed by my freakish knowledge on the subject.

"Well, I'm equally obsessed with Banksy," he admitted. "I saw his movie fourteen times."

"Fourteen?" I asked.

He nodded. "And I conned my dad into taking me to London so I could secretly see his work."

We both just started laughing. Laughing at our dorkiness or our wonderfulness or maybe just the welcome relief of finally sharing our secret obsession with somebody else.

"What I'm really jealous of is Banksy's mystery," Malcolm added. "What I'd give to be nameless. Faceless. Invisible."

I wanted to say: *That's exactly how I feel at Wickham Hall: nameless, faceless, invisible. Except when I'm with you.* But then I felt it again. A chill. I whipped around. Nothing. I thought again about Gabe and his ghosts.

"What's the matter?"

"I just got a chill, I guess."

He wrapped his arm around me. "Maybe your clothes are still damp."

"Maybe."

I looked around again and then hesitantly asked, "So, there are rumors . . ."

"That the school's haunted," he said, finishing my sentence.

I nodded.

He said, "Who knows. Maybe it is."

WE ENDED THE DAY (I can confidently say it was the best day of my life) in my studio at the Art Center, working. As usual, it was a ghost town—all the other studios were empty—so we had total privacy.

I started a collage, a picture of the two of us jumping off the cliff. I played with the blur of our movement, so you couldn't really tell if we were falling or floating. Floating or falling. This was being with Malcolm. The picture was more an impression than an actual depiction of the moment.

He sat near me, working on his own piece. We were silent. Just being together and creating. We were Alfred Stieglitz and Georgia O'Keeffe. Jackson Pollock and Lee Krasner. Diego Rivera and Frida Kahlo without all the philandering and substance abuse. It was the kind of scene I might have conjured as the Perfect Boy Scenario if I was the kind of person who sat around and thought about things like that.

He closed his sketchbook, put it down, and came over to me. He looked at my collage.

"It looks like we're flying."

I smiled. He leaned closer, studying the details carefully. It made me both thrilled and uncomfortable, as if he were examining me. Or looking *into* me, because that's really what he was doing. However cryptic and controlled, every single thing I drew revealed something about me. *I'm afraid. I'm lonely. I feel invisible. I feel out of sync with the world.* But this one, the one he was looking at, said: *I like this boy. A lot. I feel so free I could fly with him.* I wanted him to see that. I wanted him to understand what I could never say out loud.

He turned to me. "Draw on me."

"What?"

"Draw on me. Tomorrow we'll be in classes. Apart. And who knows when I'll get you to hang out with me again. I want to have you there with me."

After he said that, he took his shirt off. His body was

perfect. I don't mean "six-pack" perfect. I've never understood why girls even liked that so much. No, Malcolm's
body was perfect in a different way. His shoulders were
broad and strong, from rowing I guess. But he was skin-
nier than I'd expected. Lanky. Not much hair on his
chest. And his skin was like warm cream—smooth and
soothing—except for a single mole on his right shoulder
just beyond the clavicle. I guess his body was perfect the
same way every other part of him was perfect, in that it
wasn't. His flaws perfected him.

I chose a plum-colored Bristol marker. "Are you sure
you want to be my canvas?" I asked in a French accent for
no particular reason.

"*Oui,*" he replied.

I laughed. "It won't come off for days."

"Good."

I paused. "Will you draw on me, too?"

"If you want me to."

I nodded. So he reached over and selected a marker—a
deep green. "Like your eyes," he said. I looked down, and
my face went hot. No boy had ever noticed the green in my
eyes before. On first glance they appear brown, and I guess
most guys had only ever given me one glance.

I positioned him on his back on the floor, like a patient
on the operating table. And I stretched out on my stomach,
propping myself up on my elbows right at his shoulders.

He looked straight up at the ceiling. "I can see us," he
said.

"I do that, too, sometimes. It's like I fly out of myself
and hover, watching."

"No, I mean I can *literally* see us," he said, chuckling and gesturing above.

I looked up and there we were, a faint reflection. I lay on my back next to him and put my arms over my head. "Look, it's like we're flying. Superman style."

"It is."

I noticed our reflections were speckled with the stars that shone through the glass ceiling. "Or like we're nothing."

"Just vapor," he added.

Then I turned back onto my stomach and started to draw. I had to start at the mole. I placed the marker right on it and wrote *vapor* up across his shoulder. Then I wrote *invisible* down his upper arm, moving the word with the curve of his muscle, defined but not bulging. Solid. I gently leaned on top of him, and a wing took shape across his chest and bloomed—not into a bird as I'd first intended, but into an angel. Rather than have the angel spread her wings across his chest, I made her kneel, one wing pulled into herself. A resting angel. Banksy frequently did those.

He couldn't really see what I was doing. He looked up at the reflection to get a clue, but it was too far away for him to decipher much. "Is it you?" he asked.

"Maybe." I kept drawing. Words folded into wings. A tree sprouted, poised on a cliff that hung over water. And in the water were his hands. His strong fingers. Eventually everything I associated with Malcolm figured across his chest. Our story. I worked slowly and he lay still, receiving. He trusted me. He watched my face and seemed to enjoy feeling every mark, as if each one was a stroke of affection. And each one was.

When I finished, I lay down on my back next to him. "Thank you," he said and turned on his side to face me.

I turned my head and looked into his eyes. They were an almost unreal, saturated blue as if painted by Yves Klein himself.

"I really want to kiss you right now," he said.

"I really want to kiss you, too," I confessed, not even embarrassed to say it. But, just then, we heard the footsteps approaching, padding across the concrete studio floor. I sat up. It was Ms. Benson.

"I saw the light on. You're just about to miss curfew. You need to go. Both of you. *Now*."

She saw his shirtlessness. It was a major infraction— to quote section 4, part 2e of the student handbook: "Under no circumstances should a student disrobe in the presence of a student of the opposite sex." But Ms. Benson just said, "Interesting canvas, Liv. However, not exactly what I meant when I said your art should live and breathe."

MINUTES LATER MALCOLM AND I were briskly walking across campus along with many other Wickies rushing to make curfew. But I doubt any of them had just drawn all over the chest of someone they were falling in love with.

Suddenly we were at Skellenger. Abigail stuck her neck out, looking for latecomers. She pretended not to see me—or him—and stepped back inside.

"Let's sneak out," he blurted.

I hesitated. Wickham Hall's campus security was omni-present.

"Not tonight. But when the time's right. Then I can draw on you."

He held up the green marker, which he hadn't had time to use. He'd pocketed it. But I was still reluctant.

"It's the only way to have any time together. Alone."

"Okay," I said and then turned to run into my dorm, not looking back.

CHAPTER 5

I wanted to know more about the Wickhams, specifically how and why they'd ended up with a William Blake. So I did some research. The Wickham archives were preserved at Old Homestead and all the school records were maintained at the Headmaster's Quarters, but there was a tiny section in the library dedicated to the early history of the school.

Minerva Savage met Wallace Wickham in 1849. Wallace was thirty-four and Minerva twenty-four, which was already considered an old maid back then. Wallace was a lot higher on the social spectrum than Minerva, and so his family was not pleased. They'd chosen another woman for him, but Wallace loved Minerva and insisted on marrying her. Apparently it was so scandalous it even made the cover of the Sunday edition of *News of the World*. (Yes, *News of the World* was already peddling gossip way back when.) Wallace's parents practically disowned him, but because he was their only son, he received his inheritance when they passed anyway.

Wallace married for true love. And truly love he did.

Among their papers—mostly handwritten notes on curriculum and school traditions—was a series of love letters. I'd read some pretty good love letters in my sixteen years. None addressed to me of course. I'd never received anything more elaborate than a drugstore valentine from Doug Caswell in the fifth grade. But I'd read letters by Van Gogh and Beethoven and dozens of poets—yes, I know, I spent far too much time on the Internet—and these Wickham letters ranked right up there. They were written when Wallace set off to the United States in search of land for a school. They desperately missed each other and constantly referenced lines from their beloved poets. In one letter, Wallace listed numerous names of poems for Minerva to read—Lord Byron's "She Walks In Beauty," "Love" by Wordsworth, and Keats's "A Thing of Beauty"— almost like an old-fashioned playlist for her.

In the letters, Wallace and Minerva detailed their dream of creating a school steeped in nature and wilderness. A place to study the humanities—poetry, literature, the fine arts—and embrace Romanticism. A place where they could seek peace from his overbearing family. A place where society wouldn't disdain them for their choices.

Wallace found this land in 1859 and purchased it immediately. He wrote to Minerva, calling it "a wildlife sanctuary where ideas could be explored and minds opened." I imagined them hiking through the nature preserve and being the first to discover the mountain and its glorious view over the lake. I wondered if they'd kissed there or jumped off the cliff.

And, finally—when I'd practically forgotten what I was looking for—I came across a reference to the Blake. Minerva's father, a blacksmith, had been Blake's neighbor when Blake moved to Felpham in Sussex. They'd become friendly. Minerva's father had done some work for Blake, and Blake paid him with the drawing, a sketch for *Milton*, which he wrote while in Felpham. Minerva had always loved the drawing and, in one of her letters to Wallace, instructed him to "please build a small chamber for its viewing" in Old Homestead.

Minerva died in an accident ten years after founding the school, so she never saw Wickham Hall rise to its place as one of the top preparatory schools in the country. And poor Wallace didn't last long after her death. One article mentioned that he "continued to talk to her and to write her love letters until the day he died." He believed that her spirit lingered and that he communed with her. Apparently he'd even attempted to take pictures of it. It was sad but somehow beautiful. The poor guy really couldn't bear to live without her.

Their only child, Elijah, became a teacher at Wickham Hall. He took over the school until his own death many years later. There were numerous articles about the awards Elijah had won, details about how he'd brought the school into the twentieth century—embracing technology and instigating Wickham Hall's rigorous academic testing.

What would the Wickhams think of their school now? Sure, it still had the nature preserve, but it now stood against everything they had believed in. It had become the most elite of the elite. It *was* the society that disdained people like them: people foolish enough to marry for real love. There was no time to enjoy nature. No time to stand in awe. No time to find that person you couldn't live without.

There were no Minervas here. I might have been close, but I didn't belong.

I ARRIVED IN MY studio the next day and found a large canvas, freshly stretched and gessoed. Oil paints and solvents were already placed on a palette nearby. I could smell the turpentine from five feet away.

Ms. Benson stood nearby looking quite proud of herself.

"Subtle hint," I said.

She chuckled but kept her eyes trained on me, urging me to approach the giant canvas.

"Go on! Make it big and messy! Give me some heart, some life!" she cackled.

I paused. Then she moved closer to me and got quite serious.

"You are so talented. Do you understand? Your skill is *exceptional*. If you unleash and add true emotion to your work, it will sing, Olivia! It will fly!" She started to walk away but then paused. "I understand it's hard. From what I know of your past, your story's not so different from my own. But if you don't do this—explore your emotions and truly open yourself up and put yourself out there—well, then, you're not truly alive."

The studio door shut behind her.

I stared at the canvas. I tried to pretend I didn't know what she meant. But I did know. I understood her completely. I just wasn't ready yet.

AT OUR MONTHLY WORK-STUDY meeting, Mrs. Mulford kept me and Gabe waiting while she updated and dispatched all the other duos. Once we were alone with her, she finally told us that, yes, we were still assigned to the bricks in the catacombs. I could feel the anxiety mounting in Gabe, so I tried to see if good ole Pitchfork Lady would cut us a break.

"I was wondering, Mrs. Mulford, if maybe you might want to assign us to a different task?" Gabe shot me a "shut-up" look, but I continued, "Considering the laptop incident and everything. Maybe we'd be more productive in a different environment."

"No way!" Gabe protested. "We *love* our job, Mrs. M! Best job ever."

She flashed a brittle smile. "Good. Because this task *must* be completed before Fall Festival. No discussion. With regards to the laptop, I've temporarily procured Mr. Nichols's personal computer as part of his punishment. And as for you, Miss Bloom, I spoke to the headmaster. Consider yourself officially notified of your First Warning. You are now excused."

WE ENTERED STUFFY NAMES from years past—more unreal ones like Elias Higgenbotham and Edward Britteridge. I tried to entertain Gabe, acting like I had before, like everything was normal. But he wouldn't laugh, so I stopped.

"What exactly do you see?" I asked. I *was* curious.

"Just stop. I know you don't believe me."

"But I'm trying to understand. Do you see one right now?" I demanded.

"No. If I saw one right now, we wouldn't be here. She's usually down the hall in that nook place."

"She stays there?"

"It's the only place I've ever seen her. But I can hear her other places sometimes." He started to say more but stopped himself, biting his lip as if to hold himself back.

"But not right now?"

"No."

"Good." I kept reading names: "Herbert Carver, 1874. Elizabeth Brewster, 1873." And then, "Balthazar Astor, 1885. Wait, do you think he's related to Malcolm?"

Gabe scowled at me. "Duh."

"It says 'V.P.' at the bottom. Was he like vice president of the school?"

"Guys like that aren't *vice* anything. They're presidents. I bet it stands for Victors President."

"What's Victors?"

His eyes narrowed. "Seriously?"

"Come on, I'm new, remember?"

"The Victors. It's a secret society. And your friend Malcolm belongs."

I winced. "What do they do?"

"I don't know. Like I said, it's secret. You think they'd tell me?" He shook his head, disgusted. "I've heard they have rituals. But I'm not kidding, it's all seriously secret. They take oaths and shit."

"Oaths?"

"Yeah."

I shivered. *Oaths.* That's what Malcolm had said. Suddenly, it all made sense: all that talk about him having to be a part of things, those mysterious "things" he couldn't talk about.

"And Malcolm's definitely in it?"

"Um, *yes.* If there's one person I *know* is in it, it's him. And that's proof right there," he said, gesturing to the brick. "That's how you get in, supposedly—blood. You have to share blood with someone who was in before."

Something washed over me right then, a feeling of sickness and powerlessness. I was Christina in Andrew Wyeth's *Christina's World*: stranded in a field, helpless and alone. Faceless. And Malcolm was the house: safe, secure, poised on top of the hill. I knew it had all been too good to be true, that there was something wrong with him, there *had* to be.

Gabe saw my face. "Don't tell me you *like* him." He said *like* as if it were the most disgusting verb in the dictionary.

I paused for too long.

"I thought you were different," he snapped. "Otherwise, I never would've told you."

"I *am* different. *He's* different, too, I swear—"

"He's *not* different. He *is* them. In fact, he's worse than they are because he pretends to be something else." Gabe turned and started to walk away.

"You can't say that! You're just pissed because I don't believe you!"

He stopped and turned back to me, fierce. "Believe this: There is something evil here, and they're all part of it."

"That's ridiculous!"

He opened his mouth, but closed it. His eyes widened. His face went pale. He shook his head. "Lydia's coming," he whispered as he backed away, then turned and ran down the hall, leaving me alone.

I remained because I didn't believe in ghosts. There was nothing to be afraid of. And part of me kept thinking that this might be some elaborate prank on Gabe or *by* Gabe. I checked my watch. Our shift was not done, so I started to pack up the computer to go after him. As I zipped up the travel case, I felt it again—that chill. I hurried toward the steps.

When I arrived at the top of the spiral staircase, I saw Malcolm immediately. He was hanging out with Kent in "their" area, the cluster of leather chairs that looked ideal for pipe smoking. Kent was always smiling. He was the polar opposite of his twin, Abigail. I guess he got all the fun genes when their chromosomes split, if that's even what happens.

Malcolm's back was to me. And Kent, on his other side, was too busy listening to his own voice to notice me. I wanted to talk to Malcolm, but approaching him when he was with Kent felt too awkward. Also, I needed to find Gabe. Insanity aside, we had work to finish. We were both now on "warning." So I kept walking.

As I passed, Malcolm turned and saw me. "Liv!" he called.

I gave a little wave and rushed along. But he jumped up and followed.

LIV, FOREVER   81

I paused and looked down. I felt naked talking to him in front of his friends. "Hey, sorry. It's just I'm busy with my work-study job."

He leaned in close and whispered, "Tonight. It's a full moon. And security will be distracted because the head-master's having an event."

When he spoke to me, Kent disappeared. So did Gabe. So did our job, so did whatever "warning" had been threatened. Thinking about a night alone with him, I couldn't help but smile. He knew it was a yes.

"I'll text you details."

"Another military mission?" I asked with fake spy seriousness.

He nodded.

"Ten-four," I said with a smile, then turned and left Main, heading down the dramatic stairs into the chilly night.

THE PLAN WAS QUITE complicated. All the dorms had alarm sensors on the doors, so the only way to get out was through a first-floor window. Most of the first-floor windows were permanently locked, but the dorm prefects lived in the rooms with windows that opened to the outside. It was a sign of trust (and a fire safety thing). Since Malcolm, of course, was a dorm prefect, he could easily get out. And he'd figured out a way for me to. He said he knew Abigail wouldn't be in her room at 11 P.M., and he'd leave a master key under her doormat. All the prefects had master keys.

At exactly 11 P.M., I was to come down the back stairs of the dorm, at which point he would provide a distraction so no one would be in the common room. Then I'd use the key to enter Abigail's room and climb out the window. It terrified me so much: the thought of being caught and punished by Mrs. Mulford, promoted to Final Warning like Gabe, or even expelled. But it was also exhilarating. I'd never even considered doing something so dangerous before, something that could jeopardize my life here, my studio, my luck. And best of all, I'd be—quite literally—stepping all over Abigail Steers as part of my escape.

As I climbed down the back stairs, I heard music blasting. As a distraction, Malcolm had placed some speakers in front of the dorm and was playing "Come As You Are." From the stairs, I could hear my dormmates tittering, rushing to the front windows to see who was playing this potentially romantic gesture and speculating for whom. If they only knew. I smiled to myself as I snatched the key and slipped into Abigail's room.

It wasn't what I expected. It was a mess, actually: piles of her clothes, discarded shoes. I stepped on a hairbrush—a particularly sharp one—and, in order to keep from yelping, I collapsed on her bed. Also, I couldn't help myself; I had to snoop. Just a little. This was a military mission, after all. I looked in her bedside table drawer: Elizabeth Arden Eight Hour Cream, Kleenex, iPhone charger. Boring.

I went to her computer, woke it up. Her calendar was on the screen. It detailed her every move, all color-coded. Tonight at ten thirty there was a "meeting." In purple. There were numerous purple "meetings" across September and October, always in the evening. Sometimes quite late, even after curfew. Unless there was a secret

Alcoholics Anonymous program on campus, I was pretty sure they involved the Victors.

I heard voices returning to the common room. I dashed out her window, carefully pulled it closed and crept away into the darkness.

Malcolm had texted me extremely specific directions, taking into account which parts of campus were the most brightly lit (to be avoided, of course). In certain places, he even told me how many steps to take. I held my phone in my hand, cupping it to minimize the light, as I stole through the darkness.

I snuck around the back of the Art Center, along the tall wall that looked down on its spacious outdoor theater and fire pit, and then rushed past the old well. Following his instructions, I dashed into a grove of pine trees but stumbled on a pinecone and fell at the foot of a majestic weeping willow tree. As I stood up, I felt it again: a chill. It rushed past me, through me, almost. I turned. Nothing. Silence except for my noisy heart—frightened or perhaps just filled with anticipation.

When I finally arrived, I found Malcolm waiting for me, pacing between two trees. He wore his class blazer over a fully untucked oxford shirt; somehow he made the Wickham Hall garb look cool. And his even-messier-than-usual hair formed a silhouette like a wild and dark crown.

"Thank God you made it," he whispered. His blue eyes popped in the moonlight, looking anxious. I laughed quietly. Everyone at Wickham Hall was so terrified of getting in trouble.

"Your comrade-in-arms wouldn't abandon you in the field," I assured him as he led me silently through some trees to a clearing where he'd spread out a blanket.

"Look," he said. He lay down on his back. I lay down next to him and followed his gaze. There was an opening in the canopy of trees where we could see the brilliant moon. And stars. Hundreds of them. He took my hand. He held it strongly—with commitment. We lay there silently for a long while until he spoke.

> *"Bright star, would I were steadfast as thou art—*
> *Not in lone splendour hung aloft the night*
> *And watching, with eternal lids apart,*
> *Like nature's patient, sleepless Eremite,*
> *The moving waters at their priestlike task*
> *Of pure ablution round earth's human shores,*
> *Or gazing on the new soft-fallen mask*
> *Of snow upon the mountains and the moors—*
> *No—yet still steadfast, still unchangeable,*
> *Pillow'd upon my fair love's ripening breast,*
> *To feel for ever its soft fall and swell,*
> *Awake for ever in a sweet unrest,*
> *Still, still to hear her tender-taken breath,*
> *And so live ever—or else swoon to death."*

Of course I knew the poem; we'd just studied it in English lit. But I'd known it before Wickham. John Keats. "It's beautiful. And impossible," I said.

"You think so?"

"That's what it's about, right? The paradox. You wish a

moment could last forever. But it can't. We are not stars. And if we were, we'd be distant, immaterial. Alone. It's pretty bleak actually."

"I was trying to be romantic."

"Mission accomplished."

He smiled and turned over onto his stomach. "It's one of my favorites. Always has been." He took my right arm in his hands, pulled out the green marker (he'd remembered it!), and carefully started to draw along the inside of my forearm. I didn't look until he was finished. Two stars. But stars like you've never seen before—expressive, singular—more like Van Gogh's than Rihanna's. I smiled, and he knew I loved it.

Then he reached into his pocket and slipped a ring onto my finger. My right ring finger. My breath caught in my throat. I lifted my hand to examine: a gold Wickham Hall band with *B.A./V.P. 1885* inscribed in Wickham Hall's trademark font below the insignia. It gave me a weird feeling in my stomach.

"It was my great-great-great-grandfather's."

"Balthazar?" I whispered.

"How did you know that?"

"I have my spy ways," I said, trying to lighten the mood, which suddenly felt very heavy. "Ways that involve my scholarship work-study assignment to record every name inscribed in the bricks in the catacombs."

"Oh."

"1885. And V.P.—that means Victors President, right?"

He looked right at me. Silent.

"I know you can't talk about it. And I'm not going to

ask you to. But can you just tell me there's nothing sinister about it?"

He laughed, surprised. "Yes, I can confirm there's nothing sinister about it. Just snobby. Elitist. Stupid."

I stared at him. "I'm trying to believe whatever that secret society is and does has nothing to do with us. And you remain *steadfast*." I felt better. I'd said it.

"It doesn't. And I will," he said. We were face to face. Again. So close that his breath warmed me. We looked into each other's eyes. Without thinking, I reached behind his head and pulled his lips to mine. And we kissed.

Had I thought first, I never would've done it. I'd never done anything like that before. Of course I'd fooled around with boys, but I'd always been passive. I'd never felt like that before. It felt urgent. Essential. I forgot about all the things I'd always stressed about during a kiss. Stupid things. In fact, there was no thought at all. I just kissed him. And he kissed me.

I have no idea how long it went on for, but when it ended—as effortlessly as it'd begun—he said it: "I love you." Those three words every girl dreams about hearing. Every girl except me. I was terrified of those words, and he could see it on my face.

"It's too soon?" he asked.

"No, I mean, yes, it's just . . ." How could I explain I'd never said those words before? Not to anyone. Ever. Not even my parents. How could I explain I'd been moved from foster home to foster home for seven grueling years? How could I explain that, as obsessed as I was with the Romantics, I did not really believe in love?

I considered telling Malcolm everything, all these words and thoughts and feelings I'd kept to myself for so many years. I really did consider telling him, but right then we heard a faint crunching sound.

We froze.

"What was that?" I asked.

He lifted his finger to his mouth.

I heard the sound again. Footsteps on fallen leaves. Someone sneaking up on us—probably campus security.

"I'm already in trouble with Mrs. Mulford," I whispered.

He blinked a few times, concerned. I hadn't told him. He thought for a moment, then said, "We need to split up. You go that way. I'll go the other way and try to distract them. Okay?"

I nodded.

"*Now!*" he urged.

I jumped up and ran back the way I'd come. Around the graveyard, under the pines. Too scared to look back. A vision of being sent back home flashed into my mind. I couldn't do it. I couldn't go back. As horrible as Wickham Hall could be, it was better than home. I had my studio. I had Malcolm. I ran for my life.

I paused at the old well to catch my breath. I told myself how silly I was—this was not life or death.

How silly I *was*.

I looked around—no one was coming—so I leaned on the well, trying to calm down. I looked into its blackness. Abyss. Then something suddenly rushed up from the dark, and that cold chill slapped me in the face. My head whipped back from its force. And that's when everything went black.

FALLING INTO NOTHINGNESS. DARKNESS. But I see skulls. Bodies. Velvet. Starched white linen stained with dried blood. Ribbons.

Fingernails scraping the stone walls. Dirty fingernails, clawing at crude drawings on the stone. A ring on her finger.

Landing on lifeless bodies with a thud. Flesh, unaware.

Screams of girls. Terrified. Terrorized. Deeper voices chanting words I don't know but sort of recognize. Latin, maybe. A song emerges, high pitched. Voices in unison. A chorus singing the Wickham Hall alma mater.

Florence

I'd had designs on Willfred Pinfolds since coming to Wickham Hall. He was a fizzing beauty but wishy-washy when it came to the fairer sex. That is, until this particular night, when he had some whiskey his roommate smuggled back from Manhattan. It must've been quite potent because Willfred was off his chump, and I was quite happy to indulge his desire for a little caper.

What place more romantic to meet your paramour than the Skellenger cupola? It was so tiny two people had to rub skin just to squeeze in together.

I gazed into the sky, streaked with slivers of clouds that looked like claw marks. It was exceedingly bright, as there was a plump full moon. And we were up so high, practically next to it.

"Let's pretend we are atop that glorious Statue of Liberty! Peeking out from her headband!" He was silent so I continued. "My parents came over from Dublin, you know."

"Oh, I know," he said, as if it was something distasteful.

"Everyone came over at some point."

"Some more welcome than others," he muttered.

"Apologize," I demanded.

He just chuckled.

"Apologize right now, you!"

"No. Let's climb out the window, to the very tip top."

"You're pretty well over the bay."

"I'm fine. Just do it. I dare you. Then I'll kiss you."

Who wouldn't want a kiss from Willfred Pinfolds, even if he was a nasty drunk? And I was always one for a dare.

Little did I know, I was en route to my earth bath. My eternity box. At least my body was.

CHAPTER 6

I found myself still slumped over the side of the well, panting and unsure what had happened. Shaken but okay, I heard some feet skittering away over pine needles—I knew the sound by then. Surely it was Malcolm, but I couldn't see him. I called out for him. No response.

When I turned, I suddenly came face to face with a pale girl. She was faint, as if painted in watercolor. She started to say something to me, but when I saw the gash across her neck, I turned to run.

I abandoned all attempts to hide myself. In fact, I ran toward the light and anyone who could save me from that horrible girl. It wasn't just that she was bloody and faint— what frightened me most was that I *recognized* her. I'd met her. I'd talked to her. It took me an instant to remember; I'd seen her in that dream. It was definitely her, the one with red pin curls and that bloody flapper dress. I ran so fast I could almost feel the air rush through me, constantly glancing back to see if she was there. She was not.

I took the shortest possible route to the center of campus then headed toward the dorms. My mind calmed. I realized it was probably another prank. But this one was too real. I needed to tell Malcolm what I'd seen. I saw him moving through the shadows along the side of his dorm.

"Malcolm!" I cried in the loudest possible whisper. But it wasn't loud enough. If I was any louder, I knew I'd wake someone, so I ran toward him as fast as I could and nearly caught up with him as he was approaching his window.

"Malcolm!"

He turned and looked right at me. He was so clearly fed up with me. Sick of my dead heart. Sick that he had told me those three words, and I hadn't even managed a response. His eyes didn't even meet mine.

"It's so complicated. Please believe me. There's so much I need to explain to you. But just now, I saw something terrible. A dream or something . . ." But he turned away from me.

"Malcolm?! Please! Don't just ignore me!"

He opened his window and climbed in. I ran over to the window as he pulled himself through. I looked up at him. But he slammed the window closed and shut the curtains.

I collapsed on the ground, waiting for I don't know what. Before I knew it—as if I'd fallen asleep or time had magically fast-forwarded—the first inklings of dawn were starting to break. I needed to get back to my dorm before sunrise. I needed to keep myself in Wickham Hall long enough at least to see Malcolm and try to explain things to him. It wouldn't be easy. I'd never told anybody those feelings before. Explained how I'd been given up, dumped, handed off, passed around, and forgotten. I'd been unloved so long I could hardly even say it to myself.

I hurried toward my dorm, my mind racing. Not really paying attention, I reached out to turn the doorknob but recoiled from a shocking pain. Confused, I tried again, this time watching myself. I gently placed my hand onto the metal. I noticed it felt different—softer, almost like clay except I couldn't shape it. And when I moved my hand to turn the doorknob, it stung and seared my palm. Shaking my hand out, I stepped back from the dorm to check it out, suddenly imagining a high-tech security system involving electro-shock doorknobs that punish dormitory escapees. I wouldn't have put it past Wickham Hall.

As I was backing up, I noticed how quiet it was. I looked down and saw I was stepping on dry fall leaves, but they weren't crunching beneath my feet. I kicked my foot through them, but instead of fluttering up off the ground they barely trembled. And I felt a burning pain seep through my shoes.

Something was terribly wrong.

"Help! Somebody help me!"

Nothing. No response. So I cried louder, "Help! I'm stuck out here! Somebody come help! Please!"

I collapsed onto the ground. I swung my arms and felt stinging pain as they whipped right through the dead leaves. *Through* them. Not possible. I paused—calmed—tried to pick up a leaf. I focused intensely. I *had* to pick up that leaf. It would mean everything was normal. I managed to manipulate it between my fingers, but touching it caused a burning sensation on my fingertips as if its orange-red color was actual fire. I moved it barely—almost imperceptibly. Then I dropped it and slumped over, my whole being exhausted and weakened as if I'd just carried a heavy piece of furniture up a flight of stairs.

"You fool," a voice hissed from above. "Save your strength!"

I looked up at the massive dorm and caught a glimpse of a girl—up in the cupola, the tiny room atop the roof. Even from where I stood, I could tell she looked different, almost airy and grey.

"You! Up there? Can you help me?!" She just stared at me so I kept at her. "What are you doing? How did you get up there?" We'd been told the cupola was sealed off because of an accident many years before.

"Go away!" she yelled.

Before I could protest, she hurled herself from the cupola and came soaring down toward me. I lurched backward, stumbling, trying to avoid getting hit. *My God, this girl just committed suicide.* I looked away and winced, afraid to see the point of impact. I expected to hear a thud, a scream, the cracking of bones. All I could hear were birds chirping.

After a moment, I dared to look. She was as gruesome and bloody as I'd expected, but she was standing on her feet. Alert. She wore a black jumper over what was once a white blouse, with large, billowy sleeves—like out of a Mary Cassatt or Renoir portrait, except the large collar was caked with dried blood that had dripped from her ears and nose and big blue eyes. As she walked toward me, I could see, like the other girl, she was not made of flesh.

I jumped to my feet and ran, not looking back. I ran straight to Malcolm's dorm, trying to contain my desperate fear that this was *not* a Wickham Hall prank. As I approached his dorm, two crew team members were heading out for rowing practice. They ignored me, as usual. But that meant Malcolm would probably be getting ready for practice, too. I slinked in the door before it closed. I rushed to his room. I knew it was in the same spot in the building as Abigail's—on the first floor, off the central common room. His door was cracked open, a light on. I slipped in.

He was shirtless, standing close to the mirror, staring into it intently. As I got closer, I saw he was tracing the lines that I'd drawn on him.

"Something terrible's happened, Malcolm. Something's wrong. It's like I'm invisible. *Really* invisible. And there are girls, gruesome girls—one at the well. Another at my dorm. And . . ."

He wouldn't look at me.

"*Malcolm.*" I walked up to him, stood right behind him, and gazed into the mirror.

I was not there.

Before I could scream, he turned and walked right *through* me. It hurt. It stung like brain freeze but all over my body. I realized it must be a dream. Of course! That's why I'd seen the girl from my dream, because *this* was a dream. A nightmare. Just like the ones I'd had as a kid. I tried my wake-up technique—blinking my eyes. Nothing.

I shook my head vigorously. Wildly, even. Still nothing, except I felt dizzy. I collapsed on Malcolm's bed.

"Am I . . . ?" I couldn't say it. You're not supposed to be able to say those words. It's against science. Against nature. "I can't be because I'm here. Right, Malcolm?"

No response.

I could feel my head in my hands. I could even feel the hair on my head. And I was sitting on a bed, wasn't I? For a moment I smiled—all this must prove I existed, I was alive— until Malcolm leaned down and reached through me, grabbing his backpack. Again, a burn ripped through me.

I started to panic. "Malcolm! You *can* hear me!" This time I yelled, certain that because he loved me, he would hear me. "You *have to*!"

I grabbed at his shoulders to shake him, but my hands whipped right through him—stinging, as if his body were made of flame. He slung on his backpack and left the room.

He couldn't hear me or feel me or have any clue I wasn't safely back in my dorm. But in my panic, I suddenly remembered I knew someone who possibly could.

THERE WAS A CHANCE I'd find Gabe in the Pit eating breakfast, so I headed toward Main. As I crossed the quad, I searched for clues that might tell me what was happening, what I'd become. I walked on the earth. I felt lighter but was still affected by gravity. I could look down and see my legs, my body, my arms—I could even see the stars that Malcolm had drawn on my forearm—and it all looked pretty much normal. I put my hands together, and I could feel myself. It wasn't quite like before, but I could feel *something*. And at least it didn't hurt.

Clearly nobody else could see me. They walked straight toward me. I kept moving out of the way, protectively, because of the pain I felt when I crossed with someone or something.

One thing I couldn't feel was my heart. If the old me had been racing across campus, trying to figure out if I was dead or alive, my heart would've been pounding so hard I'd hear it in my ears, feel it in my temples. I felt nothing physically, but my emotions were rushing and raging and battling with my poor panicked brain.

I climbed the stairs to Main and approached its doors. I reached for the handle but couldn't push or turn it. The more I tried, the more it burned and stung. I gave up. I could feel the physical world. I could walk on it, but I could not affect it, at least not easily. I waited until a Wicky bustled past, and I followed in her wake, rushing all the way back to the Pit. No Gabe. As I headed back out, I paused in the clearing in the center of the hall where Malcolm and I had danced. I closed my eyes and heard the waltz again. I felt him holding my waist. I wondered how he'd feel when he found out what had happened to me, whatever *had* happened. I wanted to cry, but there were no tears.

I was startled from my reverie when a Fifth Former swiped through my arm with her tray of empty dishes. I screamed from the pain. Of course she didn't hear me. But then I screamed again, just because it felt good. Then I screamed *again* to see if anyone might hear me. I kept screaming, looking in every direction to see if a head cocked or eyebrow raised. They didn't.

I collapsed on the floor.

Out of habit, I imagined what I must look like from another angle, from above. I must look like a pathetic pile of a girl on the floor in the dining hall. No, I realized. I looked like nothing. I *was* nothing.

I DIDN'T KNOW GABE'S schedule, so I wandered from the Science Center to the Mathematics Complex to the Language Arts Compound. I checked in at the Art Center. I knew he didn't take studio art but thought he might be in drama or music. No luck. But there was Abigail on stage, rehearsing.

> *"Unhappy that I am, I cannot heave*
> *My heart into my mouth. I love your majesty*
> *According to my bond, no more nor less."*

Pop quiz: How do you know you go to a school full of chilly, unfriendly people? When Abigail Steers is cast as Cordelia in *King Lear.* She's the best they could find for Lear's compassionate, loving daughter? Please. And yet there was the drama teacher coddling her and complimenting her performance.

I went to the Tuck Shop. No Gabe. But I had to pause when I saw the booth where Malcolm and I had shared the grilled cheese and milk shake. I sat in the booth. It wasn't until then I realized I felt no hunger. No lightheadedness from not eating. And when I paused, time seemed to slip past me.

Finally, I went back to Main. I'd have to wait until our work-study period after classes. There was no way for me to get into the catacombs until someone opened the door, and I could follow them down. So I sat in one of those big leather chairs where Malcolm and his friends congregated. Time started to blur again. Students came and went in bursts of motion like Duchamp's *Nude Descending Stairs*. Two hours seemed to pass in an instant, and suddenly the lobby was flooded with the lunchtime crowd.

Malcolm's friend Kent plopped onto the chair next to mine. He kicked back and clicked away on his phone, his persistent smile now more of a grin. I moved to look over his shoulder and saw it was just Facebook. He was posting a status update:

feeling on top of the world. psyched 4 fall fest.

Another guy, Amos, walked up and sat next to him.

"Meeting today," Kent said under his breath, certain that none of the passing students could hear. "Four P.M. Spread the word."

Amos nodded and disappeared into the crowd. It was only then I noticed a blonde girl had approached, peering at me from across the room. She was translucent, but she had a perfect blow out. And she wasn't bloody like the others. Her neck was bruised, but otherwise she looked almost normal, eerily blending in with the crowd. I realized it was because she wasn't from the past—at least not the far past—she looked like someone you'd see on *Gossip Girl*.

Her stare grew intense. I got up, backing away. My heart may not have been pounding, but I was no less frightened than I ever would have been. Luckily, a teacher was approaching the door to the catacombs. I raced over, barely slipping through in time.

I followed the teacher down the stairs then lingered in the hallway, looking at the bricks. Name after name. Names I'd laughed at just a few days ago now frightened me. Standing in that hallway, looking at those names, I felt surrounded by some kind of conspiracy. What was this place? Who were these people?

It was close to our regular meeting time, so I retreated to the nook where Gabe had seen Lydia. I braced myself as I approached, thinking perhaps I might see her now. After all, I'd seen those other girls. But it was quiet and empty. I positioned myself in the shadows and waited.

I could hear his feet creeping down the spiral staircase. His fear was palpable as he reached the long winding corridor.

"Gabe," I whispered.

Nothing.

"No! Gabe, you *have* to hear me! Tell me you hear me!"

He turned toward me and snapped, "Stop trying to freak me out!"

"You see me?!"

"I wish I didn't." He turned to walk away. He was still mad at me for not believing him and for liking Malcolm. "No, Gabe, stop! You have to listen to me. Something happened to me. I need help."

He huffed. "I refuse to discuss that guy with you. All I can say is I told you so. And can you please get out of that corner? That's where I see *her.*"

"I know. That's why I'm here."

"What do you mean?"

"Something happened to me. I don't know what exactly. I was at the well. Everything went black. I saw terrible things, like I was falling into the well . . . and since then, I'm different. Nobody else can see me now. But I think I see those girls you see . . ."

"Don't make fun of me!"

"I'm not! I *need* you," I insisted as I got up and moved closer to him. As I did, his face drained of color. His eyes widened and he edged away from me—afraid—and started whimpering. Sobbing almost. Saying "no" again and again. And "not you."

"What happened?" I asked.

"You disappeared." His voice trembled. "I can only see you in that corner. Just like *her.*"

"What does it mean?" I asked.

"It means . . . you're dead."

Hearing it out loud hit me in the face, as if saying it made it more real. I finally said the three words one is never meant to say: "I am dead."

Now that I'd crossed out of the nook, Gabe couldn't see how I wilted, shaking with fear and grief at hearing those words out loud. I'd never thought I'd have to *know* I was dead—I just thought I'd be gone one day.

But then Gabe lurched back. I turned and saw her. I knew immediately it was Lydia. She was just as he'd described, Smiths T-shirt and all. She had a wild, raging look in her eyes.

Gabe jumped to his feet. "Run, Liv! Come with me!" And I followed.

AS WE WHISKED ACROSS campus something kicked in, a drive to figure things out. I hardly knew my adoptive grandmother, but when she died, I remember fixating on my mother. I don't think she cried once those first few weeks. She immediately started taking care of business—making calls, folding clothes, cleaning the kitchen, posting the online obituary. She couldn't really deal with her loss so she started doing other things instead. I felt like that.

"Can you still hear me?" I asked.

He nodded. Classes had just ended, so students were crawling all over.

"Can you see me?"

"No, I told you, I can only see the—" he started to say "ghosts" but stopped himself—"*them* in certain spots."

"I need to know what happened to me."

He nodded, with his head down. We crossed through the Art Center's outside atrium, passing a cluster of students.

"Just follow me," he muttered.

"Are we going to the well?"

He kept his head down as we passed another set of Wickies, then quickly ducked behind the dumpsters by the Art Center. "I can't just talk to you out in the open. You understand? They'll lock me up. They'll send me away somewhere. They're desperate to get rid of me!"

"Okay." Of course, I hadn't been thinking of him at all.

"And, *yes*, we're going to the well. Of course we're going to the well."

Gabe walked so fast I had to run to keep up. I noticed

I was lighter on my feet than I had been before. I could move fast, and I didn't lose my breath.

As Gabe arrived at the well, he squinted over the edge. "Nothing. I can't see a thing." He scoured the ground at its base. He studied its sides and its edges, looking for any clue, peeking over his shoulder nervously. As I approached, his gaze shifted to me, and he stepped back, almost as if awed. He looked directly into my eyes.

"You can see me?"

He nodded.

I smiled. I never thought I'd feel so delighted just to be seen.

"So well, too. You look so much more real than the others. More solid. Less . . ." he stopped himself again.

"Don't edit, Gabe."

"*Ghosty*. You look less ghosty. And that's a good thing. It means you're different from them." He heard a sound and lurched around, looking, then turned to me to explain, "Sorry it's just there's a girl, the one with the bloody neck, who's always hanging around here near that tree." He gestured to the weeping willow.

"I saw her here." I paused. "And not just here, I saw her in my dream a few weeks ago."

He tilted his head, puzzled. "Okay, now *you* sound crazy."

He was right—*he* was supposed to be the insane one. "It's true, though," I insisted. "I mean, I think it was her."

"Well, I don't know. That never happened to me."

"Tell me what *has* happened to you," I said urgently. I drew closer, but not too close. I didn't want to risk touching him, feeling that burn. "You have to tell me *everything*. I want to know everything you know. *Why* am I here?"

He shook his head. "I don't know why you're here. I don't know why any of them are. I don't think *they* know."

"Well, what *do* you know?"

"I'll tell you, but not here. I don't feel safe."

He glanced one last time at the well, then led me through the woods, explaining as we went. "I only see them in specific places, in charged spots. But I've heard them pretty much everywhere. Same way I hear you right now. But they mostly linger in the places where they died I think."

"What do they say?"

"I don't listen to them. I can't stand to. I bolt every time I hear one."

"Can you think of anything you've heard them say?"

He took a deep breath. "I think Lydia's the only one who knows I can hear her. But she doesn't make sense. She mumbles and laughs like a maniac about being powerless and weak. Losing her strength. She says they're stuck here—lingering, that's the word she uses—and she wants out."

I didn't feel powerless or weak. Not exactly. I mean, I felt different—and there were clearly different rules and constraints—but at least I was able to talk to Gabe.

"Who did it, Liv? Why were you out there? What were you doing?"

I hesitated, and Gabe immediately knew. "You were with him. I *told* you about him! I warned you."

"I was with him. But it *wasn't* him." Of course it wasn't him.

By now we were approaching the cemetery. He looked

around cautiously. "There's another one who lingers here, so let's hurry."

I moved quickly, again getting that floating feeling. With little effort, I got several paces ahead of him.

He looked up, amazed.

"What?" I asked.

"You're coming and going as you cross the graves. Appearing and disappearing."

I couldn't feel a thing. Nothing looked different to me; I could always see myself.

"It's magical," he mused, sounding almost unafraid for the first time since he saw me. "Or really creepy. I'm not sure which."

"So you could see me in that nook, you could see me at the well where I died, and now here." I was trying to make sense of it all. "You can see me where there's death."

He nodded. "I guess. Wait, stay there. So I can see you."

I paused on a grave. He slumped down beside a headstone nearby.

"Tell me what happened last night," he demanded. "You snuck out?"

I nodded.

"You met him?"

"In the woods near the well. Then we heard something. We ran in opposite directions. He was *protecting* me, distracting whoever it was so *he'd* get in trouble, not me."

Gabe didn't buy it. "And then what?"

"I paused at the well, to catch my breath. And I guess I was hit from behind."

"By Malcolm."

"No. It *wasn't* him." I wanted to tell him what Malcolm had said—that he *loved* me—but I couldn't. It was too private. I scrolled through my memory trying to think about who might want to kill me and why. Suddenly I saw flashes of a face—glowering at me as I arrived on the steps late to the tour, a look of disgust as I danced with Malcolm, laughing at me in Old Homestead, hiding in the shadows as Malcolm and I arrived back at my dorm or ate in the Tuck Shop. It was so obvious.

"Abigail Steers!" I knew it was her. "She's hated me since the moment I interrupted her tour. And then Malcolm's interest just made it worse. There's something seriously wrong with her. I *knew* it."

Gabe waved a hand dismissively. "She doesn't have it in her. Getting her hands dirty like . . ." He stopped abruptly when he saw something past me. I looked over. It was Headmaster Thorton, leading a team of police officers with sniffing dogs.

The headmaster scowled. He'd just seen Gabe talking—talking to nobody. "Mr. Nichols, do you not have a shift you should be working at present?" he called.

"I do, but . . ." He shook his head, dangling his long hair over his face.

One of the dogs started to growl, perhaps sensing me. Sensing *something*.

"Tell them to check Abigail! Tell them!" I yelled.

Gabe ignored me, but I needed them to know. At that moment, I didn't care if they all thought he was crazy. They *had* to know. "Tell them to look in the well and that it was Abigail Steers! You have to tell them! *Now!*"

Then I turned and saw a girl had appeared, standing on a gravestone silently beside me. It was the same girl I'd seen here that Headmaster Holiday night, the one like Warhol's *Jackie O.* I was certain of it. Only now she didn't look alive at all. She looked faint and translucent like the others. But her wrists were still cut open, and her skirt and jacket were now covered in dried blood. She recognized me.

"You," she said as she started toward me. I screamed and lurched away.

Gabe shouted, "Stop!"

"To whom are you speaking, Mr. Nichols?"

"No one," Gabe snarled.

The headmaster exchanged a look with the police. "I'd like for you to go to the infirmary, Mr. Nichols. Immediately. I'll inform Nurse Cobbs of your pending arrival."

"Yes, sir." Gabe stood and shuffled away.

"I'll meet you there, but first I want to go with these guys and see what they find," I said. His lips tightened in anger. All eyes were still on him, including the police dogs. "I'm sorry, Gabe. I won't do that again."

THE DOGS BARKED DOWN the well as if a cat were in there. But it wasn't a cat. It was my dead body. While crime scene investigators dusted the roughhewn stone, other officers designed a contraption to hoist my corpse up the deep, narrow hole.

My body was cold and dull. Plump with death. My eyes were clouded, but I looked almost serene. My dark hair spread around my head, kind of like that famous painting of Ophelia floating in the river. Funny, I'd made so many self-portraits and yet I'd never really looked at myself and realized I was actually kind of pretty.

A female officer inspected me and quickly ascertained I'd been hit from behind, knocked out, and I'd died from the fall. She jotted a note that read "blunt trauma to the head."

The dusters found some fingerprints. They were delighted. I jumped up, also excited, until I realized they were probably Gabe's. I had to do something. I pushed their makeshift table with all my might, but it did nothing except gently shake as if from wind. I recoiled, palms stinging as if I'd touched a hot stove, and collapsed on the ground, sapped from the effort, powerless as they sealed up evidence.

As I sat there with my head slumped, recovering, I looked down and noticed my body—my ghost body—looked different. It was slightly less opaque than it had been before. The fall wind stirred around me. I heard a gentle murmur from the trees nearby. "Preserve your strength, girl," a female voice warned.

I looked up, trying to locate the voice, then heard feet approaching through the pines behind me, leaves crunching. That same crunch I'd heard last night. I feared it might be the bloody girl, so I backed away from the well and hid behind a tree.

It wasn't her. It was Malcolm. His face was drawn and haggard. Dark circles under red eyes. He exchanged a few words with the headmaster then pushed past into the crime scene. And that's when he saw me—my body, at least—stretched out on the damp ground next to the well.

He recoiled, shocked. He'd had no idea I was dead. Perhaps he'd heard I was missing and had gone to look for me. But this was clearly not what he'd expected to find. He made a sound that wasn't quite human and gathered his strength to look at me again. His eyes searched my body as if looking for a sign of life or a clue of some kind. When he realized there was none—no breath, no life, no clues to anything—sadness set in. But his eyes weren't just sad, they were guilty.

"It wasn't your fault!" I yelled at him, pointlessly.

He kneeled on the ground next to my body and kissed my cheek. I felt my cheeks—my ghost cheeks—start to quiver as they always did when I was about to cry. But, again, there were no tears.

The crime scene people were all over him of course, telling him to move away from the body. But he resisted and quickly whispered some words to the dead me that I couldn't hear. I felt sick. What a lousy ghost, not even close enough to hear what her first love, her *only* love, tells her dead body.

The crime people gently picked him up. One of the officers approached him, notepad in hand, and asked his name ("Malcolm Astor"). His relation to me ("friend"). Where he was last night ("in my dorm"). A lie. Obviously. So he wouldn't get in trouble, right? Of course that was why.

Then they sent him away. They had work to do, they said. And, as desperately as I wanted to go with Malcolm, I had work to do, too. As I walked away, I glanced back toward Old Homestead. In one of the second-story windows, I saw the red-headed girl from the weeping willow tree—the one with pin curls and severed neck—standing with a dark figure. But when they saw me looking, they quickly shifted out of view.

I WAITED OUTSIDE THE entrance to the infirmary, but nobody came. I knew from my visit there on that first day of school that it wasn't a popular destination. Unless somebody opened the door, I wasn't going anywhere.

Stuck outside, I thought about my capabilities, reviewing everything that had happened. If someone was able to walk through me, surely I could walk through something, too. It might hurt, but I was fairly certain it was possible if I used some force.

I tried to push myself through the thick metal doors but immediately fell back. The pain, that all-encompassing burning—it was unlike anything I'd experienced while alive. I collapsed on the steps. My energy and capabilities were clearly limited, but I didn't quite understand in what way. I waited until a student with a nasty cough arrived and followed her through the doors as she was buzzed in.

Over the years, plenty of kids must have died there, so I assumed it'd be chock full of people like me. As I wandered down the hall looking for Gabe, I braced myself for an apparition. But there were none. It was oddly quiet. I found Gabe in an examination room. Alone. Door open. He sat up suddenly, so I knew he saw me. It proved my theory that he could see me wherever someone had died—there had certainly been death here.

"Gabe, I'm so sorry."

He shrugged. "Hey, you lost it. You just died, so you have a pretty decent excuse."

I smiled, noticing he was hooked up to some monitor. "What are they doing to you?"

"Psych profile. Don't worry. I'll pass. But you need to go. If they hear *this*, I'm toast."

Right then, Nurse Cobbs entered, startling me. I withdrew to the corner of the room. "Yes, Mr. Nichols? Something about toast?"

Gabe was unfazed. "Oh, yeah, I'm starving. *Desperately* need toast."

"Saltines should suffice, I think."

"Sure, salt me up, corn on the Cobbs."

She was so obviously annoyed with him that it was clear she thought he was sane. So I suspected he'd be okay and get out of there soon enough. He'd had experience with this, after all.

CHAPTER 7

Luckily, the door to Skellenger was propped open. I entered and found a swarm of police officers interviewing students in the common room. Abigail's door was closed, so I stopped to listen to what Sloan, Abigail's best friend, was saying.

"She just seemed really depressed. She had no friends. She didn't fit in. She was clearly, you know, struggling."

"I never even *spoke* to you! What are you talking about?" I snapped.

They let her go as another officer knocked on Abigail's door. After a long pause, Abigail shambled out, looking a mess, like she'd been crying. While the officers walked her across the common room, she exchanged a surreptitious glance and nod with Sloan.

"Wait! Didn't you guys see that?! She's covering for her!" Obviously there was no point, but it made me feel better to speak.

Abigail sat down for her interview and proceeded to give a tearful, Academy Award–worthy speech that detailed our nascent friendship, my desperation (which she continually tried to counsel), and her heartbreak over my loss. When pressed, she confessed that, yes, I had given warning signs. "I'll live the rest of my life regretting that I didn't pick up on them and do something." At that point she began sobbing so hard they had to help her back to her room.

I watched with a strange mix of horror, amusement, and disbelief. She was so convincing *I* practically believed her. It wasn't until her door closed that I realized I'd meant to follow her. Instead, I was stuck in the common room.

Another officer, a woman, appeared in the hallway, carrying my most recent sketchbook. "I think you guys need to see this."

She opened it up to my most recent drawing—an angel, falling—and underneath it read, *I cannot take it anymore. Goodbye.*

I had made the sketch, but I hadn't written those words.

"A suicide note," the main guy said.

"Another Wicky suicide." She raised her eyebrows.

"It's been a while. What, ten years, maybe?"

The other guy nodded. "Give or take."

"No!" I screamed. "I didn't write that! Look at the other pages! It's not my handwriting!"

The female officer closed the book. I rushed over and tried to grab it. I could feel the cover, but I couldn't move it. I tried to harness all my energy. But this time the tips of my fingers went right through it, and I fell backward, fingertips searing. I had to stop doing that. The agony wasn't worth it.

From the floor, I watched as they labeled the book, wrapped it in plastic, and whisked it away.

I WENT TO GABE'S dorm, unsure of what to do next. I followed a lacrosse player through the main entrance and waited outside his room until he returned. I began to understand why that dead girl used the word "lingering." That's what it felt like, hanging around in a place where you no longer belonged, if you ever belonged at all. As I lingered, I heard the chatter about me. The "strange" girl, the "dirty" girl, the "weirdo" Astor was "slumming with," his "charity case." That last one stung only because I had wondered that myself. Of all the girls at Wickham Hall, why would he pick me? Was he just trying to make a point and defy his parents, or did he really like me? I had wondered all that constantly. But whenever I saw him, all that paranoid chatter evaporated. Nobody was that good a faker. Well, except maybe Abigail.

I also learned a new Wicky term no one had shared with me yet: "Scolly," for scholarship student. How original. Apparently everyone knew exactly who was on scholarship. We were the minority, the lower class—the 1 percent. Pretty ironic because in the rest of the world—the *real* world—we were the 99 percent. But everyone knows, majority or not, it's the real-world 1 percent that rules. Here at Wickham Hall and everywhere else.

Gabe finally came along and opened his door. I slipped in with him and followed him to his bed, where he collapsed, head slumped over the side.

"I'm here. Just so you know, before you do something weird or embarrassing."

"Figured." His voice was monotone.

"Are you okay?"

"They gave me some electroshock. And some medicine."

"Oh no!" I was desperate. I felt my lifeline swinging out of my grasp.

Then he cackled. "Just kidding. I mean, they gave me something, but I didn't take it." He pulled two pills from his pocket and tossed them in the garbage.

"Don't do that," I snapped.

"Oh, come on. This is the first time I've been able to joke about this . . . whatever it is I have, whatever's wrong with me. Consider it progress."

"Well, we have work to do. Abigail lied to the cops, told them I was suicidal and I'd told her so. And she doctored my journal."

"No shit," he said, with a touch of awe.

"Don't be *impressed*."

He looked up, toward the sound of my voice. "I truly didn't think she had it in her. What about Astor? What'd he say?"

I didn't want to send Gabe off on a tangent, so I ignored the question. "You need to go to Headmaster Thorton about Abigail. Now!"

"They think I'm crazy!" he shouted back. "They gave me fifty milligrams of Olanzapine, not messing around. They won't listen to me."

"Well, you have to."

His shoulders sagged, and he sighed. "I know."

THE NEXT MORNING—AT least I think it was the next morning, but it's hard to say because time is as fractured as a Cubist painting when you're lingering—Wickham Hall held a morning Chapel in my memory. Of course I went. Who would give up the chance to attend her own memorial? But I was unsure what to expect. How could this school possibly eulogize me? I'd only been here six weeks. I hardly knew anyone. It wasn't exactly going to be the kind of cryfest one likes to imagine. I entered the silent, somber building, intending to wander through, find Abigail, do some research. But I didn't get past Malcolm.

Malcolm sat toward the back, away from everyone. Word had spread of our blooming romance. Several Third Formers kept glancing at him, whispering. Abigail and Kent approached together, Kent's perma-smile tastefully subdued. They gave Malcolm big hugs and invited him to sit with them. But he wanted to be by himself. He was a faded being, slumped over in the hard pew. It would've made a beautiful painting—a Vermeer or Velásquez—but it was unbearable to see in person.

As the dreary organ music began, Ms. Benson entered and swept over to Malcolm. She didn't say a word but wrapped her tiny arms around him, enclosing him in her kaftan. I saw his chest heave from behind. I desperately wanted to tell him I was still there; I was okay. But I wasn't okay. And I couldn't tell him anything.

I wasn't really listening or paying attention to the

service. In fact, I didn't even realize it was my actual *funeral*. It only hit me when Headmaster Thorton mentioned my casket. I moved up to the front to see it, placed right at the pulpit. Closed, thank God. And there were my parents! They'd come all this way. They sat front row and center. My mother looked like a ghost herself—dark hollow eyes, pale skin. My father was even more stoic than usual, but my mother's body shook with silent sobs. They looked so small and out of place.

Being in front of everyone, I was instinctively uncomfortable, insecure. I had to remind myself I was invisible. No one could see me. No one.

While the minister, whom I'd never laid eyes on, extolled on the goodness of my heart, my joy for living, my artistic spirit, I turned to take in the crowd. Most of the kids looked squirmy and bored. I couldn't blame them. Only Malcolm looked devastated.

When the service was over, my parents walked with the pallbearers, dour grown-ups I'd never seen before. Were they from the school? Or perhaps at Wickham Hall they got pallbearers for hire. The casket was loaded into a hearse, and my parents started to get into the limousine. Suddenly I realized I might never see them again. I hadn't thought about that. There had been too many other things to think about. I wasn't ready to never see them again. I hadn't even said goodbye. On instinct, I jumped into the limousine with them.

As I sat into the car, I heard a girl's voice shriek, "Don't go!" But before I could see who it was, that man in the black suit—the very man who'd driven me to Wickham Hall—slammed the door behind us.

My best friend in the fifth grade had told me she some-times cried herself to sleep thinking about how sad her parents would be if she died. I'd always wanted to say I cried myself to sleep thinking about how *not* sad my par-ents would be if I died. But I never told her. I'd never told anybody those feelings, because they were too true. Or so I'd believed. Now I saw my parents were far sadder than I ever would have imagined. My mother lost it when the door closed. She yelled to no one in particular, "I knew she shouldn't have come to this place with you rich people!" My father put his arm around her shoulder, silently nod-ding in agreement, fighting back tears. I thought they'd wanted to get rid of me. Maybe I had meant more to them than I knew. Maybe our disconnection had all been my fault. Maybe they had loved me all along.

And suddenly, for the first time, I was overwhelmed by the sadness of my own death. There were no tears, but I wept, feeling my parents' pain. Feeling Malcolm's pain. And most of all, regretting I'd never let myself love them or *anyone*. I'd spent all those years feeling sorry for myself, feeling unloved, when really it was my fault—at least partly. How stupid. What a waste.

I started to feel weak and unusual, foggy almost. I fought to compose myself. Maybe ghosts weren't supposed to cry. Obviously I needed to learn about what I could and couldn't do now. I needed to start paying attention so I could figure out this new world. But then I looked down and saw my limbs were fading away. Rapidly. As we got closer to the school's gate, parts of me actually started to disappear. Evaporate. Even my mind felt weak, as if I were alive but short on oxygen. And I realized what that girl had been trying to tell me: I was bound to Wickham Hall. I *had* to get out of that car.

I started to bang on the windows, palms searing, and scream, "Stop! Now!" My mother's sobbing increased, as if she could feel me. I reached at the door handle with all my strength, and my hand just went through it, stinging. I searched through my dwindling mind for an idea. Parts of my body had crossed through objects. I *had* to be able to push my entire body through the door. It was my only hope. Positioning myself against the far side of the limousine, I steeled my nerves and threw myself at the car door with *all* my strength.

It felt as if my body were being ripped apart by a hot poker, cell by cell. It was intense and excruciating but mercifully brief. And when I emerged from the whirl of motion and noise and pain, I was outside, soaring through the air. I tumbled onto the ground, my entire body stinging. But I was free, and I was whole. Well, as whole as I could be, given my condition. I watched as the limousine, and then the hearse, pulled through the gates of Wickham Hall and turned onto the country road, saying goodbye—probably forever—to my parents and to my body.

IT'S HARD TO KNOW exactly how long I sat and recovered from the pain. I watched surges of students bustle to and from classes on the horizon. Again and again, like sped-up time-lapse photography. It might've been hours.

I was jolted from the blur of time when someone crossed

through me. He approached silently from behind. I didn't have a clue he was coming until he'd already walked through me. As I got up and walked toward the lake, I realized something: it hadn't hurt. When I'd thrown myself out of the limousine—and when I'd crossed with other people—it'd been unbearable. But when this random Third Former crossed through me unexpectedly it hadn't hurt at all. Clearly my body had a whole new set of rules. If only I could make sense of them.

SEVERAL STUDENTS WERE OUT rowing, but I instantly recognized Malcolm. He was the most elegant. I stood on the dock beside the boathouse as he rowed his scull in, got out, and placed it on its rack. He was doing his best to go through the motions.

I walked right next to him as he crossed the campus just as I had on the Headmaster Holiday, only this time he didn't know I was with him. He ended up at the cemetery. He paused and then entered the Founders Tomb. I followed.

He sat and looked at the painting, the lake landscape with my angel ascending from it. It took on a new meaning. And he cried. He didn't have that embarrassed look guys usually have when they cry, like the way my dad had struggled against his tears. Malcolm let go, without shame.

"Is that you, Liv? Are you an angel now?"

"I'm right here," I said, desperately hoping that in this charged moment, at this private place, he might somehow hear me. But he did not.

GABE HAD AN APPOINTMENT with Headmaster Thorton the next day. As I waited for him in front of the Headmaster's Quarters—a daunting Gothic mansion near Old Homestead—I noticed a small plaque posted on the front of the building:

> *This structure was erected by Elijah Wickham in 1875 upon his return to Wickham Hall after five years abroad. While traveling in Europe, the younger Wickham discovered Gothic architecture, which he brought back to Wickham Hall. He desired for the following statement to be posted on this edifice: "Let it be known to all the students of Wickham Hall that I intend for these buildings to celebrate Infinite Intelligence and our ability to embrace such a power and use it to heal the world."*

Weird statement. Pretty arrogant, too, though that wasn't a huge surprise. Maybe that's why there was never any religious talk in the so-called chapel; he must have been an atheist or something.

When Gabe arrived, he told me quietly and firmly under his breath that I was not to speak in the meeting. I agreed.

Headmaster Thorton answered the door promptly and invited Gabe into his living room, gesturing for him to sit on the couch. Thorton, or someone who had lived here over the years, was quite a butterfly collector. There were framed collections on the walls. And even some taxidermy butterflies hanging from the ceiling— less a mobile, more like a swarm hovering around a sweet plant.

The headmaster sat in an upright medieval-looking chair.

Gabe jumped right in. "It has come to my attention, sir, that Abigail Steers lied to the police about Liv, er, Olivia Bloom. And others lied as well, backing up her story."

"How did this come to your attention?"

"I can't say."

The headmaster sighed loudly. "I'm not going to play games with you, Mr. Nichols. This is a serious accusation leveled upon one of our top students."

Gabe stayed cooler than I would have thought. "It's not a game. I swear. She needs to be questioned again and fingerprinted or DNA'd or whatever it is they do."

"Mr. Nichols, you have documented mental illness."

"I know that's what you think, sir. But . . ."

"And you have a record of defiance and, I might add, *dishonesty*. So why would I believe you?"

Gabe swallowed, losing his confidence. I was losing mine, too. Forget Thorton. No one at Wickham Hall would believe Gabe.

"The fact is, Mr. Nichols, the police are quite interested in *you.*"

"*What?*"

"That's all I can say." The headmaster shrugged, as if it was classified information. "Now you may be excused."

As Gabe was leaving, I noticed something through a door at the far end of the room—a strange old photograph of a man. I whisked in. It was a tiny sitting room, dark, with no windows. There were other photographs hanging nearby, but I heard Gabe opening the front door so I raced out to catch up.

He walked swiftly, visibly upset, and I couldn't blame him. He finally stopped behind the Art Center dumpsters. "They're framing me," he whispered. He kept shaking his head. "I'm so screwed. I touched all over that well right before the police got there."

"Do you have an alibi?"

"I was in my room. Useless."

"You didn't talk to anyone or see anyone?"

"I don't leave my room at night."

I wanted to reach out to him, to touch him. "It's gonna be okay."

"They won't listen to me. They won't ever believe me."

"We have to get someone on our side, someone they *will* listen to."

"Like who?!"

"Malcolm."

"No way!"

I had to convince Gabe. Who else would help us? Plus, I had to let Malcolm know that I wasn't gone. "Would you rather go to jail? Let Abigail go free? Just because you don't like the guy?!"

His shoulders sagged, and I knew he'd do it.

MALCOLM WAS SITTING IN one of the oversized leather chairs in the lobby in Main. Abigail, Kent, Amos, and several others were hanging around him, trying to cheer him up. He stared straight ahead at nothing. I stared at him, waiting for Gabe and hoping he hadn't decided to blow off our plan at the last minute.

"Tonight," Kent cajoled. "Eight P.M. You gotta come.

We miss you." He playfully gestured to his heart, trying to make light of the situation.

"No."

"You have to."

"I can't. I don't want to."

"It's your *responsibility,*" Abigail chimed in, annoyed. Clearly she'd used up her acting skills pretending to care.

"Then I quit," Malcolm said evenly.

"It doesn't work like that. You *can't* quit," Kent said. "Come on, it'll make you feel better. You gotta get back in the swing." Kent patted Malcolm on the back.

Malcolm sighed and turned away from him, just as the door flew open. Gabe was approaching. I breathed a sigh of relief. Gabe jerked to a stop, startled. He looked right into my eyes.

"You can see me?" I asked.

He nodded.

"Don't talk to me. They'll hear you," I said. "Now go."

He nodded again, looking around—probably afraid of seeing the *Gossip Girl* who lingered there—and proceeded toward Malcolm.

Abigail snapped, "Um, seriously? What are you doing here? This is *our* area."

Gabe laughed harshly. He shot me a glare and turned to walk away.

"No! Go talk to him! Now!" I yelled.

After a final moment of hesitation, Gabe whipped around, turning back. The whole clique looked at him like he was crazy. And he did look crazy, with his ripped clothes and lurching movements. He smiled at Abigail. "Nice pumps."

"Shut up, perv."

He plopped down into the leather chair next to Malcolm, a parody of trying to act cool. "Hey, man. What's going on?"

Malcolm turned to him, more baffled than upset.

"Seriously, get out of here," Kent said, smiling all the while as if to soften the blow.

"He's allowed to sit here if he wants," Malcolm said.

"Yeah, I'm with him," Gabe spat at Kent. "This is the form my grief is taking."

Kent laughed. So did Amos and Abigail. That's how preposterous the situation was to them—that an Astor would deign to hang out with Gabe, no matter what the circumstances.

Malcolm ignored his friends and smiled at Gabe sadly, knowing they now shared something: my death. *Well played,* I thought. Gabe smiled back, then leaned over and whispered, "She's still here."

Malcolm stood up with such force that his chair fell backward. He froze up as if to keep from punching Gabe. "Get away from me," he barked.

"What'd he say?" Kent demanded.

"Nothing." Malcolm grabbed Gabe's T-shirt and pushed him. "Go away and *stay* away."

"We mean it, freak!" Abigail yelled after Gabe.

Gabe stormed to the door, then turned back to them, suddenly simmering with a rage that frightened even me. "Fine, push me away," he bellowed. "But we will reveal the truth! *All* of it!"

When I turned to follow, I was face to face with her—the *Gossip Girl*—close enough to see the mascara clumped to the lashes around her brown eyes and the lip gloss shining on her airy lips, slightly upturned in a smile. I choked back a scream and rushed to catch up with Gabe.

Brit

Me and Haley Pinfolds ruled the school. And even she didn't know I was white trash. At least I didn't think she did. My daddy had struck it big with a time-share property scam. I'm not real sure how it worked, but we went from a dump outside Gainesville to a house in Miami that was so big I constantly lost my dog, Gucci. When my momma asked what I wanted now that we had piles of money, I said I wanted class. So my daddy made a big fat donation to Wickham Hall, and I was accepted the following year.

I studied magazines—not like Us Weekly *but classy ones like* W *and* Marie Claire*—to figure out how to dress. I got a dialect coach to work on my voice. A tutor to prepare me for the classes. I even read* The New York Times.

I really thought I had them fooled. I certainly had myself fooled. I fully believed I was one of them.

*But then I started to get IMs and texts—*i know who u r, i know what u r, u don't belong here*—and stuff like that. My Myspace page got overrun—people accusing me of being dirty and trashy,* *just like my namesake Britney Spears.* u r a liar, u suck, go away. *They even put my name on the definition of "rich white trash" in urbandictionary.com. Haley wouldn't talk to me. She said I lied to her.*

I started to feel like they were right. I had lied and faked it. Maybe I was still white trash. I didn't know who I was anymore. All I knew was I was a liar.

On my last day, I took a shower after dinner. While I was in there, it suddenly got dark, and the fire alarm blared. I got out of the shower and reached around for my towel. It was gone. I ran out in the hall, but it was empty. There was no light. I called out for Haley. For anyone. No one was there, and the alarm kept ringing so loud. I didn't know what to do but run outside.

They were all there, surrounding me, laughing at me. All the girls in the dorm and even a few guys. A few of them pushed me around. Haley said she was going to "pop my fake tits." One of her new friends groped me. Then everyone tried to get a grab. My boobs weren't fake, by the way.

I ran back inside. I curled up, crouching on my bed until the power came back on, then I got out of bed. I blew out my hair, put my face on, and got dressed in my bestest outfit, including my new Marc Jacobs dress and Tory Burch flats. I packed up my Birkin bag and marched up to their hangout spot in the Main lobby, now empty. I tied together those crisp Wickham Hall sheets, attached them to that big metal chandelier, stood on one of their footstools, and then kicked it out of the way.

They had won. They didn't get their hands dirty, but they're the ones who killed me.

CHAPTER 8

I soared alongside Gabe as he marched across campus with a new purpose. It wasn't until we were passing the Art Center that he'd calmed down enough for me to ask him where we were going.

"To the woods and the well," he snapped.

"Why?"

"To look for clues. Anything."

"Like?"

"They never found your phone. Maybe we can find it."

"But you'll go back to Malcolm later?"

"No, Liv. No, I will not."

Right. Not the best time to try to push that agenda. Anyway, we did need to look in the woods. The police hadn't known the "military operation" route I'd taken to the well. They probably hadn't even looked along the path Malcolm had so carefully planned. And maybe there *would* be some kind of clue on my phone.

I led Gabe to the clearing where Malcolm and I had met. While he scoured around, I stretched out on the pine needles in the spot where Malcolm and I had been. I stared up at the sky. It was mid-afternoon so there were no stars, of course, but the leaves were every possible orange and the clouds were perfect puffs. I thought of the poem Malcolm had recited to me right in this spot, and I looked at the stars he'd drawn on my arm. It wasn't that long ago, and yet everything had changed.

Bright star, would I were steadfast as thou art—
Not in lone splendour hung aloft the night
And watching, with eternal lids apart,
Like nature's patient, sleepless Eremite . . .

Wasn't that me now? Isolated and watching, with eternal lids apart? I didn't sleep, and time didn't really exist anymore (at least not like it had when I was alive). I was separate from the world. I had become the star, hadn't I? That tragic, lonely thing.

"Am I going to be stuck like this forever, Gabe? Here, at Wickham?"

"I don't know. Seems like the others have been."

"What if I don't want to be?"

"One thing at a time. Step one: let's try to make sure I don't get locked up for the rest of my life, because I can't be much help to you behind bars. Step two: we'll figure the rest of it out."

"Okay."

He started into the tall pines. "You went this way?"

"Yep." I followed him, a few paces behind. "No, to the right of that tree."

He went right, his eyes pinned to the carpet of leaves and dead pine needles with laser focus. Suddenly he picked up his pace. "And bingo!"

"You're kidding. You found it?!"

He picked my phone up. "Unless somebody else has *Starry Night* on their iPhone case."

I laughed. It was my first laugh as a ghost. It felt good.

"Anything?" I asked Gabe.

He pushed the home button but the phone didn't light up. "I don't know. It's dead," he said, slipping the phone into his pocket. "We'll have to charge it up and check it later."

That's when I saw her: sitting on a branch of the weeping willow tree several yards away, red hair still set in perfect curls and blackened blood still caked down the front of her beaded flapper dress. She looked off in the other direction, singing to herself. I shushed Gabe so I could hear the words; it sounded old and bluesy or jazzy or something like that. Gabe went pale.

> "I went down to the river, sat beneath the willow tree.
> The dew dropped on those willow leaves,
> And it rolled right down on me.
> And that's the reason I've got those weepin' willow blues."

She seemed at peace. In a strange way, I felt connected to her. I was like her, wasn't I? But then she turned in our direction.

"Here you are," she muttered.

Gabe was off and running before I could stop him. I followed right after.

GABE AND I TOOK a little-used path back to the main campus so he'd feel safe talking to me.

"How can we find out more about Abigail?" I asked.

"All the student records are locked up in the Headmaster's Quarters."

"Malcolm has access to those places. He's got a key."

"I'm sure he does. He's got a key to whatever he wants. The whole friggin' world."

"You have to talk to him."

"I *won't*. I think he's part of all this."

"He's *not*!" I wanted to punch Gabe right then.

"Can you just leave me alone for a little bit? Just go away!" Clearly he wanted to punch me, too.

"No!" My mind was spinning. There was so much I needed to know. Pieces that needed to be put together. "Did you ever notice they're all girls?"

"Who are?"

"The ghosts."

"Can we not talk about them?" He lurched away from me, scowling.

"I'm one of them."

"You're different. I know you. You don't taunt me."

"We could try to talk to one of them," I said hesitantly and, as expected, Gabe went ballistic.

"I lied. You *do* taunt me. Just go away!"

I wouldn't go away. And he knew it. I did give up on

trying to get him to talk to one of the ghosts, but I would not give up on finding out more about Abigail.

MRS. MULFORD HAD IMPOUNDED Gabe's computer, so I convinced him to go to the library to research. He positioned himself in the most abandoned and farthest away corner next to a bank of old steam radiators. They hissed, spooking me, as he Googled "Abigail Steers." He scoured her Facebook page, her Instagram, her Twitter. He even checked her criminal history—there was none. Yet.

Gabe was so engrossed he didn't notice what I noticed: Malcolm approached the same deserted corner of the library. But when Malcolm saw Gabe, he quickly turned away from him and headed toward another vacant spot nearby. I wanted to follow him, but there was too much work to be done. We still hadn't even looked at my phone, which was plugged in to the wall next to Gabe, charging.

Gabe got pretty deep into the Steers family history, discovering that Abigail and Kent were sixth-generation Wickies. Their relatives had been railroad barons, CEOs, US Ambassadors . . . billionaires.

"So, they're rich and powerful. We already knew that. But come on, let's look at my phone," I urged.

Gabe grumbled as he turned his attention to my iPhone. He checked my emails first. Nothing unusual there. Then he scrolled over to the messages icon.

"You have one new one!" He selected it. "From Malcolm . . . from the night you died . . . at 2:07 A.M.," he said excitedly. He started to read the words of the text, grunted, slammed the phone down, and turned back to the computer.

I leaned over and read the words myself.

you don't have to say it back—just text back a single * if you want to be together. and then maybe someday you'll say the three words. i'd wait for you, liv, forever.

All at once I was aching. The pain was different than the burning sensation I had when I crossed with objects, but it was no less terrible. I did want to be together, I did! And now he'd never know. Not possible. Not fair! I refused to accept it. I had to respond. I had to let him know I was there. It doesn't take much force to push an iPhone key. I had to try. I knew if I was too forceful my hand would go right through the phone, so I tried to focus instead. Of course the * key wasn't right there on the initial keyboard screen (thanks, Apple). First I had to press the *?123* key. I reached for it, strong and steady. I'd never even noticed that key before, but in that moment, it was the only thing that existed in the world.

"Holy shit! Their grandfather was Secretary of State!" Gabe blurted out. Then more silence as he kept reading.

I didn't reply. I couldn't break my focus. I made my finger rigid, as if that would make it more solid, and stared at that key, concentrating as hard as I could while I pressed it. It burned but it worked! The numbers screen popped up. It was only then I realized the * key is on yet another screen. *Oh, Malcolm, of all keys, why the * key?* Of course, I knew why.

Once again I focused, this time on that #+= key, praying that's where the * was hiding. Once again, my fingertip scalded, but a new screen popped up—this one with the * key, that beautiful, bright * hanging aloft! I focused again, trying to ignore the pain in my fingertip and the weakness I was beginning to feel all over my body. I only had two more buttons to press. I pushed both in one swift, focused effort—the * key and then SEND. As the phone chimed, indicating the text had gone through, I collapsed on the chair next to Gabe, completely drained. I felt sick and weak, like I had a high fever.

Gabe heard the chime and looked down to the phone and saw the sent text. "Was that you?" he whispered, glancing around.

"Yes," I murmured.

"Not a good idea, not at all." He banged the cubicle desk. "Why didn't you ask me?!"

"I had to do it. Why does it matter?"

"You reached into the real world. Who knows what doing something like that means? How it affects you? How it affects us?!"

I looked down at my hands and saw he was right. Gabe couldn't see me in this spot, but I could see what I'd done had made me—my consistency—a little more faint. I was dwindling. I recalled those girls telling me to save my strength, first when I was trying to lift the leaf out-side my dorm that first night, and then again when I was pushing the investigator's table. I was *changing* every time I affected the real world.

"And now we have to get rid of the phone!" He snatched it up and shoved it into his pocket. "What if they trace it back to me? I would—" He broke off.

Malcolm appeared from around the corner of the

cubicle, *livid*. He grabbed Gabe by the shirt. "Did you do that, you psycho?"

"No," Gabe croaked.

"Where is it?" Malcolm was possessed. He dumped Gabe's bag out on the floor. "Where's the phone?!"

Malcolm seized Gabe's left arm and twisted it behind his back, then started patting down his pockets. Immediately he felt the phone. Gabe tried to wriggle out of his grasp, but Malcolm got it out of his pocket. Shoving Gabe aside, he clutched it with trembling hands, certain it was proof that Gabe had sent the text.

"*She* did it," Gabe insisted.

Malcolm paused and looked at Gabe with horror. "You're cruel."

"And you're evil."

That set Malcolm off. He pushed Gabe again, hard. But Gabe—far scrawnier—did not withdraw. He straightened. "I'm not cruel. I'm not messing with you. She's here. Right now in fact!"

"Stop!"

Gabe shook his head. "It's true."

"Tell him about the ring," I said, desperate. "He gave me a ring that last night."

"You gave her a ring that last night," he echoed.

Malcolm paused.

I continued, "From his great-great-great-grandfather Balthazar."

Gabe repeated the information: "From his great-great-great-grandfather Balthazar. I mean—from *your* . . . you know what I mean."

Malcolm blinked.

I started spewing memories at Gabe. "Tell him about the drawing on his chest. It said VAPOR and INVISIBLE. The angel. And he drew in green, like my eyes, on my arm—the stars. That night. It was a military mission. And the painting in the tomb at the cemetery. I drew over it. And jumping off the cliff, with our clothes on and . . ."

Gabe struggled to keep up, spewing these random moments Malcolm and I had shared. "See, she's here, telling me these things. That proves it!"

Malcolm's face flushed with rage. "All that proves is that you're a pathetic stalker!"

I looked around, desperate, and noticed the steam forming on the window nearby. I whisked over to the window and climbed atop the wheezing heater.

"Tell him to watch."

"She says watch. She's somewhere over there." Gabe gestured over to the bank of windows.

I put all my focus on my hand, reaching out to the steamy glass. Focus, not fury, I reminded myself. Focus, not strength. *Calm, pure focus.* Malcolm *had* to know. He *had* to believe us.

I touched the glass and moved my finger through the thin film of moisture. It burned, but I was able to ignore the searing pain because I could see it! It was working! The excitement broke my focus, and my finger stopped working. I calmed down. I swallowed my thrill. I concentrated once again on moving the steam. It hurt, but I went on. I had to.

I drew the very same angel I'd drawn on Malcolm's chest—kneeling, with one wing pulled into herself. When I finished, completely drained, I leaned against the wall, turned to Malcolm. I found him approaching me, slowly, cautiously with awe and fear.

He stepped up onto the heater, quivering, and focused on the marks with the same intensity that I'd drawn them. He lifted his own finger up and made a mark in the steam. I summoned my strength and copied his mark.

It was only then that he smiled.

And then, for a moment, we drew together—a duet of lines and strokes. For an instant I felt as if he could see me, as if I were alive.

"You're really here," Malcolm said. It wasn't a question. It was a statement. He finally believed. Gabe nodded.

But I had to stop. It hurt too much. It took too much from me. I collapsed onto the heater. I looked at my limbs, and I was definitely fainter. I still didn't know the rules. Would I eventually end up like the others—barely visible? Powerless? Angry? Haunted? I had no way of knowing.

Malcolm turned to Gabe, shaking his head, still trying to absorb the unbelievable truth. He had no words. There were no words. After a long silence, Malcolm went to Gabe and gently patted him on the back, silently apologizing.

CHAPTER 7

We were an unlikely trio: the handsome golden boy, the conspiracy theorist of questionable mental health, and the ghost. And we had some pretty serious communication issues seeing as the golden boy couldn't hear the ghost, leaving the conspiracy theorist to be the go-between. Not to mention, just minutes prior, the golden boy had thought the conspiracy theorist was an insane stalker and the conspiracy theorist still suspected the golden boy to be the ringleader of some kind of evil scheme. However, we needed one another. Kind of like a mini-ecosystem or a triptych painting or the premise of a wacky TV sitcom.

We retreated to the dreary stacks of the library. We had much to discuss. First of all, Abigail. We told Malcolm we thought she had killed me.

He shook his head. "I don't think so."

"Then why did she lie about me and try to make it seem like I killed myself?!" I yelled.

Gabe repeated my question for Malcolm in a respect-fully calmer tone.

Malcolm looked down, silent.

"And her friend Sloan?" I continued. "And that guy Amos . . . and . . . you."

"Him?" Gabe asked. "You didn't tell me that."

I instantly regretted having said it. "But he only lied to keep from getting in trouble."

Gabe turned to Malcolm. "She says you lied, too."

He nodded. "The Victors . . . They didn't want my name associated with what happened."

"But why would the others—all Victors, I might add—lie?" Gabe pressed, now speaking for himself. "Why would they try to make it look like a suicide?"

Malcolm stared ahead, silent.

"What did they—*you*—have to do with Liv's death?" Gabe demanded.

"Nothing."

"Then why lie?!"

"Don't you understand I am *sworn* to secrecy?"

"Let me guess." Gabe sneered. "It's a blood oath."

"Exactly," Malcolm confirmed, deadly serious.

Gabe stared at him as if he were speaking a different language. "But Liv got killed and came back as a ghost. Don't you think that means pretty much all bets are off?"

Malcolm ran his hands through his messy hair, frus-trated, then finally caved. "The Victors covered it up to protect the image of Wickham Hall. Murders can't happen here. It'd ruin our reputation. Suicide's different. Suicide has happened before. It's a tragedy, but it doesn't tarnish the school. That's the way the Victors see it, at least. The society forced each of us to say what we said. When you join the Victors, you take an oath that you will do *anything* in your power to protect the society, and the society only exists to protect the school."

Gabe glared at Malcolm, his disgust palpable.

Malcolm met his stare. "I know you think I'm awful right now, but the Victors did not kill Liv." He turned away from Gabe and now spoke to me, looking blankly into the air in my general direction. "They did not kill you, Liv. I would know if they had. It's not what Gabe thinks. It's not some evil empire aimed at ruling the world. It's just a bunch of rich families who look out for each other."

It all added up. I believed Malcolm. "But what if Abigail did it solo, knowing the Victors would cover up for her?" I asked, and Gabe repeated.

Malcolm thought it through. He buried his face in his hands. "It's possible, I suppose."

THE PLAN: MALCOLM WOULD go to Abigail in her room seemingly seeking consolation. We'd pick a time when Pitchfork Lady was not in the dorm, knowing Abigail would invite him in. I'd be with him, follow him in, and look for clues while they talked.

So, Malcolm knew I was right next to him when he knocked on Abigail's door. As he waited for her to answer, he turned toward me. "Military mission," he quietly joked. "But this time it's kind of for real. Good thing we got all that practice. " I smiled, not that he could see me.

Abigail's face lit up when she opened the door and saw

it was Malcolm. He told her he "just wanted to talk." She was clearly delighted, but remembering I'd just died and everything, she quickly shifted to melancholy. She said Mrs. Mulford was at the Science Center and, as anticipated, quickly pulled him into her room.

I followed, sweeping through the doorway.

The room was now extremely tidy. "Spring cleaning?" Malcolm asked, looking around, surprised. So, he'd been in her room before and knew, as I did, that it didn't usually look like this. But of course he'd been in her room. They were both Victors.

"I had Mariska come up from the City and give it a once over. You know how dusty these rooms can get."

"Mariska?"

"Mum's live-in."

He nodded, sitting on the edge of her bed. There was nowhere else to sit.

"You must be devastated."

"I just wish I knew what happened," he said, truthfully.

"What we said happened is probably what happened."

"I don't think so. And because we lied to the police, we'll never know."

"It's for the greater good. You know that. You're just sad." She crossed and sat down next to him. "I'm sad, too." She put her hand on his leg. But he didn't seem to notice. His eyes were darting around the room, looking for something, anything. I was looking, too. Whatever incriminating evidence may have been was now long gone. Thanks to Mariska. She was smart, this girl.

Then Abigail put her head on Malcolm's shoulder. He

looked uncomfortable but didn't move. She nestled her head into his neck, summoning tears. "I really liked her. I did," she sniffled.

"Liar!" I yelled. "This was *not* part of our plan. Are you really falling for this?"

But, as if he could hear me, Malcolm said, "This is all part of the plan."

I paused. Was he talking to me or her? He turned his head away from Abigail and glanced at the door. He'd said it to me. I calmed down.

"What plan?" Abigail asked.

"I was just saying, this is all part of the plan, the Victors' plan."

"I know," she said, snuggling in even closer to him. "But I also know this is all so hard for you. You're so sensitive and kind. I'm here for you, Malcolm." They were face to face now.

I watched in disbelief—powerless—just praying this was, as he'd said, part of the plan. Then she leaned in to kiss him. He stopped her.

"Don't," he said.

"Why?" she breathed.

"I'm too confused right now," he said, as if in a few days he might not be, as if he might actually kiss her then.

Abigail nodded, satisfied. And she nestled her head back into the crook of his neck. I couldn't take it—I stormed right at them. Abigail shivered. I'd given her a chill, so she pulled in closer to Malcolm. I sighed. Nice. Perfect backfire.

"You understand why I'm doing this, right?" He turned his head away from her and mouthed *"for you."*

Again, he was speaking to me, but Abigail answered, "Yes."

"Where were you that night, really?"

"At the meeting. Same as you."

"Until eleven. But what about *after* that?"

She hesitated.

"I just *need* to know, if we're gonna . . . you know, move forward at some point." Malcolm looked down as he said that. All at once I felt mortified and blissful. He sounded like a bad actor in a worse movie, but she didn't seem to notice.

She sighed and finally confessed. "I was in the infirmary. Lady things, you know. You can check the logs if you don't believe me."

He hopped up. "I think I should go."

She walked him to the door and gave him a hug. A *lingering* hug. He pulled away and pushed open her door, careful to hold it open long enough for me to follow.

We checked the infirmary logs. And, yes, she had been there immediately after the Victors meeting, during the time I was murdered. Nurse Cobbs had administered prescription-strength Advil and let her lie down for two hours. It was all documented. And seeing as it was impossible to imagine any conspiracy involving crotchety Nurse Cobbs—even for Gabe, who thrived on such theories—the three of us agreed unanimously that Abigail was not guilty.

AT DINNER, MALCOLM SAT with Gabe in the Pit. They both pushed their food around on their plates. Students shuffled past, rubbernecking as if Malcolm's sitting with Gabe was a horrific car accident. Time blurred again, and in an instant, their plates were nearly empty.

As they started to get up, I noticed Malcolm's lips twist as if he was wrestling with something. Finally, he said, "Listen, I was wondering if you'd ask Liv if she wants to go to the mountain tonight."

"Yes!" I yelped without thinking.

But Gabe just said, "You won't be able to hear her."

"I know. But I want to be with her. Alone."

"Yes, yes, yes!" I shrieked.

But Gabe completely ignored me.

"Did you hear me, Gabe?!"

He nonchalantly told Malcolm, "She said yes. She'll meet you there."

"Hello?! Don't you still hear me?" I was nearly yelling as Malcolm got up and walked away. Gabe finally turned to me and whispered, "Yes, God. *Relax*. I was trying to play it cool for you."

"Oh," I quietly chuckled. "Thanks."

I GOT TO THE mountain before Malcolm and watched the sun set. I walked to the edge of the cliff and looked out. The setting sun was cold and muted. The lake was nearly covered with fog. I felt like Friedrich's *Wanderer Above the Sea of Fog*. That intrepid wanderer atop a cliff, seen in silhouette from behind—triumphant. But I wasn't. I wasn't even the meager and practically incidental *Monk by the Sea*.

I looked down. The fog rolled, revealing slivers of lake. I wanted to relive that moment. I wanted to know what it'd feel like. So I jumped.

Gravity did affect me but only so much as I let it. When I focused on slowing down, I slowed down. I spun around and slowed down so much I could see every crag, every rock. Finally I landed on the water. I started to descend into it. But, as my feet dipped into the still water, they seemed to dissolve into the darkness. It suddenly reminded me of disappearing in the limousine—that horrible moment when I felt myself evaporating, losing my limbs and my thoughts. So I pulled myself out, terrified of what might happen, and tumbled unceremoniously onto the shore.

I looked down to see if I'd changed, if I'd become more faint. I hadn't. It seemed I could jump and fly and run without even getting tired. But if I crossed with something—a person or a door or even a piece of paper—it caused that searing pain. And if I so much as tried to lift a leaf or draw in steam on a window—*affecting* the real world in any way—it didn't just hurt, it also depleted me in the scariest possible way: I could *see* it. I was fainter now than I had been when I first died.

I climbed back up to the top of the cliff and sat down against the tree where Malcolm and I had sat together. Now I was alone. I mean, truly alone. I'd always been a bit of a loner, but this was different. I had no guide, no understanding, and most of the time no one could hear me or see me. I didn't know why I was trapped here or where I might eventually go.

When Malcolm arrived, he came right to me as if he knew I was there and sat next to me. Silent. I looked at him. His eyes were tired and muddy. They looked out onto the landscape. As I stared at him, I replayed that day we were here together. Why hadn't I just let him kiss me when we were in the water? If I'd let him kiss me then, maybe we never would have made the plan to sneak out. Maybe I'd still be alive.

And why hadn't I told him how I felt, then or later? Why hadn't I told him that just looking at him made my stomach implode? Why hadn't I told him I'd never been in love? That I was afraid to be in love? Why had I always acted so tough? So withdrawn and ambivalent? Why had I pretended? Because, *now*, I couldn't tell him anything. Not a word. And it only made every word I'd faked or wasted or swallowed all the more heartbreaking.

He slid down from the tree onto his back. "Liv, if you're here, will you lie down next to me?"

Yes! Of course I will. And I did.

"Lie right next to me and we'll both just look up, like that last night. Okay?"

I was already there, exactly as he requested, which of course made his plea even sadder and made me feel even more alone.

"I'm so sorry, Liv. It's my fault you're gone. *I* suggested we sneak out. *I* picked the place. *I* said we should run opposite ways. I don't know what happened to you, but *I made you vulnerable.* And then I lied to the police. I'm so sorry. But please tell me you understand why." He started to cry but then quickly pulled it back. "The Victors seem stupid to you and Gabe. And I get it. But you have no idea how this club has been inculcated in me—by my father, my grandfather, my uncles—my *entire* life. It *is* my entire life. It's part of me. I have this sense of duty and responsibility that I now see is so skewed. So wrong. Somehow the meetings, the chants, the oaths—I got lost in them. And I'm so sorry I lied for them. But I've decided I'm going to go to the police and tell them the truth, help them find your killer."

I lay my head on his chest, which was heaving by now, and he shivered. "Is that you?"

Yes! I proclaimed, unheard.

He wrapped himself up in his jacket. I wanted to think he heard me, but he didn't.

"You know what I wish?" he asked.

What?

"That I could just see you one last time—hear your voice. Hold you."

I'd give anything for that. Anything.

After a long time, he fell asleep. Not me, though. Sleep was for the living, not possible for me. No dreams. No nightmares. Only time expanding and contracting. I felt Malcolm's chest rise and fall. I listened to his breath and heard his heartbeat. It echoed in my own empty chest. *I am hollow,* I thought. And time just slipped past. I'm not sure how many minutes or hours.

IT WAS STILL PITCH black when I heard feet approaching. I lurched upright, afraid of being discovered, until I remembered panic was pointless. Panic was a luxury. A gift. I only *wished* I could be caught in the middle of the night at the mountain. I only *wished* I could be sent to the headmaster or even suspended or expelled.

It was Kent Steers. He shook his head when he saw Malcolm sleeping. He paced for a beat and quickly sent a text:

found him.

Finally, he sat down next to Malcolm and gently shook him awake.

"Malcolm, what are you doing? You can tell me. I'm your best friend."

Malcolm rubbed his eyes. "She's here, Kent."

"Who?"

"Liv."

"Malcolm, you gotta let go of her." Kent's voice was surprisingly tender. Given his perma-smile, I didn't think he was capable of real emotion. "She is gone. Forever."

"No, she's not. She's here. Her spirit is here."

"You can see her?"

"No, but I know."

"Do you hear her?"

"No, but I'm telling you she's still here."

Kent smiled strangely.

"What?" Malcolm asked.

"Nothing. It's just . . . I don't know. Sweet." Kent turned away. "Look, I know you think I'm a douche sometimes. What's your nickname for me? Lil Payne?"

Malcolm laughed. "Who told you that? Abigail?"

"We have no secrets here, man," Kent said.

Malcolm's face became stony. "We do. Liv was murdered, and we covered it up."

Kent shook his head. "It sucks. And we owe it to ourselves to find the killer. But we did what was right."

"Not right for *her.*"

"We have a responsibility."

"To *her,*" Malcolm insisted.

"Yeah, we do. But we also have a responsibility to the Victors.

To this school and its history. Its position. It has to stay that way. *Always.* Our children will go here, Malcolm. And our children's children. They'll heal the world. You know that."

Malcolm sat up. He ran a hand through his mess of hair. "I'm going to the police. I'm going to tell them the truth."

"Don't say that." Kent placed his hands on Malcolm's shoulders, staring into his eyes. "You're losing it, man. If you go to the police, all that's going to happen is everyone's gonna think you're crazy. They'll send you away. *Again.*"

Malcolm shuddered.

I shuddered, too. *Again?*

"And what is the truth anyway?" he continued. "What exactly would you tell them? That you were with her in the woods? All that's going to accomplish is getting you in trouble. Probably even make you a suspect in the case. What can you say that you think will help?"

Malcolm shrugged.

"Just get some sleep, buddy."

"I can't sleep anymore."

"Well, try to relax. Maybe go rowing. Clear your head. We have a big weekend ahead. Isn't your dad coming?"

Malcolm nodded, and Kent gave him a big hug.

I'd kind of come around to Kent. Like he said, he was a douche, but at least he knew it. And all that really mattered was that he cared for Malcolm. Still, as he walked away, I just kept hearing the word *again.* He'd said it with such weight. Like a bag of sand. Where had Malcolm been sent?

Malcolm paced. He stressed. He talked to himself and to me. "I don't even know if you're still here, and I'm talking to you. Maybe I *am* crazy." On and on he rambled. He said he didn't know what to do anymore. He needed to think. Kent was right; he needed to clear his head, he needed to row. He started down the ridge, and I followed him. As he pushed through the brush, I caught a glimpse of a faint girl through the fall foliage—one I hadn't seen before. She had long blonde hair, but before I could really see what she looked like, she noticed us and turned and ran the other way, vanishing into the curtain of bright leaves.

Malcolm climbed purposefully around the edge of the lake to the boathouse. The fluorescent lights automatically clicked on when he opened the door. In a pool of green light, Malcolm took down his scull, put it in the water, and prepared it.

I screamed when I noticed another girl had appeared in the boathouse. She had dark hair, delicate features, and no visible wounds, but her skin was a sheer grey and she looked at me with unmistakably dead eyes. She wore dark-colored full-length bloomers and a dress; the outfit looked somewhere between clothes and pajamas. She paused somewhat awkwardly, as if trying to cover herself. Thankfully, Malcolm had finished prepping the boat. I jumped onto it just before he pushed off.

I looked back and saw her pass effortlessly through the boathouse wall out onto the dock. She didn't even wince, as if passing through the wall had been painless. As we glided away into the lake, she hissed, "Soon you'll be like us!"

What did she mean? I looked back at her. She lingered on the dock watching me with her dull eyes until I had to look away. I wondered if my eyes looked like that.

BALANCING ON THE NOSE of the boat, I watched Malcolm row. He was a champion—an award-winner—and now I could see why. He had perfect rhythm. The oars moved like music. But he was stoic. I don't know how long we were out there, but all of a sudden I noticed his clothes were drenched with sweat. The sky was still pitch black. How much time had passed? Who knew. It might have been hours.

He was so deep in thought he didn't notice—or perhaps he didn't care—that the boat was wavering and slowing. He just kept rowing and rowing, like a machine. But I looked and saw a side panel of fiberglass was cracked.

"Malcolm!" I yelled, but it was no use. He just looked out into the darkness with glazed eyes, absorbed in his own thoughts and sadness.

Before long, the nose of the boat was fighting to keep above the water. Of course he had to notice that. He dropped the oars and inspected the boat. When he spotted the crack, he looked around—we were in the dead middle of the lake, miles from land on every side. And his body was already shaking from exertion.

"Hello?!" he yelled out. "Help! I need help!!" His voice echoed out across the water.

Silence. No one was out there. It was the middle of the night at Wickham Hall, so if anyone was out, the *last* thing they'd do was admit it and attract attention. The water started streaming over my feet, making them invisible to me, and I became almost as frightened for myself as I was for him. What happened to me in the water? Did I just evaporate like ice in the sun? Would I ever even come back? I did not know.

I walked to the bow of the boat, careful to balance. I imagined myself an angel. I kind of was, wasn't I? I was immaterial so of course I could fly. Like that girl who had flown from the cupola! I must be able to fly. Not just float, but actually span a distance. I focused, picturing myself as a real angel—not a Raphael or a Banksy. No wings. Nothing bird-like. No real body, even. Something more like pure light. Suddenly I soared up, flying over the lake. I stayed focused on one thing: getting to land. And land I did, in an instant. This time it was fast motion, not slow, and I stumbled onto the grass on the water's edge.

But I had much farther to go. I needed Gabe. So I focused again. I sprung up into the darkness, this time more easily. I glided over the pines and the willow and the old rooftops—it was practically effortless if I let it be, like a dream—and landed at Dorm Row, just a few yards from Gabe's window.

"Gabe!!" I yelled out. "Gabe! Help! Now!" I screamed bloody murder, doing whatever I could to frighten him, wake him.

It worked. His second-floor window creaked open.

"Malcolm is stuck in the middle of the lake! Now!"

He shook his head. "What am I supposed to do?" he whispered.

"Call security! Tell them to send a boat out. Now!" Every dorm had a phone dedicated for use in emergencies. But our 911 calls didn't go out to the police; they connected to Wickham Hall's own 24-hour security.

Gabe paused. He shook his head again. "We can't do that. He'll get in trouble for sneaking out, breaking into the boathouse. He'll get expelled. We can save him. Wait there." The window slammed shut.

WHEN WE ARRIVED AT the edge of the lake, dawn was breaking. We could see the dot of a figure in the water, slowly treading toward land. Gabe stood on the bank and yelled out, "You can stop swimming and just float! We're coming!"

Malcolm raised an arm acknowledging him, too weak to yell.

On the dock next to the boathouse, Gabe quickly prepared a small motorboat, lowering it into the water. The Boathouse Girl appeared right next to him. I backed away toward the boat, away from her. Gabe saw her, too, but he just clenched his jaw and started up the engine. She had a slight smile, as if relishing our peril.

We found Malcolm floating facedown, breathing only when he had to. The survival float: I remembered it from swimming lessons in that horrible, soupy Las Vegas public pool. Gabe cut the motor and leaned down, hoisting him up onto the side of the boat. Malcolm didn't even have enough energy to get on his feet. He stayed seated, slumped, catching his breath. Once his breath had calmed, he looked up at Gabe and said, "Thank you." He paused. "Is she here, too?"

Gabe nodded, and Malcolm managed a smile. "Thank you, too."

"You're welcome."

"She says you're welcome." Then Gabe turned to me. "You're going to stick with him. All the time now. Whoever killed you just tried to kill him."

Malcolm protested. "No, it was probably just an accident."

"It was no accident," Gabe said.

"Let's go to the police," Malcolm said. "I'll tell them I lied. Let's let them handle it."

"The police can't help." Gabe was certain.

"Why not?" I asked. Malcolm asked the same thing almost instantly, like an echo.

"Because it's the ghosts. The *ghosts* are the killers."

"What do you mean?" Malcolm demanded.

"Think about it. They can see us. They can reach over to us. And they're *invisible*. No one else knows they're here. Think of how much power that gives them. All this time I was focused on the Victors, thinking they had all the power on this campus but, really, it's the ghosts who have the power."

Malcolm ran his fingers through his hair, trying to make sense of it.

Gabe wouldn't let up. "Who did Liv see at the well *right* after she died?"

Malcolm shrugged.

"Weeping Willow Girl with the bloody neck. And then, who was there, in the boathouse just now while you were stranded?"

Malcolm was silent.

"I saw her. She was smiling," I said. "And she was there before, too."

"The Boathouse Girl," Gabe told Malcolm. "And she was *smiling*."

"But how could the ghosts kill?" Malcolm asked.

"They can reach over to the real world. Liv did."

"But I can't imagine committing a murder," I said. "It hurts so badly to interact with the real world in any way. And it's so depleting."

Gabe shrugged, undeterred.

"And let's say they were the killers. Why would they just hang around the scenes of the crimes?" Malcolm asked. I had the same question.

"What do they have to lose? They're *dead*," Gabe barked.

It was a chilling thought because I was trapped in this in-between place *with* them. Was I surrounded by killers? "Why don't we try to talk to one of them?" I asked.

"NO!" Gabe was emphatic. He turned to Malcolm. "She wants to talk to them."

"You're fearless," Malcolm said toward me with near awe.

"Or just stupid. We're not doing that," Gabe snapped.

I was not fearless. I was terrified, but I needed to know.

"Who are they?" Malcolm asked. "And why?! Why are they here, and why would they do it?"

"Former students? I don't know—all I know is they scare the shit out of me—but that's what we need to find out."

"I can get us into the Headmaster's Quarters to look at the student records," Malcolm volunteered.

"But first we need to figure out when each girl was at Wickham Hall, so we at least know where to start looking in the records," I said.

"All right, she's pretty clever, that one," Gabe said, repeating what I'd said.

Malcolm smiled. "Yes, she is."

Clara

I'm afraid I cannot recall every detail regarding the occurrence of my death. In fact, I regret to report that I can recall very little. It's been such a long time. Or has it? I am not entirely certain.

I was new to Wickham Hall and searching for my proper place on campus—a friend, a group to which to belong. A girl named Henrietta, who seemed quite popular, asked me to meet her at the boathouse for a swim. I thought it odd, but she assured me it was a bit of a tradition for the new girls to take a cold swim during fall term.

Considering it was warmer than usual for October, I ventured to the boathouse on the evening she requested. When I arrived, I changed into my swimming attire. It was a new bathing outfit—a splurge we'd made when we heard Wickham Hall had a lake for swimming—and one I was quite excited to show the girls.

The girls, however, did not arrive. Rather, it was two boys. I was terribly embarrassed for them to see me in such improper attire, so I hid in the bathroom. They knocked on the door—jolly as can be—and said Henrietta had asked them to row me to the swimming hole. It did seem odd behavior and quite inappropriate, but to be honest, I was having a hard time making friends at Wickham Hall. If I were to let down the one girl who had shown an interest in me, I might never make a friend. And I had promised my mother I would make friends, not just study, as I tended to do. I was, after all, one of Wickham Hall's first students to receive financial assistance, and I intended to show Mr. Wickham I was a worthwhile investment. But my mother, of course, was more interested in my finding a proper husband.

I had brought a blanket in case we might decide to sit along the bank, so I wrapped myself in that as the boys and I set out upon the chilly ride.

The temperature dropped with the sun as the boys rowed and rowed. After some minutes, I realized they were rowing me straight into the middle of the lake. When I asked about our destination, they just chuckled and said, "We're just taking you where you belong." I told them I was cold, and one of them told me I deserved to be. I realized they were pulling some kind of cruel prank, and perhaps I wasn't terribly welcome at Wickham Hall. I stopped my protestations—I had prepared myself for this kind of ridicule. I was, after all, from the lower class.

Finally it was dark, save for the moonlight, and they pushed me into the water. I did not put up a struggle because I wanted to save my strength for swimming back to shore. What I did not expect was what happened next. They put their hands on my head and pushed me under the water, holding me there.

Somehow I caught a glimpse of one of their hands—a Wickham Hall ring, and beneath the insignia an inscription read: B.A./V.P. 1885.

CHAPTER 10

We retreated to a remote corner of the library and started to compile information.

Gabe and I came up with a list. We had seen seven ghosts: Weeping Willow Girl, Skellenger Girl, *Gossip Girl*, Boathouse Girl, *Jackie O* Girl, Lydia, and the blonde I'd caught a glimpse of in the nature preserve. If we could find names, or at least dates, for each ghost, then we'd know where to look in the student files for their records.

First, Weeping Willow Girl. She was usually at the weeping willow tree near the well. She was wearing a beaded dress, something formal for a party, maybe. Her throat was cut. And she was singing that song. I remembered the chorus: *And that's the reason I've got those weepin' willow blues.*

Gabe Googled "weeping willow blues" and easily found it was a Bessie Smith song that had been a hit in 1924. So Malcolm asked the librarian for the microfilm of any state newspapers from that year. She had *The New Hampshire Gazette,* which she boasted was "the nation's oldest newspaper," as if it were her own. Malcolm scoured the editions—day after day, week after week—looking for a death announcement, while Gabe used the rolling library ladder to pull the 1924 and 1925 yearbooks from the shelves and examined them on the long worktable. I stood behind him, studying the class pictures, hoping to identify her.

Malcolm and Gabe both flexed the serious deductive reasoning they'd learned and honed at Wickham Hall. And I couldn't help but notice that they worked surprisingly well together. They were alike in more ways than either would care to admit.

"Death reported at Wickham Hall, February 1924!" Malcolm blurted excitedly, reading from the microfilm. Then more silence as he read. "But, damn, not a student. A male teacher. Natural causes."

We couldn't find a picture we recognized in the yearbooks, but seeing as how she was singing that Bessie Smith song and wearing a flapper dress—like the girls were wearing in the mid-twenties—we could safely place her in 1924 or 1925.

Next: Lydia in the catacombs. She didn't have a visible wound, but there was definitely something wrong with her neck. And she was erratic, with wild eyes, as if she'd gone mad. She was wearing that Smiths T-shirt with a black-and-white image of a young guy in profile. We Googled and found it was for the Smiths album *Hatful of Hollow,* released November 1984.

Gabe and I pored over the 1984 yearbook. We both

recognized her immediately in the Fifth Form group photo, where she lurked in the back with a few other goth and hippie types. Then we found her again in the literary magazine photo—Lydia Korn was her full name. In the picture she looked typical-teenage angry, but not crazy like now.

And Skellenger Girl—the one who jumped out of the cupola at me—had blood coming out of her nose, ears, and eyes. She'd probably been pushed to her death. She was wearing what looked like a school uniform—a black jumper over a white blouse with large, billowy sleeves. Malcolm discovered the girls' school uniform matching that ensemble was adopted in 1907. Malcolm checked the yearbooks from that time while Gabe scoured microfilm from *The New Hampshire Gazette* starting in 1907 to see if there was any mention of a death at Wickham Hall. Gabe eventually discovered an article about a suicide in 1915—a Florence Kelly had thrown herself from the cupola of her dorm. Malcolm cross-referenced her name in the 1915 yearbook and, yes, it was definitely her. Florence Kelly.

The *Gossip Girl* I'd seen in Main was easy to date. I remembered she was wearing leopard-print flats with a distinct metal emblem. A quick Google search revealed the shoes were designed by Tory Burch and rose to popularity in 2005. Assuming she died in 2005, we looked through the 2004 yearbook and there she was—a trendy but sweet-looking Third Former named Brit McLean.

Boathouse Girl was wearing those bloomers and that dress. It reminded me of some Monet paintings of bathers I knew had been painted in the 1870s. We learned her outfit was indeed a bathing suit, the style that was worn in Victorian times—the kind that modestly covers the entire body. So, Boathouse Girl must have died sometime between 1865 and 1900. She was the most elusive.

As for the Nature Preserve Girl, there was no way of knowing. I hadn't seen enough to have any idea when she might've lived. And Gabe, who never visited the nature preserve, hadn't seen her at all.

"I don't do nature," Gabe boasted.

"That's like saying I don't do air," Malcolm replied.

Gabe shrugged at him. Yes, they worked well together, but that certainly didn't mean they agreed on much. Or anything. But we were actually making progress. At what? We didn't exactly know, but we were getting somewhere.

Finally, there was *Jackie O* Girl. She was the one I'd somehow seen—or at least thought I'd seen—in the cemetery on that Headmaster Holiday night before I died. She was undeniably sixties, had slit wrists and a blood-soaked jacket and skirt. Gabe and Malcolm studied the yearbooks from the sixties, trying to identify her, or at least date her uniform. No luck.

"I swear it was her who I saw that night in the cemetery. Maybe we should try to talk her," I proposed again.

"No! I told you—"

Gabe was about to go postal when, out of nowhere, Kent and Abigail appeared. Standing side by side, their twin-ness was almost eerie, like that famous Diane Arbus photo of the two girls, *almost* identical but not quite.

"What are you doing?" Abigail asked Malcolm. Her tone was unreadable. She deliberately ignored Gabe.

"Just looking at some old pictures," he said. His knee twitched, his foot bouncing up and down. I wished I could stop it. Gabe noticed, too, his eyes flitting toward Malcolm.

"With him?" Kent pressed, visibly concerned that Malcolm was with Gabe.

Malcolm nodded.

"You feeling okay?" Kent added. "Did you talk to the grief counselor? You don't want them to tell your dad."

Malcolm stiffened in his chair.

"When's he coming?" Kent pressed.

"Tomorrow."

"We missed you last night," Abigail said.

"At some point we need to discuss the absences," Kent went on. "I—"

"In case you didn't notice, we're kinda busy here," Gabe interrupted.

"Right." Kent didn't take his eyes from Malcolm. "New friend?"

"Yep."

Kent shrugged. "Just talk to the counselor, okay?" And then he drifted off, his near-mirror-image shadowing close behind.

"Your friends are assholes," Gabe said, loud enough so that they'd hear. "Just for the record."

"Kent's not bad. I swear." Malcolm looked down, ashamed. "I had some issues last year. I got really depressed. I isolated . . . so I took some time off."

Gabe frowned. "That's why you left? I heard you went abroad."

"That's what everyone is supposed to think," Malcolm said. "Kent kind of saved me. He helped spread that lie. But he also helped me get help. I owe him. And anyway, I'm stuck with him. He's a Victor. We're all stuck with each other. But with him . . . I don't mind. I know he's kind of a dick, but he's a friend."

Gabe put his hand up like he was taking an oath. "I do solemnly swear to befriend all the stuck-up pigs and jerks heretofore known as the Victors."

"Stop it, Gabe," I snapped. I couldn't help it. Malcolm had just confessed something huge; he'd made himself vulnerable. Why couldn't Gabe back off?

Gabe swallowed. He nodded toward me. "Sorry, man. That was harsh. I just . . ."

"Whatever," Malcolm said. "Anyway, it's not like that, at least I don't *think* that was what we were swearing. I wouldn't exactly know."

"*Because?*"

"It's not in English. It's all in Latin and some old Celtic dialect."

Gabe barked a laugh. "So, wait, you sit and make all these oaths, and you don't even know what you're swearing to?!"

"I heard a rough translation. Once." Now Malcolm looked ashamed. "But yeah, pretty much."

AS WE WERE LEAVING the library, three police investigators approached Gabe, blocking his exit. They just wanted to talk, they said. They knew he and I had become friends, and they wanted to learn more about me. At the station. He said he was busy, he had homework, but they assured him it wouldn't take too long. It was clear he didn't really have a choice in the matter.

"Fine, but can I at least take a pre-interrogation whiz?" he asked in true Gabe form. The officers stepped back. Gabe scurried off to the bathroom. Malcolm followed. As did I. And in that bathroom, we quietly made a pact to sneak out and meet that night at 1 A.M. outside the Headmaster's Quarters to pull the girls' records.

AS MALCOLM AND I approached the Headmaster's Quarters, I worried Gabe might have been detained. Or gotten caught sneaking out. I missed him the same way you'd miss your hands or your voice. He was both of those things to me, particularly the latter. As we waited, Malcolm paced, looking at his watch. "He's my connection to you," he said, echoing my thoughts. "He better be here."

Gabe slunk from out of the shadows. *Thank God.* He looked tired, but relatively unscathed. He shook his head, making it clear he didn't want to talk about the questioning—or risk anyone overhearing us.

Malcolm's master key got us into the house. I lingered at the foot of the headmaster's stairs, standing guard, while Malcolm and Gabe crept into the records room and rifled through the files, searching for the dead girls' Wickham records. As I waited, I studied every detail around me. Next to the door was another historical plaque. This one detailed every headmaster who'd resided here, starting with Elijah Wickham.

There were several holes above the front door, as if there had been bolts of some kind to hang something above it. Something heavier than mistletoe. And, looking closely, I could see the door had been damaged and carefully repaired and repainted. The door frame and even the walls on either side of the door had *all* suffered some damage—marks or streaks of some kind.

I drifted into the small room attached to the living room; I wanted to look more closely at those strange photographs I'd seen before. Each photograph was labeled. The first read: *Elijah Wickham and the spirit of his mother, Minerva, 1877.* Elijah was a handsome young man, maybe thirty. Posing thoughtfully, a halo of light above him. Looking very carefully, you could see the faintest eyes looking out over him. I guess that was supposed to be her. It was spirit photography—obviously a hoax, right?

I'd learned about spirit photography in a multimedia class I took at a community college last summer. Hilariously, the whole movement started with an accident: a photographer mistakenly double-exposed his film. When he realized that it looked like a ghost, he decided to capitalize on the booming Spiritualist movement and market himself as a spirit photographer. Spirit photography became quite a thing—think *JibJab* of the nineteenth century except people actually seemed to think it was real.

Another, *Elijah Wickham with female spirit, 1886,* revealed an older Elijah, now standing with hand to chin, pensive. A trace of a girl swirled above him. She reminded me of Boathouse Girl. Her peaceful smile was hardly recognizable, but I wondered if it could be her or, more likely, a super-imposed photo of her.

Elijah Wickham with three female spirits, 1916 portrayed a greying Elijah with a swirl of light and three ashen smiling faces around him. One of those faces looked distinctly like Skellenger Girl, with her big blue eyes. He'd used her Wickham portrait—the one I'd just seen in the year-book—for the double exposure.

And *Elijah Wickham with many spirits, 1930* portrayed an elderly Elijah outdoors in the woods, arms raised as if in victory, surrounded by six bright "spirits." Now I saw another familiar face—Weeping Willow Girl.

The final photo—this one much smaller—was *Wallace Wickham with Minerva.* An aged, kind-looking Wallace was seated in a sumptuous room, enveloped in a blur. There were no eyes or faces, but he genuinely seemed to be wrapped up in the spirit of Minerva in this one. Perhaps this one was real. His eyes were closed, but the expression on his face reminded me exactly of the way Malcolm looked when I was around—peaceful but deeply sad.

I was so engrossed in the photo that at first I didn't hear the footsteps coming down the stairs. It wasn't until the *thunk* of two slippers that I was shaken out of my daze. I flew out of the small sitting room into the vestibule. Head-master Thorton was there grumbling, "Hello?"

I panicked. This was my fault. I was supposed to be at the foot of the stairs. I was supposed to have alerted Malcolm and Gabe if anyone was coming. I needed to dis-tract him, draw him away from the records room. I surged past him. He shivered and shook his head as if he'd felt a chill, mumbling, "Damn drafts." As he went to check the window in the living room, I looked around for more to do, grasping for something light enough for me to affect. The butterflies.

I rushed at the hanging butterflies and pushed myself through them. I ignored the burning pain as best I could—the swarm began to swoosh and flutter in the air. The metal contraption that held them up squeaked. But I had to collapse against the couch, drained.

Thorton went over to the butterflies. He touched the delicate strings, calming them. Then he checked the other windows—none were open, of course. He was confused and unsettled now.

I had another idea. I lifted myself up and rushed past the old steam heater, chilling it, causing the thermostat to turn on. The radiator began spewing steam and hissing. Somehow that made him feel better, convinced everything was the fault of that noisy heater. He padded over and turned a knob. As he started back up the stairs, I collapsed on the bottom step, still stinging and exhausted. Once I recovered and was certain the headmaster was back in bed, I crept in to find Malcolm and Gabe.

The records room was something out of the past, long before computers, musty and stale: rows and rows of floor-to-ceiling files, documenting every student who ever attended Wickham Hall. Malcolm and Gabe were so deep into a heap of folders they hadn't heard a thing.

"Thorton came down, but lucky for you guys, I did some deft ghost interceptions."

Gabe chuckled.

Malcolm asked, "What's funny?"

"Liv's back. She saved us from Thorton."

"For now," I grumbled, angry at myself. "Any progress?"

"Progress?" Gabe beamed. "We struck gold. We found a file for *every* one of them. Boathouse Girl took forever, but we just found her."

Malcolm started gathering up folders. "Let's get out of here. We can go over it all at my dorm."

THE THREE OF US climbed through Malcolm's ground-floor window. Gabe and Malcolm now knew to leave the window open a few extra seconds for me to follow. "In," I announced. Gabe shut the window as Malcolm spread seven school folders out onto his bed.

"Seven?" I asked. "You found Nature Preserve Girl?"

"No. The six we identified and . . . you," Gabe explained.

"Me?!"

"We thought it might help us look for commonalities," Malcolm said. He was getting good at guessing my side of the conversation and responding to it. Sometimes it even seemed like he could hear me.

"Okay. I guess. But please tell me that's not the end of this story. That I become some murderous ghost."

"You're not going to become a murderous ghost," Gabe assured me.

Malcolm followed Gabe's stare and said firmly, "We know you're not that, Liv. You will *never* be that. And that's why we're doing this—to end it. To make things right."

"Okay. Tell him I said okay."

Gabe grumbled. "She said okay."

"Say it nicely."

"She wants me to say it nicely."

Malcolm flashed a brief smile, but I was frustrated with Gabe. We all felt that way. Gabe was sick of having to repeat everything I said. I would have been, too. And Malcolm was clearly frustrated he couldn't hear me. But we got back to the task at hand. Malcolm moved all the folders into chronological order and started to review the facts.

"Clara Dodge, aka Boathouse Girl, disappeared in 1885. Technically, it was an unsolved missing person. Florence Kelly, aka Skellenger Girl, died in 1915. Suicide. Ruth Bookout, aka Miss Weeping Willow, died in 1925. Suicide. Cut her own throat."

"How is that even possible?" Gabe grumbled angrily.

"Just let him keep going," I said.

Gabe growled, shaking his long hair down over his face, as Malcolm proceeded. "Mary Bata, aka *Jackie O* Girl, died 1965. Suicide. Cut her wrists. Lydia Korn, died 1985. Suicide brought on by a bad reaction to LSD."

"Shit! No wonder she seems so insane," Gabe proclaimed. "She's tripping."

He had a point. That could explain her belligerence and wild eyes.

"And, finally, Brit McLean, aka *Gossip Girl,*" Malcolm finished. "Died in 2005. Suicide. Hanged herself in the lobby of Main. So . . . those are the facts."

"According to Wickham Hall," Gabe added.

"Yes," Malcolm concurred. "The facts *according to Wickham Hall.*"

"So what does it all mean?" Gabe pressed.

"Well, for starters, they're all girls," Malcolm said.

Exactly. I moved next to Malcolm, studying the papers. "And, look, we all died in October."

Malcolm echoed the same thing without knowing I'd spoken, adding, "Usually late in the month. He turned to Gabe. "You wanna write this down?"

"I'm not your personal assistant, Mr. Astor."

"Just do it," I urged, and Gabe grabbed a pen off Malcolm's desk. He wrote "late October" on the back of some crew-related handout. I couldn't help but notice the trophies and awards on Malcolm's desk. I glanced around and saw they were everywhere—trophies, awards, plaques, certificates. Malcolm was a winner. At everything, it seemed. "And look at the years," Malcolm noticed. "Each death is in the fifth year of a decade!"

"No way *in hell* those are all coincidences." Gabe stood and started pacing.

"But every death was reported as a suicide." Malcolm leaned back. "Except Boathouse Clara—I guess her body was never found."

"*Reported* is the key word. Liv's death was also reported as a suicide, but we *know* it wasn't. Come on! There's a pattern here, some kind of ritualistic killings happening at pre-determined intervals, right?!" Gabe wasn't taking notes anymore. He was exploding with conspiracy ideas. "Maybe each ghost kills the next one?"

"Don't say that to her. It's not necessarily the case," Malcolm insisted. "Let's keep studying the records." He again bent over the papers, reading. "Help me, Liv."

I stood next to him, examining each girl's file.

"All good students," I noted. "Especially Mary." But

something else caught my eye. "Look! Every one of these girls—except Brit—was on scholarship, financial aid, or charity of some kind, including me. Look here at the letter attached to Clara's file. It's from her parents, asking the Wickhams for help before Wickham Hall even officially had scholarships."

Gabe repeated every word that tumbled out of my mouth for Malcolm, then his focus suddenly shifted. "Wait a minute. What about the Wickhams? We've all read that thing about Infinite Intelligence and healing the world. It's our friggin' school motto. And weren't they into some weird occult shit? What if they started all this somehow?"

I nodded, thinking of the spirit photography. "There are some really strange photos of Elijah Wickham at the Headmaster's Quarters," I confirmed. "Creepy pictures of him with spirits. Most of them looked pretty fake, but there was one of Wallace and Minerva that actually looked real."

"See?!" Gabe jumped all over it. "What did I say?! They were way into ghosts and shit!"

"See *what?*" Malcolm groaned. He was tiring of always being one step behind.

Gabe repeated what I'd said then asked: "And didn't Minerva die young?"

"In an unexplained accident," Malcolm said. He stood. "Let's go to Old Homestead."

"Now?!" Gabe asked.

"While we still can. This place is going to be crawling with alumni in about four hours."

AS WE CROSSED CAMPUS to Old Homestead, Malcolm told us everything he knew about the Wickhams. They'd come over from England to open the school, supposedly with the idealistic aim of bringing Romanticism to the New World. Malcolm said it was widely known, at least among the Victors, they were into mysticism and the supernatural. He'd heard there was a special room in the basement of Old Homestead where Wallace communed with Minerva after her death.

"Like a séance room?!" Gabe asked. "I knew it! They did something dark, something weird. A curse or something . . . we need to get down there."

Gabe was energized. Of course he was. After all, he'd spent two miserable years at Wickham labeled a freak—most of all by Malcolm and his friends. Now every paranoid thought he'd had was being vindicated. It was like giving Van Gogh his happy ending—as if everyone had recognized he was a genius (or at least not insane) before he died.

As we rushed through the cemetery, Gabe stopped. He caught a glimpse of me crossing over a charged headstone. "Stop!" he hissed.

I halted.

"What?" Malcolm demanded.

"She's changing more," Gabe told Malcolm, distressed. He stared at me. "You're fading. You're disappearing. What did you do at the headmaster's house?"

"I had to distract him. I moved the butterflies."

"Stop doing that! Stop trying to move things and change things!"

"Gabe," Malcolm said, trying to calm him.

"I don't want her to become like the others. Or disappear," he murmured.

"Neither do I." Malcolm patted Gabe on the back, gently pushing him to continue on. Together the three of us kept moving.

WE DEVISED A PLAN of who would do what, but when we arrived at Old Homestead, we discovered Malcolm's key no longer worked. He looked as agitated as Gabe. He kept shaking his head, shoving the key into the lock. "This is the master prefect key. It should work everywhere, *especially* here."

"What do you mean by especially?"

"This is where the Victors meet. In that hidden room on the fourth floor."

"Yeah, I think I know the one, where Abigail so kindly locked me up."

Gabe chuckled. Malcolm just looked at him. Instead of asking him what I'd said, he turned and started walking back toward the dorms. "It's late. I need sleep. I'll get us into Old Homestead in the morning."

"You shouldn't be alone, man," Gabe called after him. "It's not safe."

He looked in my general direction. "I won't be alone, though. Right, Liv?"

WHEN WE ARRIVED AT Pitman, Malcolm opened the window and extended his arm, gesturing for me to go first. Always the gentleman, even to invisible me. He climbed into the window after me, closed it, pulled the curtains, and collapsed on his back in bed.

"It's so hard not being able to hear you. It's so unfair."
He paused, then laughed at himself. "I can't believe this.
I'm talking to air."

It's not air. It's me.

"But it's not air. It's you," he added, once again seeming
to read my thoughts. "I know you're here. At least I *believe*
you are. Let me know you're here."

I looked around, desperate to show him a sign but
knowing I shouldn't use my energy. I rushed past Malcolm
as fast as I could, skirting his flesh by only an inch or so.

He felt my chill. A sad smile played on his lips.

"You are here," he said.

I am.

"Maybe it's good I can't see you. I don't know if I could
say what I want to say. When I told you I loved you . . .
you're the only girl I ever said that to, Liv. And I meant it."

I wanted to show him I was still present, but I was frozen.
Rapt. I could only listen.

"I imagined us together. You're the first person I ever
felt really myself with. I don't know what my point is. Maybe
I'm just feeling sorry for myself. But I shouldn't—you're
the one who's gone." He paused. "My father is coming
tomorrow, er, today I guess. You'll see me with him. I'm
already a little embarrassed. You'll see . . . I'm weak."

"You're not weak!" I shouted silently.

He squeezed his eyes shut and blurted, "I need to hear
your voice!" He grabbed his phone and clicked his voice
mail. "I have one message from you. I saved it, thank God.
I think I've listened to it a hundred times." He put it on
speakerphone, and I heard myself. *"Hi, Malcolm, it's Liv.*

Um, I was thinking . . ." I sounded so young, so far away. I remembered how I'd had to call five times just to get his voice mail. And how nervous I'd felt. How I'd practiced exactly what I wanted to say but then said something completely different. *"There's one word missing in the drawing I did, the one I did on you, I mean. Free. I should've put the word 'free' in there."*

He stood up and unbuttoned his shirt and checked. A faint, ghostly trace remained. He took his shirt completely off and approached the mirror. "I don't want it to fade away."

I stood next to him. I wanted to see us together, but there was no me. It was still shocking to peer into a mirror and see nothing. I fell away, unable to look. He lay back on his bed. "I think I should probably get a little sleep." He closed his eyes, and I watched him gently doze off.

CHAPTER 11

Malcolm hadn't exaggerated: alumni started to arrive on campus before he woke up. It was day one of Fall Festival, the school's anniversary weekend celebration. They celebrated Wickham Hall's anniversary every year, but this was a particularly big one: the big one-five-oh.

Malcolm slept though the voices and car-door slams. I even heard a helicopter and wondered if the president had arrived on Marine One. It wouldn't have surprised me. Malcolm needed the rest; he was so spent. He slept right through first period, although his phone kept buzzing. He slept until his door was swung open by a handsome man—a taller, sturdier, older version of Malcolm. When Malcolm saw him, he sprang up, instantly awake.

"Dad!"

"Shouldn't you be in class?" His father's eyes immediately dropped to the fading ink on his chest. "What's all that?"

"Just a drawing."

"Put a shirt on, son."

As Malcolm followed his father's orders, Gabe burst in. "I found Brit's old MySpace. Serious creep-o-rama . . ." He trailed off as he noticed Malcolm's father, then quickly tried to cover up. "*Creep-o-Rama,* have you seen it? On Hulu? So realistic, that movie was *so* realistic, man!"

Malcolm's father ignored Gabe as skillfully as Kent had in the library. "I have business to tend to. I'll see you at the Ball this evening."

Malcolm nodded, not that his father waited for a response. He turned on his heel and walked out of the room, without even so much as a nod to Gabe.

The door slammed.

Gabe exhaled. "Sorry, man. But Brit's MySpace is outta control. They kept writing on her profile and harassed the crap out of her. Even after she died."

"And that's probably *why* she died," Malcolm grumbled. He already looked tired again.

"Exactly. But, anyway, what's the plan for Old Homestead?"

"The Victors Ball."

"Yay for you," Gabe muttered.

But Malcolm started to smile. "No, that's the plan. That's it. *That's* how we're going to get in."

"*We*?! As in you and me?"

"Yes, *we.* But first we have some work to do."

Gabe eyed him suspiciously. "What do you mean?"

"Making you presentable, my friend."

BOTH MALCOLM AND GABE went to see Nurse Cobbs to get out of classes for the day. They figured it'd be pretty easy to get a medical excuse after a friend had died, and they were right. Although she was prickly, Nurse Cobbs was, it turns out, a bit of a sap. Not that she didn't loathe Gabe for his "ceaseless shenanigans" (her phrase, not mine), but Malcolm charmed her (of course) and she also remembered me. Apparently she'd noticed a drawing in the notebook I was carrying that first day and thought I was very talented.

As Malcolm was leaving, Kent passed him on his way in.

"What's the matter?" Malcolm asked.

"Stomachache. And you? Seeing the counselor, I hope."

Malcolm shrugged, avoiding an answer.

"I've been calling you. And texting. See you tonight?"

"Yeah, I'll be there."

I wanted to linger to see what Kent was up to. He didn't seem to be in any pain. But Gabe was still in the examination room and I couldn't leave Malcolm alone, so I ran over to Gabe's door and whispered, "Watch Kent."

"HE DIDN'T GO INTO an examination room," Gabe told us when he got back to Malcolm's room. "He went into Nurse Cobbs's office and left with a bunch of big envelopes."

"Big envelopes," Malcolm repeated.

"Maybe he takes some medication," I offered.

"These didn't look like medication envelopes. They looked . . . I don't know. They weren't labeled. It was weird."

"Weird, yes," Malcolm interjected. "Who knows what

they were. But we have work to do to get you ready for the Ball."

"*A lot* of work," I added.

Gabe stuck out his tongue.

Malcolm looked at him. "I really hope that was meant for Liv."

"Yeah. She's a little dubious of this alleged makeover."

Malcolm turned to face my general direction. "Well, Liv, please weigh in. I could use some girl-help here." Then he turned to Gabe. "And you, take a seat."

The facial scruff was first to go. Then his long hair. While Malcolm chopped off Gabe's locks, he studied his face. It was pained, no doubt. You could maybe even say tortured. Like I said before, very Van Gogh. Finally Malcolm asked, "When did you know you had it?"

"Lice?"

Malcolm whipped his hands away.

"Kidding. Damn. Seriously? Just because I'm not filthy rich doesn't mean I'm infected."

Malcolm sighed and got back to chopping. "I was asking when you knew you had the gift or whatever? Hearing voices."

Gabe sighed. "Just since I got here."

"How? *Why?*" Malcolm asked cautiously.

"I . . ." Gabe paused, uncomfortable, but he continued. "My older brother died two years ago. He was my hero. I . . . I don't know. I wanted to talk to him again, so I focused. I prayed, I begged, I cried. I don't know how it happened, but I guess I just opened myself up to it. Or maybe it was always there, and I just wasn't listening. I don't really know. There is no explanation, I guess."

"So you just heard his voice one day?"

"No, he was never there. But when I came here last year, I started hearing the girls. And seeing them. I told my parents, but they figured—still figure—it's all in my head. They're too wrecked over my brother. They can't deal with me. That's why they sent me here in the first place."

Malcolm nodded as he snipped off a lock of hair.

"What?" Gabe said.

"Nothing," Malcolm said. "It's just that we all end up here for a reason."

Malcolm turned back to the task at hand, studying Gabe's hair. Or maybe just pretending to. He was a pretty decent stylist. Who would have known?

WITH THE SCRUFF AND the long hair gone, Gabe already looked like a new man. "Turns out you're not terrible looking," I said, quite serious.

"Ha. Ha." Then he told Malcolm. "Turns out your lady friend has a real sense of humor."

"Yes, I know. Now for styling."

"*Styling*?!"

"I know I don't look it, but I'm very in touch with my feminine side," Malcolm said with a smirk.

I giggled. I almost forgot for a moment.

"She laughed at your joke," Gabe said.

Malcolm smiled with a sigh as he went to his wardrobe, pulling out a starched shirt and suit. Gabe insisted on wearing his own vintage Radiohead T-shirt underneath "so there's some dignity down there somewhere," but

Malcolm's formal wear was still miserably large on Gabe. He looked in the mirror. "This looks like a joke. Like a bad music video from the eighties."

"I'll get you another one," Malcolm said as he left the room. Within moments he was back with another, smaller shirt and suit.

"So you can just walk out into the common room, tell someone you need something, and they just bring it to you?"

Malcolm nodded. "On a silver platter." His tone was dry. "Especially if they're smaller than me."

Gabe sniffed. "Seriously, though, when I walk into the common room, people flee."

"Don't take this the wrong way—I mean, I see how the people here are and they're not always nice—but you do kind of ask for it."

"*What?!*"

"You have to admit, you cultivate the image. You practically wear a sign that says, 'Go Away.'"

"You do," I added.

Gabe looked down, intending to swing his hair down over his face—as he always did when he got uncomfortable—but the hair was no longer there.

"But that's the old Gabe," Malcolm said. "Tonight you're going to be confident. Outgoing."

Gabe grunted.

"No grunts or grumbles."

Gabe huffed and looked down at the floor.

"No staring at the floor or off into space."

He jammed his hands in his pockets, squirming restlessly.

"Or fidgeting."

"So what am I *supposed* to do?!"

Malcolm laid his hands on Gabe's shoulders. "Look at me. You work the room. You pick out alumni. You notice who's bored and who's available to make small talk, and you approach them. They will assume you're a new or prospective Victor, so they'll want to talk to you."

"But what am I supposed to talk about?" he asked, his voice rising.

"College applications and visits are always a solid choice." As he continued, Malcolm instinctively gestured as if in conversation. "Harvard Square, the weather in Boston versus Princeton versus New Haven. Rowing on the Charles. Of course you'd prefer Harvard, for undergrad at least, but Yale and Princeton are great backups. "

Gabe's eyes flashed toward Malcolm's desk. He squirmed out from under Malcolm's grasp, grabbed a notebook, and actually started taking notes. I almost clapped.

"When they ask about classes, just talk about the core curriculum—how you enjoy the broad educational base. And the Harkness Method, how the round tables really help classroom conversation. They love to talk Harkness because it's one of the things that sets these schools apart."

Gabe was scrawling every detail.

"And crew, of course. If it were me, I'd talk about how much I enjoy rowing alone. How I like to go out there and think—I'd probably say I met a girl. I liked to think about her . . ." He stopped talking, suddenly reminded I was dead.

"Got it," Gabe said. "Go on."

"And the key is to hold your chin up, puff your chest out. You must *look* extremely confident but speak with modesty."

"That's how you people do it?"

Malcolm nodded.

"But, wait, who am I?" Gabe asked. "I can't just be Gabe Nichols. Don't I have to have that fancy Victors bloodline?"

"Well, you have to be Gabe Nichols because Kent and Abigail and the others will recognize you. But . . . what they *don't* know is that your mother's maiden name was . . ." Malcolm paused, conjuring.

"Goggins!" I blurted, remembering one of the old names from the bricks in the catacombs.

"Goggins," Gabe repeated for Malcolm. "It's a name we saw in the catacombs."

"Perfect! I've seen that name in the Victors charter. So there's your lineage."

Malcolm flipped open his laptop, got online, and searched the Goggins family tree. In less than five minutes, he'd presented a completely plausible scenario for Gabe. His mother would be Cynthia Goggins—Wickham Hall class of 1984, a Victor with a long bloodline and, now, a foreign ambassador's wife who almost never made it back stateside for the alumni celebrations.

Gabe scribbled every detail of "his" family tree into the notebook.

"But you can't use notes," Malcolm said, shutting the computer. "You have to memorize it all. You have to believe it. *All* of it. If you run into my friends, you know they'll question you hard."

"And?"

"You say you never talked about your family history because you had no clue what you were missing until we started to hang. Now you want to join."

"I . . . don't know," Gabe stammered.

"I can help you," I volunteered. "I can be that little voice in your head telling you what to do, reminding you of dear Aunt Mildred and poor cousin Clyde."

"She said she can help me, say things to me."

"Good idea," Malcolm said to me—to the air—then turned to Gabe. "Posture!" Gabe straightened up. "And now, let's work on the handshake."

Gabe put out his hand and Malcolm took it, shaking it firmly and giving it a sharp pat with his left hand.

"Ouch. And what's with the little slap?"

"You shake firmly. And the pat basically tells the man, or woman, that you're friends. It implies a closeness that exists among all Victors."

"Like a secret handshake?!" Gabe was elated.

Malcolm laughed. "I guess. I mean it's not something anyone's ever said out loud, but it's just what they do."

"Sweet. I always wanted to know a secret handshake."

A lifetime of dedicated eccentricity and alienation was hard to overcome in an afternoon, but Malcolm worked Gabe like a drill sergeant, tutoring him right up until it was time to go to the party. And I watched carefully, so I'd know what to look out for at the event. After all, being invisible, I was the perfect etiquette coach.

MALCOLM HELD THE DOOR open for me as the three of us were leaving Pitman. I swept out ahead and looked back at them: two handsome, clean-cut young men walking out the dorm. Once Gabe realized this was truly our only access to Old Homestead, he devoted himself to the performance of a lifetime. And, miraculously, he'd become a dead ringer for a Victor. He was almost unrecognizable. He looked more like a Victor than Malcolm himself.

"Look at those two hot Victors," I joked.

"What of it?" Gabe snapped arrogantly, the cockiness almost *too* easy for him.

"I think you were one of them in a past life."

He lifted an eyebrow suavely. "Perhaps I was."

As we were both chuckling, I caught a glimpse of Malcolm. His head drooped. Weird. It was almost as if the he and Gabe had traded places. In our trio, Malcolm was— probably for the first time in his life—the outcast. He couldn't be in on our banter, so no matter how much Gabe translated for him, he ended up the third wheel. Out in the real world, of course, I was the odd one out.

Crossing campus, we saw several alumni—men and women dressed impeccably in suits or silk dresses. Not ostentatious, though. Nothing flashy. I think it's that Old Money thing, where people are so secure in their wealth they don't have to show it off. Malcolm nodded hellos, introducing Gabe with, "You know Gabriel Nichols. His mother's Cynthia Goggins." Like the handshake, the statement "you know" told the others Gabe was one of them. Subtext: If they didn't know him, they should.

As we came through the woods near Old Homestead, I noticed Gabe fidgeting. I glanced over and saw Weeping

Willow Girl—aka Ruth—sitting at the base of her tree, singing.

Malcolm noticed Gabe's change in demeanor. "Do you see one?" he whispered.

Gabe nodded. "And she's singing. I hate it when she sings."

"Don't listen," I urged him.

But when she noticed us, she got up and came after us. "Come back! Come back here, you!"

Gabe picked up the pace, but I hesitated. However frightening she was, I wanted to hear what she had to say. But this was not the time so I rushed along. When I glanced back to see if she was behind us, she wasn't. She was back at the willow tree, and a ghostly figure in a long black dress was gripping her arms. The figure moved to conceal herself behind the trunk when she saw me looking, but I caught a glimpse—she seemed to be trying to calm Ruth, restraining her.

"Don't worry. She's gone," I told Gabe, deciding it best not to provide all the details. He nodded and puffed himself back up.

Passing the old well moments later, Gabe smiled at me. I'd forgotten he could see me here. I smiled back. It felt so good to be seen.

Again, Malcolm noticed. "You see Liv?"

Gabe nodded.

"Is she beautiful?"

"Of course. Except for a couple of bruises, she died pretty nice." He always knew how to lighten up the mood.

THE HOUSE WAS DARK against the dusky pink sky. The woodwork I'd found so beautiful at the beginning of the year now looked more like black webbing, like a snare. Limousines were parked along one side, a fleet of hatted chauffeurs at the ready.

As we entered, I was surprised to find that there was no list. No gatekeeper. Only the portrait of Wallace and Minerva watched over the entrance. Everyone seemed to know who was who, and no one questioned authenticity. We were ushered into the grand living room where the Victors mingled. Gabe started to look spooked.

"Don't worry," I whispered. "I'll be watching."

Malcolm greeted people again and again with The Handshake—people he knew, people who knew him and his father. And the introduction, "You know my friend Gabriel Nichols. His mother is Cynthia Goggins," put the older Victors immediately at ease. I kept my eyes out for Kent and Abigail and Sloan and Amos.

Malcolm's father was presiding over a small cluster of men toward the back. Malcolm greeted him the same way. Once he'd made introductions, Malcolm slipped away. That was the plan: he'd go into the basement and look through the Wickham things while Gabe worked the crowd. It seemed the safest strategy. If Gabe was caught rifling in the basement, he'd probably be expelled—or worse. And I was to stay with Gabe, coaching while trying to keep an eye on the exits to make sure no one headed down to where Malcolm was.

As planned, we looped back around to some of the older people Malcolm had introduced Gabe to. First, he approached a fit man in his fifties who'd been introduced as a friend of Malcolm's father.

"So, Mr. Maxwell, how did you get to know Mr. Astor?" Gabe asked.

"Right upstairs. In that room you know well."

"You were Victors together?"

He nodded. This man was terribly proud of himself. "I was president the year after he was. He got the anniversary year, the one hundred and tenth. Lucky fellow."

"Oh, an anniversary year. Magnificent," Gabe fawned.

"He can tell you're being snotty," I snipped.

"Forgive me, sir, sometimes I get overexcited about Wickham Hall's history. It's so fascinating." He smiled at the man and walked away.

The man watched him. He might have distrusted Gabe but not enough to do anything about it.

"I think you need to dial it back a little," I said. "They're not idiots. They can tell if you're making fun. Don't call attention to yourself like that."

Gabe sighed audibly, reaching for his nonexistent hair.

We then came across an older woman, Mrs. Slade, maybe seventy, sipping on a martini with several olives. Gabe started right in, talking about the peace he found while rowing. She was just delighted to be acquainted with him (and a good deal tipsy).

"You know you're made," she cooed to him.

"Made?"

"Being handsome *and* a Victor. Be careful, because you can have anything you want."

"She's flirting," I teased.

"Gross," he spat out, accidentally.

"Gross?" she asked.

"Gross pleasures will be avoided or at least enjoyed in moderation. *That* I assure you," he quipped.

She giggled, charmed. "Well, if you end up being president, *forget* about it."

"Forget about *what*, Mrs. Slade?"

"You'll have the keys to the world then," she said, leaning closer to Gabe. "The presidents have it *all*. They *know* it all, and they have it all, those devils."

"What do they know?" Gabe asked demurely.

"They never let a woman be president, so I wouldn't know the *real* secrets." She winked. "You tell *me* when we meet here again in a few years."

"Mrs. Slade, I take my oaths *very* seriously."

"Of course you do," she giggled. "You're just a darling, aren't you?"

"Oh, he is, isn't he?" Kent appeared from behind us, all smiles.

Abigail, not far behind, asked, "But what is he doing here?"

Right then a classical string trio started up, and Mrs. Slade tottered off to admire the musicians. But Kent and Abigail stayed put.

"Seriously, what are you doing here?" Abigail asked.

"I came with Malcolm."

"Then where is he?" asked Kent.

"Getting some food."

"Did you think we wouldn't recognize you?" Abigail smirked.

"You noticed my makeover? I'm so flattered."

"You're not welcome here," she snapped.

"Oh, but I am," he boasted with the utmost confidence. "Are you not aware that Cynthia Goggins is my mother?"

Abigail and Kent both scrutinized him, trying to figure out if he was for real.

"And why are we just hearing this now?" Abigail pressed.

"To be honest, because I didn't like you. But now I see the perks of being a Victor. So, come on, do you really want to make a scene?"

"No, I just want to know what you're up to," Kent pressed. "What are you doing to my friend?"

"I don't know what you mean."

Kent turned and walked away, searching for Malcolm. Abigail followed him, of course. And I trailed them both, telling Gabe, "I'll be back."

Kent stalked over to the food table spilling over with lobster, edible flowers, stuffed artichokes, and other stuff rich people eat. He looped around the table while Abigail cruised past the bar, where vintage Victors were getting crystal tumblers filled with gin or scotch.

A heavy-set, distinguished old man—a politician no doubt—stopped Kent, did The Handshake. "Kent Steers, good to see you, son. Is your father here?"

"Mr. Samuels, hello. Unfortunately, he couldn't make it this year. He's at that summit in Dubai."

"Of course, I knew that," Mr. Samuels said, patting Kent on the back. "Tomorrow's a big day for you."

"Yes, sir, it is. But, if you'll excuse me, at the moment, I'm looking for one of my Victors." Kent pulled Abigail over and presented her to Mr. Samuels. "But I'm sure you remember my sister, Abigail."

"Carry on," Mr. Samuels said, clapping Kent heartily on the back. He turned to Abigail. "Miss Steers, look how you've grown."

She smiled and stayed with Samuels, trapped, as Kent rushed off. He pushed through the swinging wooden door, headed into the hallway. I soared over to him, barely making it through the opening as the door swung back. Kent was wasting no time. He rushed through the rooms, looking for Malcolm. He pressed through the kitchen, where the catering staff was buzzing about how to keep the lobster properly cascading.

"Did someone go through here?" Kent asked no one in particular, gesturing to a door at the back of the kitchen.

The caterers shrugged; no one had seen anything. But Kent slowed his pace and opened the door quietly. The moment the door was open, I charged ahead, flying down the stairs in front of him. I was supposed to warn Malcolm if someone was coming.

As I raced through the cellar, I passed through a small bare room, stone on all sides. The floor, walls, and ceiling were all charred black. That room connected to another room, this one finished sumptuously in every way. Thick dark-velvet curtains draped the walls. A round table stood in the middle of the space—a billowing light fixture hovering above it. I'd never seen a séance room, but I'd say this qualified.

Malcolm sat at the table scattered with stacks of old notebooks and several odd small objects—vessels and blades of various shapes—poring over what looked like an old journal, pocket-sized and filled with handwritten notes.

I rushed at him, which I hoped would give him a chill. I pushed myself toward the table, going right through it and Malcolm both. Excruciating pain. But he looked up. He knew I was there and knew something was wrong. He quickly concealed two of the objects in his jacket pockets and closed the journal. But before he could pocket it, Kent appeared in the doorway.

"Hey, man," Kent said casually.

"Hey."

"Party's upstairs."

"Yeah, I just wanted to get away. You know, my dad." Malcolm was good.

Kent nodded. "What's that notebook?"

"I dunno. Just some weird notes and things. The Wickhams were into some pretty creepy stuff, huh?"

Kent shrugged. "I don't know. It's not really our business, is it?"

Malcolm nodded. "Probably not."

"Come on, let's go back up."

"I'd rather hang down here for a few."

"You better come back up now. I don't know why you brought that guy."

"I know it's hard to believe, but that guy is actually a Goggins."

"Lineage isn't all it takes. You know that. He's not in yet, so you can't leave him up there alone." Kent was firm.

Malcolm got up. He hung back. It was clear he

wanted to pocket the journal, but Kent kept his eyes on him. "After you," Kent said, gesturing toward the doorway.

So Malcolm went ahead, leaving the notebook behind.

That's when I saw her. It was the woman from the painting upstairs: Minerva. I recognized her dark, piercing eyes, which were now dull. Dead. And she was as faint as the others. She was dressed in a long, black dress, and I realized she was the dark figure I'd seen with Ruth. She stared at me, and I held her gaze.

"You're not to meddle here. Please, consider yourself fortunate and move along."

"*Fortunate*? I'm dead," I snapped.

"But at least you're *here*."

She rushed at me with a speed faster than I'd known a ghost could go and grabbed me. I could feel her fingers digging into my shoulders as if they were still flesh. She terrified me, but in that moment, she made me feel alive again. I had substance! Until then, I hadn't known ghosts could feel other ghosts. But then she pushed me with such force that I ripped right through the cellar ceiling and into the party, screaming.

I landed near the string trio, which continued to play, oblivious. But Gabe heard my scream. I could see him shuddering, wincing away from Mr. Samuels, whom he'd been chatting with.

"Are you all right, son?" Mr. Samuels asked him.

"Yes. Migraines, you know. Sometimes they just strike. Like that," he said, snapping his fingers. Mr. Samuels nodded but looked suspicious.

I was getting back on my feet, aching, when I saw Minerva again—in the corner, watching me.

"Go," she demanded. She sounded angry but also somehow concerned, almost maternal. It took me aback for a moment, but then she came at me again. This time, I fought back. I prepared myself for her strike, building up my own force. When she hit me, we collided more like two humans would. She knocked me down but did not push me through the wall. No, it turned out I was stronger than she was. We both tumbled across the floor. I stung all over as we skidded through a group of chattering Victors.

I desperately wanted to grab something to hit her with—anything! But I couldn't, of course, so I went at her with all I had: *me*. I could tell she was tired and weakening. I jumped up, weightless for an instant, then thrust into her with such force that she tumbled through the outer wall of the house, screaming all the way. Through the bay window, I watched her fade away, reeling into the distance.

I looked up and saw Malcolm had returned. He was at Gabe's side, backing up the migraine story to Mr. Samuels.

"He gets what they call flash migraines. They come on really fast." Malcolm looked at Gabe. "I can see your pupils dilating."

"Yeah?" Gabe asked, still gathering himself. "I better get my inhaler."

"Please excuse us, Mr. Samuels." Malcolm flashed a winning, apologetic smile. "I think I should escort Mr. Nichols here back to his dorm to get his medicine."

Mr. Samuels nodded, watching them with curiosity as we went.

Mary

I received an inter-school memorandum stating that I was to attend a small honors ceremony in the cemetery. I had been invited to several such things in my two years at Wickham Hall. I was excited to have another award to list on my college application. I hoped to attend Radcliffe.

I worked very hard to maintain the highest grade point average and avoided all possible diversions. I had not heard the Beatles album all the way through. I had not even taken time to mourn Kennedy the way everyone else had, crying and carrying on. No, I was at the library reading Anna Karenina. My book report was not going to be a day late just because the president had been shot.

So it never occurred to me that the letter could be a hoax. It appeared very real.

It was raining, so I wondered if the ceremony was going to be postponed. I checked the memo and there was no contact information or indication of what faculty member was in charge, so I had to assume it would proceed as planned. I set my hair and put on *the tweed suit that my mother had made me. It was the only upside to having a mother who labored in the garment district. She knew how to make a good suit for these occasions.*

My parents had cried when I got the envelope from Wickham Hall because it meant they had succeeded. Things were going to change. They had come to the States from Hungary with nothing. But all their work—their callouses and bloodied fingertips—had not been in vain. I had already started a letter informing them of my newest accolade. I planned to finish it when I got back to the dorm, before going to dinner.

But when I got to the cemetery, nobody was there. Then someone approached. A Sixth Former. I had never met him, but I recognized him. He was president of the student government so of course I knew his name. He was very handsome. He sat down next to me and asked to hold my hand. Of course I noticed he was wearing gloves, but I thought it was because there was a chill in the air.

He quickly pulled a blade from his pocket and slit across my wrist. As I screamed and squirmed, he pushed me down onto a headstone, covered my mouth, and cut my other wrist. He dropped the blade at my feet, looked right into my dying eyes, and said, "Fac fortia et patere." Perhaps he did not know I was an honors student in Latin, but I knew exactly what it meant: "Do brave deeds and endure."

CHAPTER 12

As we walked away from Old Homestead, I told Gabe about Minerva. I was sure it was her. I told him what she'd done. Gabe started to repeat what I was saying to Malcolm, but Malcolm asked him not to speak.

"Why?" I asked.

But Gabe just shrugged at my question and kept silent. I realized Gabe was, for the first time, actually listening to Malcolm.

We retreated to Gabe's dorm room, where we'd be less susceptible to a visit from Malcolm's father. Malcolm went straight to Gabe's desk and started writing frantically. I stood above him and saw he was scrawling phrases in Latin and other languages I didn't recognize. I looked around Gabe's room. It was bare and unadorned except for one framed photograph on his bedside table—two boys happy and full of light, one of them an almost unrecognizable Gabe looking up to his handsome older brother. Suddenly

I could see how much Gabe had changed since coming to Wickham Hall, how truly haunted he'd become. I felt even more committed to fixing things. For all of us.

Once Malcolm finished writing, he turned to Gabe. "Sorry, it's just there was an old notebook and I couldn't take it, so I tried to memorize as much as I could. Oh, and I also got these." He pulled the small vessels out of his pockets and placed them on the desk. "What'd you find out?"

"Mrs. Slade told me the Victors President knows all. She made it sound like the regular members don't know the true inner-workings of the club, only the presidents do."

"Kent's the president," Malcolm said.

"That's why he followed you downstairs," I said. "He's hiding something."

Gabe told Malcolm what I'd said, and we all agreed it was likely. "But what are the secrets?" I asked.

"Let's see if any of this tells us anything," Malcolm said, gesturing to the phrases he'd scribbled.

Malcolm borrowed a laptop from a Fourth Former across the hall and typed the first phrase into Google while I looked at the objects on Gabe's desk. They were each inscribed with an odd imagery of insects and bees and— if you looked carefully—death. Each featured a single crude-looking ritualistic murder. It all looked familiar, but I wasn't sure from where.

Finally Malcolm read a translation from the computer: "*Sacrifice to prevail* and *the weak perish for perfection of the winners.*"

"What winners?" Gabe asked.

Malcolm shrugged and dove back into the translations. But it was so obvious to me. "Winners are *victors*," I said. "The weak perish for the perfection of *the Victors*. The Victors are making human sacrifices, Gabe! That's what it says."

Gabe was silent. He looked toward me, shaking his head, terrified. I knew what he was thinking: that this proved Malcolm *was* part of it. I went to Malcolm. I got close to him and looked into his eyes as he searched the computer for more information. I knew for certain he was as clueless and scared as we were. "It's not possible," I told Gabe. "He's not part of it."

"No?" Gabe said involuntarily.

"What?" Malcolm asked.

"Tell him," I said forcefully. "He's not a part of it. I *know* that."

"*Winners* can also be translated as *Victors*, Malcolm," Gabe said slowly, fearfully. "Meaning, the Victors killed them all."

Malcolm paused to take it in. That one sentence—if true—destroyed everything Malcolm's life was built upon. It cracked his foundation. But he only nodded, his head hung low, and said, "Of course." As if deep down he'd always known something was terribly wrong.

"It means we—the ghosts—are not the killers," I added. "We were the victims."

"Except Minerva. She *is* the Victors," Gabe insisted. "She must be in league with them."

"What do we do now?" Malcolm asked.

"Well, according to what Mrs. Slade said, it's probably the presidents."

Malcolm nodded, absorbing the possibility that his best
friend Kent had killed me. He asked the question we were
all thinking: "Why?"

"I don't know," Gabe said.

"I mean, he didn't like me being together with Liv
but . . ."

"He's a selfish prick," Gabe said, finishing Malcolm's
sentence. "Why would he risk his future to kill Liv? What's
the motivation?"

Malcolm shrugged.

"Unless somehow he knew it was *not* a risk," Gabe
offered.

"We have to talk to the other girls—the ghosts," I
piped in. "So maybe we can get information. Piece things
together from their answers."

"No!" Gabe yelled, reacting viscerally.

"What?" Malcolm asked.

Gabe told Malcolm what I'd said, and Malcolm agreed.
But Gabe started to get nervous and edgy—dressed differ-
ently, but still the same old Gabe—babbling, "I can't do it.
I can't go see them. I can't talk to them."

"No, Gabe," Malcolm said firmly, with the faintest hint
of jealousy. "You *can* see them and talk to them. So you
have to."

Gabe sighed.

"I'll be there," I added. "I can protect you. I think I'm
still stronger than they are. I'm stronger than Minerva, at
least. I know that for sure."

"And I'll be there, too. For what it's worth," Malcolm
added.

For the first time since I'd known Malcolm, he sounded scared. But I knew it wasn't ghosts or even danger he was afraid of. It was the truth.

GABE COULD SEE ME in any "charged" spot where a death had occurred, so we assumed he could see all the ghosts that way, too. We knew Minerva was in Old Homestead, and the others were spread all over campus. We decided to meet after curfew that night at the graveyard, both because it was centrally located, and we knew it was charged.

In the meantime, we agreed I'd stay with Malcolm and warn him if he was in danger. But, also, he said he wanted to talk to me. Alone. Through Gabe, I promised him I would follow him, not leave his side, and I would listen.

I followed Malcolm back to Pitman. As always, he opened the door and let me enter first. I smiled, always charmed by his chivalry. That would never grow old, so long as I was still here, still with him. But I imagined how sad it must've looked to other people, this guy opening a door and holding it open for no one. Nothing. But the guys in his dorm didn't seem to notice.

Chatter about the big Fall Festival and bonfire the next day bounced around the common room—speculation on the celebrity alumni who might be there, and plans for various shenanigans like spiking the punch or tossing fireworks into the bonfire. Malcolm's buddies tried to rope him into the conversation, but he shrugged them off, saying he was tired.

He closed the door to his room and sat on his bed. He looked down and leaned his chin onto his curled up

fist, his normally broad shoulders slumped. It was pain-
fully silent. He was Rodin's *The Thinker*: a broken man
silently battling inside his own head. Suddenly I feared he
had a confession to make. I got that same sick knot in my
stomach I'd gotten when he approached me in the dining
hall that first night. Only this time, I had no stomach. I
wasn't even sure how I felt such things.

He started to talk. "Kent told me to stay away from you.
He *told* me to. If only I'd listened to him . . ." He couldn't
finish the sentence.

"Maybe he would've done it anyway," I said, although I
knew it was futile. I couldn't bear to see him in such pain.

"If I'd given you up, he might not have done it. So, I
am guilty after all, aren't I? In some ways, it was my fault.
But I promise to you, I had *no idea*. He told me to stay
away from you. I thought the worst thing that could possibly happen was that he would tell my father. Can you
imagine? Just a week ago that was the worst of my fears:
that my father might discover who I really was?! Who I
really *am*?! My life was so small. I was so weak. I'm so sorry,
Liv." He paused for a beat. He looked around the room,
searching for me. "Things can change quickly, can't they?
In life . . . in death."

He lay down on the bed, curling into a fetal position.
There were so many things I wanted to say, but I could no
longer stand uttering unheard words. All I wanted to do was
comfort him. So I lay down next to him—facing him—and
curled my knees up into his stomach. I draped my arm over
his body and looked into his eyes. And I loved him.

I love you.

Love charged through me and made me feel as if I was still a vessel. As if I still had salty tears and a throbbing heart and blood churning through my veins. I didn't know what I was made of anymore—or how or *why* I even existed—but I knew I loved him completely right there in that moment. And I always would.

He lifted his head and looked into my invisible eyes. "Thank you." He said it so quietly I could barely hear. But I could see the relief wash over his face. He knew I was there, loving him regardless of what had happened. He felt it as powerfully as I did. Then he said it again, this time loud and unafraid, "Thank you, Liv Bloom."

Right then, as if on cue, the steam heater under his window hissed on, startling us both and breaking the moment. He laughed quietly at his own skittishness. We both lay there silently and watched as steam slowly gathered at the base of the window. I knew he wanted me to write something, but he wouldn't ask me to. And I knew I shouldn't because my energy was diminishing, but I *had* to. I waited and waited until there was enough condensation for me to write a single sentence. It took every ounce of willpower to ignore the pain in my fingertip. But I did it.

I will hold u again, I wrote on the glass.

He smiled sadly, knowing that would never happen. He would never hold me—the real me, the physical me, the *complete* me—in his arms. He'd never hear me speak. I fell onto the bed next to him, hurting. It was getting harder and harder to affect the real world. Both my power and my very substance were dwindling.

AT 11:45 P.M., MALCOLM crept out his window. I followed. As we did so, he told me all the dorm prefects were Victors. The reason they all lived on the ground floor in fire-exit rooms—and had master keys—was so they could attend Victors meetings in the after hours. Of course that meant Kent could get out just as easily as Malcolm. And, as Malcolm walked away from his dorm, I saw Kent was waiting in the shadows alongside the building.

I raced up to Malcolm to warn him. As he slipped into the woods that led to the graveyard, I rushed beside him to give him a chill. But it was crisp and cold so he was already shivering. He felt nothing from me. I poured my feet through a small pile of dry leaves nearby, scorching my ankles. But, at that very moment, the wind picked up and rustled still more. Nature was conspiring against us.

I could not warn Malcolm, so my focus shifted to Kent. He had a scarf tied around his neck. I concentrated as hard as I could and attempted to tug at it—to choke him or at least slow him down—I could endure the pain, but my hand would not hold the material. I surged past him, hoping a chill would at least give him pause. It didn't. He proceeded stealthily behind Malcolm.

Just after Malcolm swept past the weeping willow tree, I heard her. *The way he treats me, girls, he'll do the same to you! That's the reason I've got those weepin' willow blues.*

I looked over and saw Ruth at her tree. She looked different than before—solid and *real.* Oil paint, not watercolor. The wound on her neck looked almost fresh. Kent suddenly stopped and looked right at her. Kent *saw* her!

"He sees you!"

She nodded. "It's that day I suppose."

She turned to him and coyly asked, "Are you the one who sent the note, handsome? Did you invite me to the willow tree? For a little nookie, maybe?"

He approached her, looking at her with awe and fascination. He reached his hand to her shoulder—and he seemed to feel her.

"Do something!" I yelled. "He killed me! He's going to kill someone else! You have to stop him, now!"

Kent was shaking with fear, but a look of excitement played across his face. "You're proof," he said. "I've heard you exist, and you come alive once a year for an instant. You're proof that what we do works."

"No! I will *not* be your proof!" she yelled, immediately enraged. She grabbed him and pulled his shirt, trying to strangle him, but as he stumbled backward, gasping for air, she faded back to her ghost self.

Kent spun around, looking for her. She'd disappeared to him. But I could still see her, once again airy and immaterial.

Kent, invigorated, turned and raced back in the direction we'd come from, leaving me alone with her. I looked around. Malcolm was long gone. By now he'd probably reached the cemetery, so I took a moment to understand what had just happened.

"He could see you. He could *touch* you."

"That was my deathday. For once, I almost got to use it."

"What do you mean?"

"Every year on the day you were murdered, you materialize. Briefly. Right at the time you died."

"Every year?"

She nodded. "But just for a moment, right at that special time."

I realized that must have been what I'd seen in the cemetery that Headmaster Holiday night, when I was still alive. I *had* seen Mary—Miss *Jackie O*—it had been her deathday.

"I saw one once," I told Ruth. "When I was still alive. In the cemetery. And . . ." I hesitated, "I think I saw you, too . . . in my dream."

She nodded. "You did. I was trying to warn you."

"What do you mean?"

"It seemed about time, perhaps, for another death. I was attempting to spare you. But I didn't say enough . . . or do enough."

"But you warned me about Malcolm. Why? Do you know something about him?"

"Not him. Not him *specifically*. But I've observed the scenario before. Too many times now. I thought I could help this time."

"Will you come with me to the cemetery?" I asked. I'd never before had to appeal to a girl with a slashed throat. She still frightened me, but I needed her. She had answers, and she seemed willing to share them. "We need to know everything. We're trying to figure it all out."

"Minerva doesn't want me to speak to you. Or anyone. She forbids it."

"She keeps you all apart?"

Ruth nodded.

"We have to figure out *why*, Ruth. Please come," I begged. "We've gathered so much information. We're so close."

She perked up. "*We?*" she asked. "I knew it! Can one of those boys I've seen you with *hear* you?"

I nodded yes. She smiled, almost exhilarated by the possibility.

"*Please* come. Together maybe we can fix this."

She looked around nervously, then nodded. And together, we—two dead girls—walked to the Wickham Hall cemetery.

BY THE TIME WE got there, Malcolm and Gabe were both waiting. Through Gabe, I explained to Malcolm why I'd abandoned him and what had happened with Kent, which we all agreed was only further proof of his guilt. Then I introduced them to Ruth, and she told us her death story, involving the anonymous note. The weeping willow. Getting pinned to the tree from behind. Gabe relayed the story to Malcolm, who was scribbling notes into a spiral notebook.

We flooded her with questions. What grabbed her? Was it a man? Who? Why? What had she observed over the years? The details were blurry. She was confused about time. She knew things were different when she had died—girls dressed differently and people spoke differently—but she didn't seem to understand it had been nearly a hundred years. She had noticed every so often, a female student, someone on the fringe, had died. Usually after mingling with Victors. She had spotted me and for the first time, attempted to intercede. But she didn't know how or why the girls died. She didn't have any details. One thing she did know: her strength had diminished, except at that magical moment on her deathday once a year. But she never knew how to anticipate or exploit her brief power.

"What do you mean your strength diminished?" Of course I'd felt it myself, but I needed to hear it from her.

"When I first arrived, I could affect the real world if I tried very hard. But it's very painful. I know you know what I mean. I can see you still have power because you're not as faint as we are yet. But your energy is limited. Each spirit has only a finite amount. *Every single time* you affect the real world—every time you do something that interacts with it or changes it—you get fainter, weaker. It is painful, and you lose reserves. I am now powerless. All I can do is give a chill. I have been this way since I can remember. I think all the other girls have lost their energy as well."

"What about going through things? It hurts, but it doesn't use my power, right?"

"No, going through an object—if you don't affect it—doesn't use your strength. We can all do that. And if you just release yourself—open yourself to the object—it won't hurt anymore. Not at all."

That's why the other ghosts could easily pass through walls without even flinching. And when that Third Former had crossed through me from behind, it hadn't hurt because I hadn't even known it was happening. Now it made sense.

I had to try. I reached out to a tree branch nearby. I tried to relax my arm and move it through the dangling leaves. I recoiled. It still stung.

"You must open yourself. Completely," she instructed.

I closed my eyes and tried my hardest to feel open, to

feel free, and swept my arm up. As I opened my eyes, I saw my arm pass though the leaves and branch painlessly. I smiled, sighing with relief.

"But your power—your ability to change things, to *do* things in the world of the living—is precious," Ruth urged. "Save it."

All my efforts flashed in front of me like slides in art history class—trying to lift the leaf that first night outside Skellenger, shaking the crime scene investigator's table, writing in the steam on the window in the library, making the butterflies flutter in the Headmaster's Quarters, writing on the steam on Malcolm's window . . . Each of those actions was marching me closer to total powerlessness. How much energy remained? There was so much left to do, but I had no idea how much power I still had. I was beginning to look almost translucent, like the others. I exchanged a look with Gabe. He could see my concern.

"Can you tell us about the other ghosts?" Gabe asked.

She shrugged. "What is there to say? We don't talk. Minerva forbids it."

"Does she say why?"

"She told me they're angry and dangerous . . . not to be trusted. She told me to stay away from them. And she's frightening. Powerful. So I just go about my own business. I sing. I watch the clouds. Time is all a blur."

I knew what she meant.

Gabe reported the information to Malcolm, adding, "Minerva must not want them to talk for a reason. If they all talk they might figure something out. And she doesn't want them to." For someone so exceptionally skilled at concocting far-fetched theories, this one actually sounded plausible.

"That's why we're going to bring them all here," I said. "Now."

RUTH WAS NERVOUS ABOUT the plan. She'd gone so many years without talking to the others. I understood. It was overwhelming. She was terrified of them. We all were. I pointed out that if we were scared of them, then maybe they were just as scared of us. After all, I'd been terrified of Ruth until I met her. Maybe that was part of Minerva's plan. Finally Ruth nodded, agreeing to proceed.

We didn't want any of the living people to hear us, so Gabe and Malcolm remained silent. I sprung up to the roof of the Founders Tomb so that my voice might boom all across campus. I shouted out each girl's name, turning to face in the direction where I knew she resided. "Clara! Florence! Mary! Lydia! Brit! I'm speaking to *all* the dead of Wickham Hall! You were *murdered*! You are stuck here—lingering—and I am, too! I need to know why! Why us?! I want to free us so we can move on! Please come! Talk to me! Talk to us! Tell us your story!"

Silence.

No ghosts. I couldn't blame them if they needed more convincing. Years, *decades* of fear must run deep. I jumped down off the crypt and looked to the notebook Malcolm held open for me with notes about each girl.

I started with Mary because I knew she lingered right there in the cemetery.

"Mary! Do you hear me?! Did you really cut your own wrists because you were depressed? Unable to hack it here at Wickham Hall? Seriously?! You were on the honor roll, and you couldn't take it here? What a lie! They said the same thing about me! Are we going to let that be the record forever? That we were quitters and losers?! I don't believe these stories! None of them! Do you even know what they said about you?!"

Gabe stepped back, staggered by my force. I was surprised, too. I hadn't planned this speech. It just barreled out of me, fueled by my anger at my own death and its cover-up, Ruth's death . . . *all* these senseless deaths. Anger I hadn't even known I had bottled up.

"Florence! Were you really so clumsy that you slipped and fell off the top of Skellenger? You were a dancer. You were graceful, weren't you? And Clara, you were a smart girl. Did you really just go out in the lake alone at night?! I don't believe it! And Brit, you did kill yourself, didn't you? But *why*? What did they do to you?! And what about the rest of you?! Where are you?! Come out! Tell us your stories!"

As I shouted, shadowy figures peeked from the trees. They started to surround us, but none drew close. Each was still dressed in her period clothing—a flapper dress, a sixties suit, a Victorian bathing costume, skinny jeans and flats—it was like being encircled by an exhibit at The Met, "150 Years of Style."

Finally, Mary, who had been lurking in front of the Founders Tomb, stepped forward. But she kept silent.

Then Florence appeared. "I was not clumsy!" she

insisted. All at once she was raving about Willfred Pinfolds and the Skellenger cupola—how he'd been disgusted with her immigrant status and challenged her to climb to the very top. Did he push her? Did she slip? She wasn't certain. The details were blurry. She'd had something to drink that night. A few somethings. He might've come up behind her. She might've slipped. She wasn't at all sure.

At some point Nature Preserve Girl arrived. I saw now that she was clearly from the seventies—with bell-bottoms and long flowing hair. But she lurked in the shadows behind the others, with her arms clutched to her chest.

Then Brit approached. She told us her story. It was devastating, but none of the other ghosts understood what MySpace or cyber-bullying was.

Then Clara—still in her Victorian bathing suit—appeared, attempting to cover herself although the bathing costume concealed practically every inch of skin.

They all hovered around us. I was partly grateful to see them and still partly afraid. But so were they. Which made me more certain that Minerva had somehow orchestrated all of this.

"And, Lydia, did you know they found ten hits of LSD in your system and said you broke your *own* neck, high on drugs?! Do you really want your family to think you took those drugs and died that way? Do you want to be remembered like that? And let people get away with murder?!"

Lydia was suddenly there. She remembered the bitter taste as Cyrus Huckle had kissed her; he'd slipped her LSD. As she lay dying, LSD was pouring into her system. It seemed to stick, making her eternally aggressive and crazy.

She was enduring every teenage druggie's nightmare: the never-ending acid trip. At least now she understood why she felt this way, as much as you can understand anything while on ten hits of acid.

I turned to them all. "What about the rest of you?!" I noticed Nature Preserve Girl slip off into the night. I continued, louder; I needed as many as I could get. "Do we want to be remembered this way?! Will we accept these murders?!"

Lydia screamed, "NO!" Then there came a chorus of *NO*s. Ending with Mary just shrieking, silencing everyone.

"I was murdered," Mary said. And the others chimed in, speaking over one another.

"As was I," Clara vowed. "They drowned me. They pushed me under."

"I can tell you one thing for certain," Florence insisted. "I did not jump!"

"And, *mon dieu*!" Ruth added. "I did *not* cut my own throat!"

I saw relief wash over Gabe. He'd spent so long fearing— even tortured by—these girls. He'd finally heard the truth: we were all victims and had no intention of hurting anyone. Not yet, anyway . . .

The chatter ended when Mary said, "I saw who did it. His name was Samuels. Burr Samuels. He looked me in the eye as he cut my wrists."

Gabe and I exchanged a look. "Burr Samuels is still alive," Gabe told her. "He's here on campus. Right now."

I watched Mary fill with rage—unsure what we could say or do to calm her—so I didn't notice we were surrounded until it was too late.

CHAPTER 13

It all happened so fast. There were more police officers than I'd ever seen in one place before. And campus security guards. And Headmaster Thorton. And there, skulking at the very far back of the crowd, was Kent.

They were there to arrest Gabe for my murder. Apparently they had "more than enough evidence to indict." They'd been to his room and discovered the strange objects. They'd found my phone—which he'd discarded in the dumpsters behind the Art Center—smothered with his prints. The clincher: his prints were all over the well. They grabbed him and held him firmly, handcuffing his hands behind his back. Through the trees I could see the flash of sirens.

"You're wrong!" Malcolm shouted. "He didn't do anything! He's innocent!"

Gabe looked at me, his eyes terrified.

I was terrified, too. I couldn't lose him. He was my hands, my voice. He was my sole connection to the earth, to the world of the living. To Malcolm. I wanted to collapse or cry or rage—I wasn't sure which—but I was the only person who could talk to him and calm him in the midst of the chaos, so I had to be strong. Or at least pretend to be.

"If they take you, we will save you. I promise we will get you out of there," I assured him.

"No! Don't worry about me," he said to me, no longer caring that a dozen cops and security guards were glaring at him. "Don't waste your energy on me! Just fix things here. You have to get them. You have to *stop* them!"

I saw the officers exchange looks. He was talking to thin air—sure evidence of his guilt, not to mention insanity.

"Don't speak to me," I hissed. "They already think you're a loon ball."

He laughed.

"And don't laugh. We *will* save you. *All* of us." I gestured to the ghosts. "We will save you. I promise."

"We will," Ruth echoed, assuring him.

One of the officers found Gabe's jacket on a tombstone nearby, another Wickham occult vessel in its pocket.

"Is this your jacket?" he asked.

Malcolm jumped in. "It's mine."

The police looked at him dubiously as they pulled Gabe's phone from the other pocket. Gabe shook his head at Malcolm. He was grateful for the attempt, but he knew it was futile. "No, it's my jacket," Gabe stated.

Malcolm glared at him. "Gabe, for Christ's sake—"

"Let it go. For now. Liv wants you to let it go," Gabe lied.

"I didn't say that!" I yelled. But Gabe ignored me. I realized it was the first time he'd misrepresented me.

He was surprisingly level-headed as the officers patted him down. "We can't say anything that will change their minds. Let them take me. They'll learn the truth eventually," he told us both as they escorted him back through the woods toward the flashing lights.

I followed, desperate. Malcolm followed as well, yelling at the police about how Gabe was different than the other students and he'd been victimized and taunted and bullied. Grasping, Malcolm told the police this was a conspiracy against Gabe created by students who didn't like him.

"I appreciate the effort, man, but let it go," Gabe said, sincerely. "You know what's most important right now: to learn the truth and bring justice. For her."

I raced to him. I was desperate to hug him or comfort him, anything. But I only had words. "I'll bring justice for you, too," I said. "But how am I going to do it without you?"

He quietly said, "Malcolm."

"But he can't hear me! I can't communicate with him."

"You have to."

"Yes," I replied. He was right. I had to.

He then turned to Malcolm and whispered, "Go back to the cemetery with Liv, try to listen for her clues. She'll come back to your room tonight and tell you what's next."

Malcolm had no choice but to agree. Especially since one of the police officers barked, "And you, don't stray too far from campus. We need to talk to you, too."

I couldn't just stand and watch Gabe being shoved into a car and disappear down the road in a whirl of flashing lights and sirens, I chased after him. But I started to feel weak. My thoughts became muddled and unclear. My limbs started to evaporate before my eyes—just as they had in the limousine with my parents. Clearly I was not meant to leave Wickham Hall. I paused on the threshold of the school, afraid of what might happen if I crossed the boundary. From a distance, I thought I saw him look back toward me through the window, his eyes unfocused, searching the air. He couldn't see me, but he knew I was there.

AS I APPROACHED THE cemetery, I caught a glimpse of Minerva peeking from her tomb. When she saw me, she withdrew into the darkness. But Ruth, Mary, Florence, Lydia, Brit, and Clara were all still gathered, tentatively talking amongst themselves. I had a flash of hope. We were united now. At least most of us.

Malcolm sat slumped on a gravestone in the middle of them, unaware of the chatter bouncing around him. He'd wrapped himself in his wool blazer, chilled from their presence, just waiting for a sign from me.

Ruth and Mary, both Type A, had collected facts. "We died every ten years," Ruth reported. "Not on the same day, but always on a full moon. In every case, it was related to a popular boy, one who was probably a Victor."

Mary piped in, "We were all scholarship students."

"Or outcasts," Brit added.

"Freaks," Lydia barked.

"I believe we were all murdered by the Victors," Ruth explained. "Could it have been some sort of ritual established by the Wickhams?"

"And the ritual trapped us here . . ." Mary paused, afraid to say *forever*.

I nodded, shrugging. I wasn't certain about any of it.

"But I want to see my mother and father. My sweet baby sister. I've been here too, too long," Clara said, weeping. She'd been here the longest, since 1885. "I want to ascend. I have seen so many others do it: the students who perished from tuberculosis, influenza. It is a beautiful thing. I want that, too."

A chorus of yeses followed. All they wanted was to stop the curse (whatever it was) and move on to where they were supposed to be (wherever that was). I don't know. I guess probably heaven. I was beginning to think, or at least hope, such a place existed.

"We're going to fix it, right?" Ruth looked to me and gestured to Malcolm. "He can help us fix it."

"Like how?" Brit demanded.

"Minerva! I know you're listening!" I yelled, then turned to address the others. "The Wickhams were into the occult. They had to be the ones who created this ritual and established the Victors, right? And, for all these years, Minerva kept you all from talking to one another, from doing anything. There had to be a reason for that. Minerva's the culprit. I think she started it all."

They all nodded. It only made sense. So I turned to her crypt. "Come tell us what you know, what you created!" I soared over to her hiding place, but she was gone.

I rushed past Malcolm. "Time to go?" he asked, feeling the chill. He got up, shivering, but his eyes wide and somehow happy. All he really seemed to care about was that I was still here. I smiled, until I looked up and saw all the ghosts peering at me curiously.

"You are in love," Florence said.

"Madly, madly in love," Ruth added, almost giddy.

I nodded, then rushed alongside Malcolm. I didn't notice Ruth following us.

BACK IN MALCOLM'S ROOM at Pitman, he cranked up the heat so it blasted onto his window, slowly forming steam. While we waited, he took out his iPhone and set it up so the keyboard on its screen was readily available to me. I needed to use the bare minimum amount of energy. So I typed dad then sam . . . every single stroke was excruciating. Exhausting. And I watched my consistency dilute as if the painter was mixing a bit more solvent into the paint.

"Samuels," Malcolm said before I finished spelling it, "I'll talk to him. Tomorrow. And my father . . ." he trailed off. The mere thought of confronting his father about *anything* made him uncomfortable. "He was president of the Victors, so he has to know something."

When the window was thoroughly steamed, Malcolm used it as a canvas. "I know you can't waste your energy drawing. So I will," he said as he drew a girl flying—not floating but flying—gliding over a small world beneath her.

He worked slowly and carefully, and I watched every stroke. I could see slivers of his reflection in the window where he was drawing. The soles of the girl's feet were in the foreground. Her arms stretched in front of her like a superhero. Her right pointer finger reaching forward . . . almost touching another hand—his hand. A boy stretched out in the far distance, connected to the earth but reaching up and up, attempting the incredible feat of touching her finger. Nearly grasping her. It was kind of like *The Creation of Adam* in the Sistine Chapel, where God reaches to Adam and Adam reaches to God, their fingertips nearly touching. That was me and Malcolm: so close to each other yet impossibly apart. Impossibly disconnected.

Suddenly I saw Ruth's faint bloody neck through the strokes in the steam. I lurched backward, screaming. She moved her head down so I could see her entire face then effortlessly pushed through the window into the room.

"*Je suis désolée*! I gave you a terrible fright! So sorry, but I wanted to share something with you."

I shook my head, trying to smile and recover my composure.

She stood there awkwardly, all social graces erased over the last hundred years.

"You can visit him in his dreams, just as I visited you that night before you died. You can be with him that way. It's just a dream, but when you're there, it feels *very* real."

Of course! I almost reached out to hug her. Why hadn't I thought of that? If Ruth had been able to do that, I should be able to also. "But I can't waste my energy."

"That won't use it. It's only when you affect the *real* world that your energy diminishes."

"How can I get there? Into his dream?"

"Settle yourself into him while he's sleeping. You have to *release* yourself. The same way you moved your arm through that branch. Free yourself to him, and you will find him. But, understand, you have no control in the dream. Now I'll go. I'm terribly sorry to bother you. But I wanted to thank you. We all do. *Merci.* Consider this our thanks."

"Well, thank you for coming and telling me."

She passed through the window—now covered with steam again, Malcolm's artwork nearly vanished—back out into the cold night.

"Are you still there?" he asked. "Will you lie next to me? Let's listen to your mix." He called up his iTunes and put on Liv, Forever. As Bright Eyes played, he lay on his side, and I wrapped around him, trying to comfort and calm him to sleep so I could be with him again.

It didn't seem long to me, but according to the clock, it was hours before he was deeply asleep, breathing heavily. He was still lying on his side, so I moved around to the other side, facing him. I got close and then kept getting closer. I tried to ignore the fear that I might disappear altogether or that I might get lost in his dream world. I closed my eyes and just kept moving closer and closer to him until . . . we merged.

I HEARD WATER GENTLY lapping. When I opened my eyes, I was at the mountain, but it was an island, surrounded by lake on all sides—now looking more like an ocean. Where was Malcolm? I turned, and he was suddenly where he hadn't been before. He was frozen, terrified to see me.

"I've been praying to dream about you. And you're here, finally."

I nodded.

"It's really you?"

"It's really me."

He nodded, smiling.

"But, then again, I'm not really real anymore, am I?" I pointed out.

"True," he laughed. At least we both had a sense of humor about it.

"Can I touch you?" he asked.

"I don't know."

He approached me slowly. I was scared he wouldn't feel me. That I wouldn't feel him. He paused. We locked eyes, and I could see he was just as apprehensive as I was. Finally he reached for my hand. He grasped me so firmly it almost hurt. Pain had never made me so happy. He felt me, and I felt him! He pulled me into his arms, wrapped himself around me. "I won't let go. Ever."

"Not even for a kiss?" I asked.

"For a kiss? Yes, I'll let go of you for that." He loosened his grip so I could lift my lips to his, and we kissed.

In the history of art and poetry and music and novels and everything beautiful that human beings have fought to describe, there was never a kiss like this. Was it the dream that made it so intense? Did it matter? We devoured each other like two starving, deprived lovers. But all at once I could feel that it wasn't entirely real. And then the setting changed. In an instant we were in the dining hall, surrounded by the entire student body dancing the waltz around us.

I pulled away from him.

"This is weird," I said. "Wouldn't an abandoned beach be better? Or a chalet in the Alps? Or pretty much anywhere else?"

"I can't really control it. We're here now . . . so will you dance with me?" he asked.

I nodded and took his hand. It was just a dream after all. And in this dream I was graceful, a skilled and confident dancer. We moved perfectly together—turning and spinning, not missing a beat—for a long, long time. Ages. Ages of perfection . . . until I noticed someone near us staring. His face was generic. I glanced at the others, all their faces bland, not even completely formed. Mouthless. Vacant. They weren't really there. I wondered if we were vacant, too. No! It was Malcolm, and it was me—but it just didn't feel completely real.

"Does this feel real to you?" I asked him.

"Real enough."

Then he took my hand and led me off the dance floor and through a door. We were in a home, one more lavish than I'd ever seen. Malcolm walked me through the marble entryway, pointing out a Tracey Emin and a Warhol and a Damien Hirst unicorn. It was like a museum of modern art.

"Is this your house?"

"My father's house. Yes."

He led me into a library much like Wickham Hall's, wood-paneled and stately but chilly and aloof. All the books were off the shelves, stacked in tall piles. Malcolm approached the stacks near the large bay windows. I followed him, glancing outside.

Down below was a place that looked like Wickham Hall—the same Mount Vernons and Gothic arches and Victorian woodwork—but also like the third panel of Bosch's

Garden of Earthly Delights. In other words: hell. Dark and soiled with violence and swarming with unrecognizable, half-eaten creatures. The buildings were in shambles, windows blasted out, roofs removed. Shanties pitched along the muddy Dorm Row. And it was dark, a winter's evening with storm clouds glowering above. There seemed to be no electricity, only small fires dotted the horizon. Crowds swirled, unruly and savage, mingling with insects and animals. Filthy. Clothes tattered. Chaotic. I heard screams of pain. Agony.

And I could *smell* it. I'd never smelled something in a dream before, but this scent was so strong—of bile and waste and death—that it made me feel sick.

There was a man who rose out of the darkness. He stood at the top of the Main steps, protected by a fortress of underlings. He was still somehow, amid all the chaos, well dressed in a dated but formal three-piece suit. He yelled out to the crowds of people as if trying to inspire or galvanize them. He was powerful. He was to be feared. His face was *very* distinct, *very* familiar. It was a Wickham. Wallace Wickham, I thought.

Malcolm pulled me away from the window. "Don't look out there."

"What is it? Something in your imagination, right?"

"I don't know. I've never seen it before." He started throwing the books out the window, which was somehow now wide open.

"What are you doing?"

"We have to get rid of the books," he said.

"Why?"

"I'm not sure, but I know it needs to happen. Please help me."

"What if we hurt someone? It's a long way down."

"They're already dead."

I looked outside again and realized he was right. They all had the look of death I'd become all too familiar with.

Malcolm became anxious and upset. "Please help me. It has to happen."

I hadn't dreamt in some time, not since my death, but I remembered how it was. Sometimes the most absurd things seemed so important and real. So I grabbed old books and started throwing them out into the misery below. Together we threw them faster and faster until I heard a booming, "Malcolm!"

I turned and saw Malcolm's father standing in the doorway—tall, so tall, in a black suit, and displeased with us. Malcolm did not turn, so his father yelled again, even louder. "*Malcolm Astor!*"

Then it ended. All at once the images erased.

Malcolm woke up. His father—the real one—stood in his doorway, his real doorway. And I was, once again, *not* real. Or at least not material.

"Malcolm! You're late. We have the trustee breakfast. And you have some explaining to do. Something about a boy arrested last night?"

Malcolm sat up in bed, covered in sweat, shaking. "Tell me about the books," he said urgently.

"What books?"

"Something to do with the Victors. There are books. Evil books."

"Do you have a fever? I think you're unwell."

"I'm unwell because a girl was murdered. A girl I *loved*. You have to tell me what you know."

"I don't have any idea what you're talking about."

"That's a lie."

"You are forbidden to speak to me like that. Now let's go. We're supposed to be at Old Homestead right now."

"Human sacrifices. Girls murdered brutally. Every ten years. Ring a bell?" Malcolm was fierce, but his father was icy and resolute.

"You need help, son."

"I only need help uncovering the truth. I need to know why this was done and how it can end. I need to know who is responsible. If you won't tell me, I'll talk to Burr Samuels. He killed one of them."

Mr. Astor kept staring at his son, unblinking. But his jaw flickered. Malcolm seized the moment and brushed past him into the common room. His father followed him, starting to look a little flustered. Malcolm burst out the front door. I soared in his wake. Mr. Astor grasped for his cell phone and started to dial a number while yelling after him, "You will not speak to Mr. Samuels!"

"Yes, I will," Malcolm spat back at his father as he ran toward Old Homestead. "You can't control me anymore."

CHAPTER 14.

Malcolm knew his father would not make a scene in front of the esteemed alumni, so he continued through campus, careful to move only through the most populated parts. He was still dressed from the night before, and as he walked he tucked in his shirt and attempted to straighten his hair. And, still being the most popular guy on campus (at least until the rumors of his association with Gabe started to spread), he did not have a problem borrowing a jacket off an underclassman he passed.

"And I don't need it back," the flattered Third Former yelled after him, smiling as if he'd just been given a gift. Malcolm swept through the Art Center, where a fleet of Wickham Hall staff was putting the final touches on the bonfire setup. As we passed through the cemetery, it fell oddly silent. There was no one in sight. Bad sign. Sure enough, as I spun around, I saw Mr. Astor striding from the road toward Malcolm.

"You will not embarrass me in front of these people! They are *far* too important. You need help. I'm taking you out of school. Now."

A slow-moving dark car pulled up alongside the cemetery. The windows were tinted. Mr. Astor grabbed his son's arm, easily pulling Malcolm toward the car. Malcolm seemed small next to his imposing father. Desperate, I rushed past his father, trying to give him a chill. I did it again and again. And still it wasn't enough. I started to panic as Mr. Astor dragged Malcolm closer to the car. Then Mary appeared by my side.

"We have to stop him. Malcolm's our only connection. Our only way to get to Samuels, our only way to fix things!"

She swooped away from Mr. Astor, suddenly fierce. Then she rushed into him, shrieking all the way. She moved too fast for me to see, but it did the trick. Mr. Astor shuddered and lost his grasp on his son.

Malcolm slipped away, whispering, "Thank you."

"To whom are you speaking?" his father demanded, getting pale.

"The girl I love," Malcolm barked, scrambling away.

"The dead one?"

"Yes, the dead one," Malcolm shouted back toward his father as he ran.

MARY COLLAPSED ON A tombstone, trying to recover. "I think that was it," she said, looking down at her body. It had been drained of its last remnants of opaque color. "I've been saving that bit of energy for so many years, but I think that might've been the last of it."

I asked Mary if she would come with us to find Samuels so she could confirm he was in fact her killer. She actually wanted to see him face to face. As we rushed to catch up with Malcolm, we passed Ruth at the weeping willow. Without a word, she joined us.

We reached Malcolm just as he was climbing the stairs to the front porch. I spotted Minerva in one of the upstairs windows, but when she saw me looking up at her, she darted out of sight. On the porch, Malcolm noticed the woodwork as if for the first time, staring at the imagery— the angels and fire and strange creatures.

"It's the same iconography that's on the Wickham objects," he said. "And in the dream. Did you see this in the dream, too?"

"Yes! I did!" I exclaimed. At least Ruth and Mary could hear me.

"I've seen it, too," Ruth said. "I think it's hell. I am afraid of that place."

"You won't be going there," I assured her. "You haven't done anything wrong. You tried to save me."

Ruth nodded, trying to believe.

Malcolm opened the front door and held it open for me. Ruth and Mary noticed. "It *is* love," Ruth cooed.

I nodded. It was true. I knew it. And I wasn't too embarrassed to admit it.

As Malcolm entered, he forced on his jovial face to greet the Victors. But I was on edge; Minerva knew we were there. What would she do? Ruth, Mary, and I drifted through the room, careful always to face in opposite directions so at least one of us could see her coming.

The place was packed with the usual suspects, the same crowd as at the Ball. Only now it was blazers instead of suits. Coffee instead of gin. Danishes instead of lobster. The same string trio played classical music. The absolutely most elite of the absolutely most elite rubbed shoulders and muttered empty pleasantries, unaware they were surrounded by spirits. First it was just me, Ruth, and Mary, but over time more and more arrived—sweet Brit, unpredictable Lydia, angry Florence, and modest Clara—a motley crew crashing the party. We were so many spirits in such a small space, we cast a chill over the entire room, so much so that old Mrs. Slade asked one of the catering staff if he'd please turn up the heat.

I stayed with Malcolm as he worked his way toward Samuels. He had to act casual and stop to say hello along the way. Yes, Harvard was his first choice. No, he didn't plan to join the family practice. Yes, he'd spent the summer on the Cape. No, he didn't know yet if he'd be rowing the Head of the Charles. In between clusters, he whispered, almost indiscernibly, "Guess they didn't hear about my new buddy getting hauled off to the clink yet." We both smiled, relieved.

Finally, he got to Mr. Samuels and shook his hand.

"We meet again, my friend," Samuels said, his expression polite but unreadable.

"We do. I wonder, Mr. Samuels, if you'd do me the favor of giving me a moment alone. There's something a little personal I'm seeking your advice on."

Mr. Samuels paused.

"My father thought you might take a few minutes for me."

His eyes brightened. "Well, then, yes, of course."

Malcolm led Samuels through the swinging door to the kitchen. "There's such a din in here." He knew exactly what he was doing. "Let's go downstairs where it's nice and quiet, don't you think?"

"I'm not good with stairs, my boy."

"I'll lend you a hand," Malcolm said, grasping Mr. Samuels to lead him through the door (and to prevent him from saying no). As they moved slowly down the stairs, we spirits went ahead, passing through the dim, charred chamber into the séance room.

I'd been in such a panic last time I hadn't been able to take much in about the room. But I could now see this place was constructed and designed for the sole purpose of communicating with spirits. Against the long wall, numerous ancient conjuring devices were lined up along a narrow table. Everything was dusty from years of neglect. A good thing: dust was something we could use. In fact, looking around, I saw the room had many possibilities for communication. I guess that was the point. The Wickhams had definitely known something about spirits. We all gathered around the edge of the room, forming a circle around the table.

When Malcolm and Mr. Samuels finally entered, the old man was winded and red in the face. He took the nearest seat to catch his breath. Mary got up in his face and stared right into his eyes. She studied him until she was sure. After a long pause, she looked to me and nodded—a strange mixture of triumph and revulsion playing on her face.

"It's chilly down here, son."

"I'll get right to the point, then. Mr. Samuels, you were president of the Victors in 1965?"

"Yes, I was."

"Do you recall there was a death that year? A Mary Bata?"

"I do." He nodded, dabbing his forehead with a handkerchief. "It was a sad story. Suicide. From what I recall she was disturbed. She couldn't handle the pressure." He was nervous, even his politician smile couldn't hide it. "Why do you ask?"

"Well, we've done some research and found there have been numerous deaths at this school. And they all seem to have quite a lot in common."

Mr. Samuels carefully folded his handkerchief and placed it back in his blazer pocket. "Is that so?"

"We believe they might have been sacrifices of some kind."

The old man's nostrils flared. "What are you getting at, son?"

"I believe you killed Mary Bata, and I want to know why."

Mr. Samuels didn't so much as blink. He chuckled, and I knew right then he was guilty. We all did.

"I wouldn't laugh, Mr. Samuels," Malcolm warned.

"Oh, would you not?"

Malcolm shook his head. "Because she's here. Right now."

"Obviously this is some kind of jolly prank, but now is not the time for it," he said, starting to stand up. "Pranks are for Orientation and Headmaster Holiday—"

Malcolm pushed him back down. "It's no prank. Please stay seated until we're finished."

"*We?*" Samuels sniggered.

"I mean the ghosts who remain here at Wickham Hall. Mary and all of them."

"Please. That's enough."

"They're here right now."

Mary, now filled with a rage, rushed at him. The old man's rheumy eyes widened. He shivered.

Malcolm smiled. "See?"

"What are you doing, son?"

But Malcolm didn't reply. He let us work our magic. Ruth and I shrieked and soared through the curtains. Lydia, Brit, Clara, Florence, and Mary joined us—all shrieking and moving in a circle through the curtains around them, using their little remaining energy—until the fabric walls of the chamber began to quake.

Samuels's lips trembled. The last bit of color drained from his craggy cheeks.

Malcolm grabbed his shoulders. "Did you kill Mary Bata!?"

"Stop!" Samuels finally yelled.

And we did. We waited for him to confess, but he was silent. Mary went to the table. She tried to write in the dust, but she didn't have enough strength left. She turned to me. "Will you write something?"

I looked down at my own limbs. I was not as faint as Mary. I knew it might sap my remaining force, but I needed to do it for her. For us. I just prayed I had enough energy. This was the moment to break him.

"I'll try. What do you want to say?"

She told me. I stood next to Samuels and leaned over

the table so the words would appear right before him. I focused intensely, channeled all my strength, and quelled the pain.

You looked me in the eyes.

Now he blinked. Several times. Rapidly. But, to my horror, he smiled as the words appeared. When he looked up, his face was less stricken than pleased, even awed.

I collapsed against the wall nearby, consumed from the effort. I looked down and saw my limbs were even more ghostly. I now looked almost as transparent as the others. It had cost me . . . and for what? The old man was delighted.

"It's a sacrifice for good," Samuels stated. "You'll find out soon enough."

"For *good*?!"

"A ritual. The spirit is sealed in the bonfire, binding it to Wickham Hall forever."

"The bonfire. Today?"

Mr. Samuels nodded. "You'll be president, Malcolm. You'll take Kent's place. You'll see the book. You'll understand."

"What book?" Malcolm demanded.

Mr. Samuels shook his head. "No more questions. I've already said too much. You'll learn very soon, son."

"We're stuck here forever. That's what he's saying, isn't it?" Ruth asked, nearly crying.

"We cannot be! I have to see my mother and father," Mary sobbed. "I have to tell them I did not kill myself."

Ruth turned to me. "But *you* are not bound forever. Not yet. The bonfire hasn't yet happened. You have to do something."

I nodded as Malcolm watched Samuels shuffle out the door. We had no more use for him. We had to get to Kent and that book.

WE FOLLOWED MALCOLM UPSTAIRS and found breakfast was over. The crowd had broken up and moved along to the next alumni event. As we passed through the entryway, I paused to look at the portrait of the Wickhams. I studied Wallace's face. He looked different here than he had in the dream. I hesitated, trying to make sense of it, when suddenly Minerva manifested in front of her own image. I lurched backward away from her.

"I told you to stop asking questions," she snapped.

"You also told me I was lucky to be dead."

"No, I said you were lucky to be *here*."

"What does that mean?"

"Leave it alone. It does not have a good end."

I held her gaze. "I will not." Then I raced to follow Malcolm out the front door.

TIME RUSHED PAST IN a troubling, hazy blur—was I losing more track of time the weaker I became?—and an instant later Malcolm was banging on Kent's door. No one answered. Malcolm told the dorm master he'd left something essential for the bonfire celebration in Kent's room. The dorm master handed him the key without further question. Membership really does have its privileges. It also meant that Malcolm's reputation was still untainted. But that wouldn't last long.

Malcolm ransacked Kent's room, opening every drawer,

kicking every heap of dirty laundry, but found nothing. Soon he worked himself into such a fury that he started overturning everything, even items that didn't have the slightest chance of hiding a book. When he dumped Kent's penholder onto his desk, a gold ring tumbled out and rolled across the floor.

Malcolm fell onto his stomach and inched himself under Kent's bed, chasing after it. He finally clenched it and pulled it back out into the light. It was the gold Wickham Hall insignia band inscribed with *B.A./V.P. 1885.*

We both shuddered, now knowing for certain what Kent had done.

"It's proof, Liv! Proof he killed you! You had that on when you died!"

But proof that Kent had murdered me wasn't enough. There was something so much bigger we needed to prove, and fast. The infamous bonfire would soon be lit, and I didn't particularly want to have my soul burning in it.

Dawn

I wanted to do something important, man. I wanted to fix things. I wanted to change the world. The feminist movement was happening—I'd read Friedan and Steinem and Simone de Beauvoir—and I was on that bandwagon already, man. I knew my power. I felt my power and found my calling—the Earth. Our beautiful Earth was being used and abused. The birds were dying. Oil was spilling into our oceans. They were testing bombs there, too, you know. I didn't want nuclear waste in my ocean. I didn't want chemicals in my food. Acid in my rain.

So, I started the Environmental Club at Wickham Hall and arranged my first protest: an anti-nuke rally. I thought I was leading a revolution, man. I even borrowed a megaphone from the gym. But no one came. And the headmaster instructed campus security to remove me. Still, I did not despair. Like they say, keep on truckin', right?

Then I heard they were gonna spray the nature preserve with DDT. Right here: our own nature preserve. I'd read Silent Spring, *and I knew what that stuff did. I tried to talk to the authorities, but no one cared they'd be killing the wildlife. They said it was supposed to keep us healthy. Man, what bullshit.*

But then finally one person joined my club. Aiden was his name. He didn't seem like the type who wanted to save the world—and he clearly didn't know much about the movement—but you can't turn away a soldier, right? Plus, he was all I had. Together we organized another rally—this time in the nature preserve.

He suggested we meet at night. He said it'd be cool. We'd make a bigger statement that way, making lots of noise while the campus was dark and silent. And I fell for it. I thought I was so smart. But he was smart, too, man. He knew how to use my cause against me. I'd do anything for my cause.

I remember my last walk through the woods as I headed to the pre-serve—smelling the night smells, hearing the owls—thinking only about their imminent death. I never even considered my own death. I was powerful. I was going to live forever, man. Forever.

When I approached and saw Aiden was not alone—there was a small pack of shadows near him—I was so happy. People had come! It meant I'd finally cut through the bullshit. The apathy. It meant Wickham Hall might change. It meant all the bees and the owls and the foxes might live. But no, we now know how this story ends.

The three others pushed me onto my back and held me down. Aiden held a knife over my chest—it was like a dagger, man. I begged him to stop. I told him I just wanted to do good. And you know what he said? He said, "You are doing good. You're dying an honorable death and doing more good in this death than you could ever hope to achieve in life." And then he ripped the blade into my chest.

They found me a few days later when the plane went out to spray the DDT. They said it was hara-kiri—the hysterical actions of a suicidal protestor. Everyone found it so ironic that the very birds and owls and foxes I'd wanted to save had picked at my body until it was beyond recognition.

CHAPTER 15

Celebratory music bled all over campus from the Art Center atrium. The string trio had been joined by a throng of other musicians to make a complete orchestra. As night fell, hundreds of alumni streamed toward the bonfire. But Malcolm charged in the other direction—back toward Old Homestead, hoping the Victors were assembled for a meeting he'd been excluded from.

The door was locked, of course. We knew the lock had been changed, but he tried his master prefect key again just in case. It didn't work. Malcolm scoped out the perimeter. All the windows and doors were sealed. He looked up to the peak of the house and saw the curtain was drawn across the Victors meeting room window.

"That means a meeting's in session. We *have* to get in."

The others rushed through the door. When I hesitated, bracing myself for the pain, Ruth reminded me instead to release. I unwound my knotted hands and closed my eyes. I tried to summon that feeling I'd had as I let myself merge with Malcolm to enter his dream. I shook off the fear that caused my body to go rigid, and I tried to believe that there would be no pain. And there was no pain. I flowed effortlessly through the door. All this time, I'd been trying to force my way through things, when all I needed to do was let go.

Once inside, we realized it was of no use. The door still couldn't be opened. I stared at the lock. I attempted to grasp it, but my fingers went right through, stinging. It still hurt when I tried to reach into the real world. I concentrated on opening the lock, but no matter how hard I focused, I couldn't turn it. I feared my energy had gotten too weak.

"I was *never* able to do such a thing, even when I had my full powers," Ruth said, trying to make me feel better. The others echoed in agreement.

Suddenly, I had an idea. "What would happen if we put all our energy together? If we could somehow merge, just briefly? Have you ever tried anything like that?"

They looked at one another, unsure. They had not. They'd barely spoken to one another before I came along. I looked at the others, and we nodded in silent agreement. Each spirit would release herself into me with the hope some small vestiges of their energy might unite with mine, and we'd somehow become stronger together. In any case, we had no choice but to try.

"You might get our thoughts, too," Ruth said, concerned.

"So everyone just focus on turning the lock. Just only think about that. Okay?"

The idea of having other people's thoughts in my head

was frightening—but, then again, so was the idea of being a ghost. I looked at every face to make sure they all agreed. Lydia seemed distracted.

"Lydia, did you hear me? Will you be able to focus?"

"I'll try." Poor thing. Who knew what was going in *her* mind? I stood at the lock, my finger poised. Ruth merged with me first—I could feel a surge, a kick, like I'd just slammed three Red Bulls. Then Lydia, Florence, Brit, Mary, and Clara. I felt more and more substantial as each spirit merged with mine. I touched the lock. It felt more solid but was still hot as a burning coal.

When we were all aligned, my body felt strong, but my mind was cluttered. I could hear the other girls' thoughts as if they were my own. Words I never used and old-fashioned phrases:

Golly, do you think she can do this?

Don't flip your wig, Mary, don't flip your wig.

And even the chorus from a song I'd never heard before swam through my head (courtesy of Ruth, I'm sure):

Always look for the silver lining and try to find the sunny side of life . . .

Now I understood why Gabe felt so crazy: to hear disembodied voices makes you feel like a certified lunatic. But I could feel the lock firmly in my grasp, searing. I took a deep breath. It felt like an actual breath! I almost felt like a real body. Then I or we—or whatever pronoun describes a spirit unified with multiple other spirits—turned the metal over. *Click.* Nothing had ever sounded as beautiful.

Malcolm dashed inside. "Thank you," he gasped.

The spirits and I separated immediately. I paused for a

moment, drained from the pain and effort. Reluctantly, I looked down and saw, yes, I was fainter still. And Malcolm's drawing on my forearm was fading with me.

As we followed him up the three sets of stairs, I looked around for Minerva. I knew she was there. I caught a glimpse of her receding into one of the upstairs bedrooms. Malcolm ascended the final steep flight of hidden stairs silently, clutching the complex skeleton key for the Victors meeting room. He knew they'd probably never change the original lock. As we approached, we heard deep-voiced chanting. Malcolm briskly slipped the key in and turned it.

The door opened.

Seven men, all in large hooded cloaks, sat around the round table. Some kind of ritual was set up on the table. Candles. A bowl of dark liquid: blood. A thick, old leather-bound book clenched with a lock. I almost laughed at how unoriginal the scenario looked, until I saw, right in the middle of the table, my necklace—the locket I always wore. I hadn't even known it was missing. I shuddered. This was not a joke. It was very, very real.

The men stopped dead and looked up. Chanting halted. Their hoods made their faces shadowy and sinister. Or they just *were* sinister. They were neither alarmed to see Malcolm nor angry. Kent, sitting in the center, smiled. "Malcolm, we thought you might pay a visit. Please come in. Close the door."

And they all smiled—warmly, welcomingly—from beneath their cloaks. Smiles had never held such horror. They were inviting Malcolm, *including* him. They *wanted* him there. I whispered for the others to wait outside, and before they could protest, I rushed in behind him.

The door closed behind us, disappearing into the wall of books.

"What is this? Who are you people?!" Malcolm demanded.

"Your family." It wasn't until then that I noticed the man speaking was Malcolm's father. "You're one of us."

"I am not!"

"True. You haven't been acting like family lately. I wasn't sure what to do about that," Kent remarked.

"You tried to kill me. You tried to drown me, that's what. My scull, remember?"

Kent ignored him. "But I discussed the matter with these kind gentlemen, and we decided rather than get rid of you, we should promote you."

"You demonstrated scruples, son—misdirected, but noteworthy," Mr. Samuels added. "And a drive that proves you capable of taking charge."

"We've voted you Victors President for next year," Malcolm's father said, so pleased and proud. "This way we can tell you everything. *Finally.*"

"You're lucky, my son. You're the next heir," another offered. I recognized him; in fact, they were all strangely familiar from the Ball.

"Welcome, Malcolm," they muttered from under their hoods.

"Please sit," Kent insisted. But Malcolm stood.

There was a man even older than Mr. Samuels, over-weight and shaky. He spoke with a quaking voice. "The

Victors were founded one hundred and forty years ago, in Wickham Hall's tenth year."

Malcolm's father took up the sales pitch. "The school had incredible potential, but the founders didn't have the necessary discipline or focus."

"They were a little lost amid the Romantics, Spiritualism . . . séances," Samuels offered.

"They understood there was another realm—and one with great power—but didn't know how to use it to benefit their school," another chimed in.

"But their son, Elijah, understood this school could be the best institution in the country," Malcolm's father continued. "And that it *should* be. Elijah had a long-standing interest in Spiritualism fueled by his parents."

"But he was also a Latin scholar," Kent added.

My eyes flitted from Kent to Malcolm's father to Samuels to the others. They were all uncannily the same—it was like looking at one man at different stages of his life.

"And in reading the writings of Julius Caesar, he became acquainted with some Celtic and Gaelic traditions," Malcolm's father said. "Such as the worship of darkness."

Samuels spoke again. "Samhain was the Gaelic autumn festival that heralded in the 'darker half' of the year. Sacrifices were made to ensure a fruitful year. They made human offerings. Burning them. Elijah believed if an offering was made to Wickham Hall, Wickham Hall could reach its true appointed potential. So he established the Victors, and in 1885 Elijah's protégé Balthazar Astor made the first offering: Clara Dodge, a sad commoner who'd managed to finagle her way into the school."

"It was hardly a loss," Kent said. "And Elijah was right. Wickham Hall and its students thrived. Thus, he created this book and established the ritual." He gestured to the large leather-bound book. I noticed that its cover was embossed with the same strange imagery from the dream and the Wickham objects and the woodwork downstairs.

"And the Victors were designated to preside over this precious tradition. Every ten years, the president oversees the sacrifice, then seals that sacrifice in the annual bonfire."

"What does 'seal the sacrifice' mean?" Malcolm finally asked.

"The soul is offered to Wickham Hall."

"You've mentioned ghosts," Kent said. "If you're telling the truth, that's proof. The souls were captured. And we benefitted. So, your little girlfriend proves what we do is real. It works."

"Son, it has made Wickham Hall the most successful school in the country. What we do benefits so many."

"We lead countries. We wage wars."

"And we bring prosperity and work to so many."

"We heal the world," Samuels added with a smile.

"We are the proud men who have carried on the sacred tradition."

Malcolm turned to his father. "You, too?"

His father was silent but held his gaze.

"You're a murderer?!" Malcolm snarled at him.

"We don't look at it that way," Samuels interjected. "It is a privilege to serve our country, our school, and our classmates."

"A privilege and a duty," Mr. Astor added.

"All students are guaranteed success, but the Victors enjoy privilege beyond imagination. And the Victors President can have anything he wants in life."

"*Anything*, son," Malcolm's father emphasized.

Kent continued. "This year was my year. I had picked someone else—another expendable—to sacrifice, but because of your interest in Olivia, I changed plans. *She* became the sacrifice."

Malcolm's demeanor withered as he absorbed the truth. "An *expendable?*" he finally asked.

"A lesser person," Samuels offered.

"The dregs and drags on society."

"The dead weight," Kent explained.

"It's our responsibility. Our *mission*." Samuels was practically beaming with pride.

"And you will be president next year, son," Mr. Astor finished.

"I will *not*."

"You *will* do it. You will not have to kill, but you will be Victors President—the *seventh* Astor to hold such position," his father said forcefully. "It ensures your success for life. God knows you need the help."

Malcolm looked down. He shook with rage but swallowed it. He looked up, all of a sudden eerily placid. "Success at anything? *Anything* I desire?"

"Anything in life. The Victors President can do anything."

"And what do I have to do?" he asked quietly.

"No, Malcolm, don't!" I yelled. He was so convincing even *I* thought he was wavering.

"You will inherit the book, care for it. Pass it on. You will conduct the annual Samhain ritual."

"Which entails . . ."

"Leading the chants," his father said.

"Collecting the blood," Kent gestured to the bowl filled with blood. "And burning it in the fire."

"Whose blood?"

"A drop from every new student—taken at the admissions physical—so each and every one is bound to the school and will benefit from the sacrifices we've made. Eternally."

"Bringing wealth and success to themselves and eventually to Wickham Hall."

"That's it?"

"Yes, son," his father assured him.

Kent smiled.

Malcolm nodded. In the next instant, he knocked the bowl across the table, splashing the burnt-umber liquid all over the cloaked men, and scooped up the book, backing toward the door.

"You cannot have this information and walk away," Kent warned.

Malcolm turned, but Kent and two others were instantly on top of him, pinning him against the wall of books. Malcolm struggled against them, but it was three against one. His own father watched, silent. I yelled for help. Ruth, Mary, Florence, Clara, Brit, and Lydia were already there.

"What do we do?" Kent gasped, his hand around Malcolm's throat.

Mr. Samuels gestured toward the window. He pulled

the curtain without even bothering to get up. Malcolm's father started toward his son, but the oldest man in the room put up his hand and simply said, "The oath."

Malcolm's father sat back down and gestured for them to proceed. Suddenly I saw a flash of Goya's hideous *Saturn Devouring His Son,* the gruesome painting Malcolm had said reminded him of his father. Now I understood why. His father was inhuman, a monster. He had already murdered once for Wickham Hall, and now he was sacrificing his own son.

Kent tried to get the book out of Malcolm's hand, but he wouldn't loosen his grip. So Kent pushed Malcolm right up against the glass of the window. "Don't make us do this to you."

"Stay, son. Agree to stay," his father urged.

Kent looked at the elders; they all nodded. Mr. Astor turned away. As the other two held Malcolm, Kent opened the window. With that, they pushed him out.

As I saw it happening, I instinctively soared after him. I didn't realize or expect—or even have time to consider— they'd all come with me. The six other spirits merged with me, and together we created enough resistance to slow his fall. It wasn't enough to stop him completely, but he tumbled gently, like a falling leaf. Somehow enough energy remained among us. Perhaps the other ghosts had more power than they'd known. Or perhaps it was that together we created something greater than the sum of our parts. Or maybe some other spirit, some greater spirit—that thing people like my parents would call God—wanted Malcolm to live. Regardless, I helped save his life. And in that last instant as he descended toward the earth, I heard him laugh over this miracle: he was *flying*.

Once he landed, I separated from the spirits and saw Minerva was there, too. She'd helped us! But before I could speak, she vanished back through the closed front door without a word. Why would she help? It didn't make sense. Unless . . . was she a victim, too? Had Elijah turned *against* his parents? Was Minerva different somehow? Did she even know what had occurred at her school? If she did, why wouldn't she have stopped it? Why keep the ghosts apart?

The Victors peered down from the window—shocked and horrified—as Malcolm stood up, unharmed, still clutching the book. He waved it triumphantly and then took off into the darkness.

CHAPTER 16

Malcolm made it through the cemetery unseen, but as he crossed through the woods, he was spotted by one of the Wickham Hall security guards. I could hear the sound of the walkie-talkie as the guard, who'd obviously been called by the Victors, alerted the other guards to the culprit's whereabouts.

Malcolm turned in the opposite direction, heading directly to the Art Center. He spoke to me as he ran, huffing, "I think I'm safer in the crowd. They can't hurt me in front of everyone, can they?"

"I don't know," I said calmly. Clearly. Not huffing. When you're dead you don't get out of breath. That's one perk, I guess.

He ended up at the back of the Art Center. He ran along its perimeter and headed toward the roar of the party. I could hear the familiar sound of Headmaster Thorton prattling into his beloved microphone, resonating against the glass-and-concrete atrium.

"And now, we light our annual bonfire—the one hundred and fiftieth such one that has burned right here in this space to celebrate Wickham Hall's birthday! When Wallace and Minerva lit that first fire, it was a modest campfire, but now we're in this elegant Art Center. My, how we've grown! Before you know it, we'll heal the world!"

There was a big round of applause for the headmaster as Malcolm turned the corner, now in sight of the crowd—hundreds of people. And he ran smack into Ms. Benson.

"Sorry, ma'am."

"I heard on one of those walkies that you stole something from Old Homestead."

He started to back away.

"Burn it," she whispered.

"Excuse me?"

"Burn it. Destroy it. Before they get to you," she said urgently.

Malcolm scanned the situation. Security guards were closing in on all sides, but he still had a clear path to the fire.

"Go!" I yelled, but of course he couldn't hear me. All the spirits surrounded him now, shouting, "Go! Go now!"

"Go *now!*" Ms. Benson told Malcolm, swatting him, pushing him. And he went.

MALCOLM PUSHED HIS WAY through the tweed jackets, tea dresses, and hats—lots of hats. While the orchestra played a cheerful tune, fireworks erupted, and Abigail, Sloan, and

Amos performed the ceremonial lighting of the bonfire. Malcolm peppered his shoves with *excuse me* and *forgive me*—ever the Victor gentleman, even as he desperately sprinted to put an end to their lies and age-old curse. In that moment, I loved him more than I ever had.

Flames shot up from the giant fire pit. Smoke swelled into the sky. As Malcolm approached the edge overlooking the fire, Kent was suddenly upon him.

"They are really here, aren't they?" Kent asked.

"Who?"

"The girls . . . the ghosts?"

Malcolm stood stone-faced.

"Come on, Malcolm—don't you see? This is proof! It's validation. We really have power. We can do anything we want. Don't give this up."

"It doesn't prove anything except you killed innocent girls."

Kent thrust a finger at the book. "If you burn that, they'll go away."

Malcolm clutched it tightly to his chest, seething. "I mean it," Kent said. "Say goodbye to your girlfriend."

Enraged, Malcolm pushed Kent and slipped away into the crowd. He looked up and asked me, "Liv, is this what you want? You want me to burn it? Is this what I'm supposed to do?! You have to give me a sign!"

Of course it needed to happen to end the murders, the cycle of darkness. Ruth, Mary, *all* the spirits had waited years to move on, to ascend—to see their loved ones, to be somewhere other than here, to reach their final place. It wasn't necessarily what I wanted, though. Because it probably meant I'd be ascending, too. Of course I knew I should go on to that place—heaven or whatever it's called—but I didn't want to. I wasn't ready yet. But this wasn't about me, I reminded myself. I *had* to let him burn it.

I looked around for a possible way to communicate. I didn't have enough energy left to affect anything solid. The smoke—it was my only option.

I leaped off the edge of the fire pit into the smoke and wove through it, chopping the smoke up into pieces, like a giant smoke signal. But I wasn't finished. I had to make it spectacular. As I dove and danced through it, I realized something: I was probably making my last piece of art.

CHAPTER 17

Malcolm crouched low in the crowd, hiding from Kent. Abigail had spotted her twin and was making a beeline for him, followed by Sloan and Amos. They knew something was wrong. From his position, Malcolm looked all around—searching for my sign—but he couldn't see a thing.

The crowd saw it first. They broke into a thundering applause. There was *oh*-ing and *ah*-ing and *only-at-Wickham-Hall*-ing. Finally Malcolm stood up and saw it: an angel in flight.

I paused on the side of the fire pit, exhausted but pleased. The smoke angel seemed alive, in slow-motion drifting up toward the heavens as she dissolved into nothingness. She was not precise and controlled like my old work—she was unbridled. She was pure emotion. She'd cost me my final bits of energy, but it was worth it.

I caught a glimpse of Ms. Benson nearby, eyes shining and with a secret smile on her lips, as if she knew it was me.

As if she knew that this was my art—finally big, bold, and seen by all.

And Malcolm knew. He rushed toward the fire until he saw that Kent blocked his path at the edge of the pit. Abigail and the others were close behind. Malcolm's eyes met Kent's. He stopped short, still buffered by a few people in the awestruck crowd. He used all his strength to hurl the book over those heads and into the fire.

Kent leaped up toward the book, a desperate lunge. And, unbelievably, he *did* grab it. It was in his hands. I saw his face—triumphant—and lifted myself to try to stop him. But it was too late. He'd missed his footing and was already falling into the flames. Abigail pushed her way to the edge of the pit and screamed, looking down in horror as her near-mirror image shrieked and spun, consumed by the raging fire.

The book seemed to hover for a moment, crackling and exploding into brightness like a sparkler on the Fourth of July.

Ruth was immediately at my side. "I think I can go now. I think we all can. I can feel it."

I smiled.

"You're coming with us?" she asked.

"Not if I don't have to. I'm going to linger if I can. There's one more thing I want to do."

"Well, thank you," she said. She swept me into a brief and intense hug.

While Headmaster Thorton whisked the hysterical Abigail away from the edge of the fire and security guards pushed the crowds away from the scene in an attempt to maintain order in the chaos, the other ghosts surrounded Ruth and me. All saying thank you. All smiling. Some probably smiling for the first time in decades.

Then, slowly, one by one—starting with Clara, who died first—they became lighter and lighter and brighter and brighter—until they became entirely immaterial and dissolved in a near-blinding light.

Nature Preserve Girl finally approached me. Dawn was her name. She told me her story, but she refused to show me her gruesome wound.

I grabbed her arm. "But why didn't you join me?" I had to ask her. "You're an activist. Why not help us expose the Victors?"

"Because Aiden's last name was *Astor*."

"Malcolm's father," I realized. Of course.

"And, they're practically twins, man," she said, gesturing to Malcolm nearby. It was true. The resemblance to his father was striking. But only skin deep.

"I couldn't trust him," she continued. "I couldn't even *look* at him. But now I see he's all right. He's breaking the cycle. He's good." And with that, she smiled—content there was good in the world and people who'd stand up for it—and departed.

Finally, it was Lydia's turn. She raised her arms up, still tripping no doubt, in complete rapture.

Only Brit was left. She seemed panicky. "What if it's not heaven? What if I go to that other place? That dark place we've seen? I stole something once, you know."

"You won't go there for that," I assured her.

"But what if it's not heaven? I'm scared, Liv. I'm scared,"

she cried. I put my arms around her and held her until she vanished.

I looked to Malcolm. He was being questioned by security guards. I *had* to stay here for him. I chanted it in my head, even out loud.

"I have to stay here for Malcolm. I have to stay here for Malcolm. I *will* stay here for Malcolm." I looked at my limbs. They remained. I remained.

My time to go had passed, and I remained.

MALCOLM REFUSED TO SAY anything until the real police officers arrived, but once he was alone with them, he told them everything, except, wisely, the part about being pushed from the fourth story window and floating to the ground. Or anything ghost-related, for that matter. Even so, the police didn't take him very seriously until they discovered the Victors had taken a trophy from each victim as a part of the ritual. There was enough evidence to demand a serious investigation—starting with my locket.

Though dead, Kent became the lead suspect in my murder. And as his prints were found on Malcolm's boat, they also suspected him of attempted murder. Cases were reopened on each of the murders. Clara had told us where her body had washed up, so Malcolm was able to point the authorities to her remains, closing her missing-person case and indicting his own great-great-great grandfather posthumously. Malcolm's father, Mr. Samuels, and the hooded others were all taken in for questioning.

Apparently Abigail had no idea what Kent was up to. Like Malcolm, she'd only covered up my death to protect the image of the school as instructed by the Victors. I actually felt sorry for her. She left Wickham Hall almost immediately—half a twin—never to return.

Gabe was promptly released and returned to campus in a police car—the *front* seat this time. Malcolm greeted him with a hug. "I don't know how you did it, but you did it!" Gabe hugged him, then pulled away, suddenly panicky. "Wait, are they all gone? Is she gone, too?"

"I don't think so, but I'm not sure. She doesn't have any energy left, no way to show me or tell me. I've felt some chills, I think, but it might just be wishful thinking."

"Or the flu," Gabe joked. Then he called out, "Liv?! Liv Bloom?!"

I was right there. I waited a moment, then said, "Boo!"

He jumped, then whipped around, pissed. "Not funny!"

"Come on, *kind* of funny."

"*Not.*" He turned to Malcolm to explain. "She scared me by saying boo."

Malcolm chuckled. "Come on, it's funny."

"You two deserve each other," he said, teasing and happy, but with a hint of envy. I could see Gabe longed to meet *his* match.

The officers asked Malcolm if he wanted to leave campus, go into some kind of protective custody. "No," he said. "I've got protection here. And I don't have anywhere else to go anyway." He'd already vowed to never again go home, to never again see his father.

LATER, WE WENT TO the catacombs so Gabe could see me as we told him everything that had transpired in his absence.

When I finished describing the girls' dramatic ascensions, he asked, "What about Minerva?"

"She wasn't there, but I saw other lights ascending in the distance. If they killed every ten years, there must've been other ghosts that we never saw, right? So I guess it was them and I assume she ascended, too, from wherever she was."

"Why? You think she's still here?" Malcolm asked Gabe.

Gabe shrugged, looking concerned. "Maybe," he said. "But maybe not. Shouldn't we go find out?"

Together we headed to Old Homestead. The campus was still crawling with police and media, even the FBI and CIA were getting in on it because so many of the Victors held office in the government.

The front door of Old Homestead was open; people were dusting for more prints. The top floor had been roped off by officials. But we found Minerva on the second floor. She was in what was once her bedroom, sitting in what was once her rocking chair. It was as if she'd been waiting for us. And, finally, she told us the whole story.

Minerva

Neither Wallace nor I established the Victors—in fact, we had no knowledge of the Victors whatsoever. The Victors were established by our son, Elijah.

Elijah attended Wickham Hall in its first three years. Of course, any institution takes some time getting on its feet. Ours did as well. We stumbled those first few years as we explored how to best run the school. Elijah was displeased with the education we'd given him. He felt very strongly that Wickham Hall was not yet what it could be.

After finishing secondary school here with us, Elijah went abroad to London to pursue his advanced degrees. He studied Latin, Celtic tradition, and history. Also, he spent significant time exploring his own history. He met with Wallace's sisters and his own cousins. He learned of their disdain for me and that his aristocratic grandparents had disapproved of our marriage. He discovered what Wallace had walked away from in choosing me as his bride.

I'm not entirely certain what other influences Elijah was exposed to in London, but when he returned, he'd changed. It pains me to recall this time. Elijah refused to look me in the eye or even address me. He called private meetings with Wallace to talk about the future of the school and the necessary changes to be made. For example, he just loathed that we insisted on taking students who could not afford to pay. He begged Wallace to dissolve our marriage and to marry "his kind." Of course, it broke my heart and Wallace's as well. And, of course, Wallace stood by my side.

Wallace's allegiance to me and to our standards of equality enraged Elijah. They had screaming fights. Elijah would throw things, smashing them. He was filled with an anger we'd never seen before, and something we did not know how to manage. Neither of us had known violence before. We were peaceful souls.

One night in October, Elijah sent Wallace to Concord to meet with a prospective new teacher. After supper, Elijah called me to the cellar. I was quite excited he was addressing me and expressing interest in my presence.

But, when I got to the bottom of the stairs, he called me into the small, dank stone chamber and quickly locked the two of us in there. He began to utter phrases in Latin and ancient Celtic dialects. I didn't know much Latin, but I recognized some words, of course. It was talk of power and death.

I asked what he was doing. I begged to know what I'd done, as a mother, to bring about this behavior toward me. Elijah told me I'd sullied the Wickham bloodline. I'd ruined his chances for aristocracy, his chances for success in this world. I assured him the world was changing rapidly, that he had every opportunity available. He silenced me and told me he intended to change things at Wickham Hall. He planned to ensure primacy and success to every student of Wickham Hall in a way I never could. When I asked what exactly that meant, he would not reply.

When I realized what Elijah was aiming to do, I assured him I loved him and forgave him for what he'd said. But he simply continued to chant, and finally, he set the fire and left the room, locking me—alone—within it.

So, there you have the truth, children. I was murdered by my own son. I did not found the Victors. Rather, I was their first sacrifice to Wickham Hall, on October 29, 1875.

After Elijah locked the door, trapping me in a chamber of fire, I watched the flames surround me and I died—not of burning, not of suffocation, but of a heart attack. A broken heart. No mother should ever have to know what it means to be killed by her own child.

Elijah never told a soul. He knew even the Victors wouldn't accept matricide. So my murder remained clandestine. Until now. Now you know how truly gruesome my own son was.

And I did commune with Wallace after my death. But I could never tell him what Elijah had done, or he'd have died of a broken heart as well. As horrid and incomprehensible as it may sound, I never wanted Elijah to be discovered. He was my son, after all. No matter what he'd done to me, I still loved him.

As the school changed, I saw he'd created something extraordinary. I loathed and mourned every single sacrifice, but I couldn't stop them. So I kept the ghosts apart—weak and divided. Until you came, Olivia.

But what you don't know, my child, is—just as I told you—we were lucky to be here at Wickham Hall. There is another place where every student of Wickham Hall goes sooner or later. Eventually.

It's no use to attempt to avoid it. Every student who ever attended Wickham Hall is bound to this place—this future, this eternity—by blood. You three are no exception. It is a world where they pay for their prosperity in this world. And where Elijah rules.

I have seen it, and I fear it. But I must go.

CHAPTER 18

It is now one year later. We've had time to absorb the horrors of Wickham Hall, but we didn't run from them.

The tabloids were all over the Fall Festival incident, of course. The school was quickly labeled "Wicked Hall" and "Wickham Hell." The involved luminaries were exposed and hung out to dry. We will never know if their successes came from the sacrifices, but one thing's for certain: their lives are now in ruins.

Much of the student body dropped out immediately. *All* the Victors retreated to their wealthy enclaves—probably enrolling in new private schools, insisting they'd had nothing to do with Elijah's plan. And in truth, many didn't. But both Malcolm and Gabe remained. And a fresh set of students entered the school this fall—they're robust, diverse, *interesting*. In fact, it feels like a completely different place.

There is a new headmaster—a woman, no less. She's

humble and straightforward. You might even call her granola. Now the Art Center, once nearly abandoned, is teeming with students.

As the Victors were investigated, it was discovered numerous faculty members had been on their payroll. No wonder they all made straight A's. But now there is a new set of teachers—ones who don't bow down to the rich and popular. They're inspiring and inspired, and they seek to fulfill the original Wickham vision of the school: "a sanctuary where ideas can be explored and minds opened."

Old Homestead and the Headmaster's Quarters were demolished. I watched as the bulldozers effortlessly crushed each building. It's extraordinary how easy it is to raze a building, to just erase it from the picture. Of course, the atrocities can never be erased, but it's nice not to have the daily visual reminder.

At the moment, I'm in the Art Center watching Malcolm paint. He's finishing a large canvas—an oil painting of a smoky angel. The angel emerges from the darkness almost imperceptibly. It's stunning.

Now that he's focusing on his art, it's clear Malcolm is talented, more so than I knew, and more than he ever allowed himself to believe. And that's not just love-goggles. Even Ms. Benson would agree. She's his mentor. But I will take some credit for inspiring him. Come on, he's painting smoke angels and all with titles like *Liv Free, Liv Apart,* and of course, *Liv, Forever.*

I watch him clean his hands with turpentine—oh, how I wish I could smell the turpentine. I can see the cracks in his fingers from painting so furiously and frequently.

I know how the turpentine burns, but he doesn't even cringe (I can relate). He won't let anything spoil this day, our last day together.

Before leaving the studio, Malcolm grabs a small velvet pouch off his worktable. He smiles as he slips it into his pocket. It's my locket. I made certain he got it when the investigations concluded. And I finally told him about it— that it was my birth mother's. It's the only thing I had from her—the only clue I ever had as to who she was. He told me he'd always keep it close. And he does.

I follow Malcolm to his mailbox in the Student Activity Center, where he goes about every fifteen minutes these days. He applied early to the Rhode Island School of Design and is desperately waiting to hear. When he opens the small metal door, the envelope is there. And it's big.

He refrains from jumping up and down until he rips it open and reads the first word, "Congratulations." He holds it up for me to see, but he's jumping up and down too much for me to read it. I don't need to. I knew he was going to get in. Of course he was going to get in. He's the next Banksy. Or better. I love seeing this joy on his face and knowing I had something to do with it.

"Thank you," he says to me.

A passing girl is taken aback and utters, "Um, you're welcome?" He smiles and rushes up the stairs to the Tuck Shop to find Gabe. In the empty stairway, he turns to me and says, "I'm so glad I found out before you had to go."

"Me, too," I say. I always respond to him, even though he can't hear me.

Gabe's in the Tuck Shop sharing a milkshake with a girl

and playfully arguing about some conspiracy theory. His hair is longish again and his face is scruffy, the way he likes it—but he doesn't carry fear around anymore. No more fidgeting or hiding. He's happy, truly, for the first time since his brother died.

When he sees Malcolm, he says, "Hey, guys." He knows I'm with Malcolm. I'm always with Malcolm, especially today. Today is the day. Gabe gets up from the table with the girl. While Malcolm and I sit down at another table, he heads to the counter to get something.

From behind I hear him singing, "*Happy deathday to you, happy deathday to you, happy deathday, dear Liv, happy deathday to you!*" And he sits down, unveiling a chocolate cupcake with one candle. It's lit and everything.

"Blow it out," he says.

"You know I can't."

"I'll do it for you," Malcolm volunteers.

"Make a wish," Gabe says.

Malcolm pauses, kind of serious, then blows out the candle.

IT'S MY DEATHDAY. AND I've decided it's my last day here. In this realm.

"I'm going to miss her," Malcolm says to Gabe. "Just knowing she's here."

"She'll always be here—here, there, and everywhere." Gabe gestures his arm out dramatically. Malcolm smiles, trying to believe it.

And I get that feeling in my stomach. Same feeling I got those first few times I saw Malcolm: fear. But this is not excited fear or infatuation fear—this is true fear. I am afraid of where I might be going, but I know I have to go. It's time.

I don't know if what Minerva said was true. She ascended just as she finished her story, dissolved right in front of us. But, if what she said *is* true, I need to help my friends. I need to help Ruth, Florence, Mary, Brit, Clara, Lydia, and Dawn. If they are there—in that horrible place—it means that I sent them. And if I sent them there, then perhaps I can help get them out. If they aren't there, well, then we'll all be feasting on nectar and ambrosia, or whatever it is they feed you up there in that better place.

I just have one final thing to do.

IT'S 11:49 P.M. AND I'm waiting at the old well. Malcolm is here, too. Neither of us know exactly what time I died, so we're just waiting for the moment. I can see Malcolm is growing impatient. It's been a long year of waiting, and now we're just moments away.

In an instant, I feel it. I feel alive. Complete. "Malcolm!"

He looks up and sees me.

"It's you." He reaches out and takes my hand, as terrified as he is excited. He feels me. I can see it on his face. And I feel him. He immediately notices his drawing on my forearm—looking just as it did the night he drew it there—and smiles.

"Forever," I say, smiling back. "It'll be there forever."

We lock eyes, and I feel as if we're dancing the waltz again—alive, unharmed, excited to meet each other for the first time. But *this* time I say what I feel.

"I love you!" I say it five or ten or maybe a thousand times. He says it back again and again.

And I grab him and hold him like there's no tomorrow. Because there isn't. There's not even five minutes from now. I hold him and kiss his face again and again. I taste salty tears in the kisses—they're mine!—tears of joy and tremendous grief all at once. Tears of love and love lost. But mostly love. I just keep kissing him and *feeling* him in my grasp—until . . . I am gone.

Acknowledgments

This book would not exist without two key people—Matt Smith and Daniel Ehrenhaft.

Matt and I had developed several teen screenplays together. He knew I was looking to write something different and suggested I think about the supernatural world, something I'd long been interested in. We had many conversations about the story before I realized it should first be a book. I owe him many thanks for guiding me into this territory and helping me find the story it should be.

Next, my editor (and old friend from boarding school), Daniel Ehrenhaft. I'm so grateful that he—and publisher Bronwen Hruska—had faith in my ability to write a book. They had a lot more faith than I did initially. Beyond that, Dan helped me define Liv's voice, helped me find layers in the story, and saved me from countless rookie mistakes. Thanks, schtoon.

And, to the entire Soho Teen team—specifically

Meredith Barnes, Janine Agro, and Rachel Kowal—as well as the Random House sales team, thanks for bearing with me.

I also want to thank my manager, Richard Arlook, for fearlessly and joyously guiding me through this entire process (among many others). And I'm so grateful my agents at United Talent Agency—Blair Kohan, Larry Salz, and Lauren Meltzner—supported this writing detour and, at the same time, kept me busy with screenwriting work.

Speaking of, we don't have to use proper grammar in screenplays, so I'm very lucky I had Aleida Rodríguez (a copy editor and accomplished poet) to help me clean up the text. I had several interns who contributed invaluable research and feedback, including Jacey Heldrich, Caitlyn McGinn, and Margaret Boykin. Most of all, Victoria Bata provided insightful feedback and boundless enthusiasm. Thank you.

I also want to recognize photographer Tereza Vlčková. Many images inspired me as I wrote the book but none more than hers. I'm so honored and thrilled that she shared her art with us for the cover.

Thanks to my friends and colleagues, to whom I've turned for favors (and with stupid questions): Abby Weintraub, Lisa Zeitz, Crickett Rumley, Gretchen Crary, Lex Hrabe, Jandy Nelson, Janet Hagan, and Katrina Dickson, who graciously took my portrait and somehow made me look a thousand times less tired than I was. And, of course, I must acknowledge the loving people who played with my children while I worked: Lorena Escobar, Nancy Gell, and all of the incredible caretakers at Oak Glen Nursery School.

Thankfully, neither of the high schools I attended—the Hockaday School in Dallas and Choate Rosemary Hall in Connecticut—bear any resemblance to Wickham Hall. I have many teachers to thank from both. From Choate: Reginald Bradford, William Cobbett, and Melinda Talkington (no relation, believe it or not), the latter of whom was the first to encourage me to write. And at Hockaday: Janet Bucher-Long; Ed Long; Dr. Dona Gower, who first introduced me to Romantic poetry; and Ruth Harrison, who was the first to encourage me to paint.

Finally, I must thank all the published and produced writers in my family, each of whom has been an inspiration to me: Wallace "The Commander" Savage; my mother, Virginia Savage McAlester; Lee McAlester; Carty Talkington; Keven McAlester; Eve Epstein; and Leonora Epstein. (Yes, I know, that's a lot of published and produced writers for one immediate family. My family happens to rock.) To that list, I must add my father, C. M. Talkington, MD, who is published only in medical journals but whose riveting storytelling has inspired me since childhood. Had you all not blazed the trail, I may never have thought of making movies or writing books or painting pictures. Thank you.

And I must thank my two young daughters—Clementine and Virginia—for almost never complaining as I disappear to write each day. I'm so grateful you already understand why it's so important to me.

And finally, Robbie, thank you for burying your head under the pillow while I typed this thing at 4 A.M. and—even more—for believing I can do anything (even make a pie).